D1158336

AN UNEXPECTED FOREST

An Unexpected Forest

A NOVEL

Eleanor Lincoln Morse

DOWN EAST BOOKS
CAMDEN, MAINE

Cover painting: *5:30 A.M.,* by Sylvia Murdock

ISBN-10: 0-89272-744-6
ISBN-13: 978-0-89272-744-5

Printed on acid-free paper by Versa Press, Inc., East Peoria, Illinois

5   4   3   2   1

Down East Books
Camden, Maine
A division of Down East Enterprise, Inc.
Book orders: 800-685-7962
www.downeastbooks.com
Distributed to the trade by National Book Network, Inc.

Library of Congress Cataloging-in-Publication Data:

Morse, Eleanor Lincoln.
  An unexpected forest / Eleanor Lincoln Morse.
    p. cm.
  ISBN-13: 978-0-89272-744-5 (trade hardcover : alk. paper)
  ISBN-10: 0-89272-744-6 (trade hardcover : alk. paper)
  1. Hospital attorneys--Fiction. 2. Ex-convicts--Fiction. 3. Vinalhaven Island
(Me.)--Fiction. 4. Maine--Fiction. I. Title.
  PS3613.O77855U64 2007
  813'.6--dc22
                                              2006037435

for bufflo

"The trees are singing my music,
Or have I sung theirs?"

Edward Elgar

1

Horace Woodruff was overworked and aware of a certain muscle in his lower back that could, if he wasn't careful, lead him to howling pain. He made his way along the corridor of the administrative wing of the hospital. He'd hardly been outdoors today, only long enough to get from his car to his office on the third floor, but in that space, he'd registered the first, soft edges of spring; he recalled it on his face now as he hurried along.

People knew him. They said, "Good afternoon, Horace." He was wanted by the president for an unscheduled meeting. He felt a twinge of self-importance as he walked. But no sooner did he have this thought than he swept it away. He was Horace Woodruff, J.D., Legal Counsel, nothing more: pigeon-toed, overweight, nearsighted, inclined toward indigestion, in love with his wife of thirty-nine years, childless.

Coming toward him down the hall was a woman in a billowing hospital gown who must have stumbled into the wrong wing. He never saw patients, even though he worked in this hospital every day. The woman had a bandage over half her face and head, and she dragged a metal stand that held a bottle connected by a tube to her arm. Through one eye, she looked straight at Horace. Her eye was hard and brown, like a nugget of bark fallen from a tree. He turned around and watched her move away from him, saw the lump of yellow-white bandage on her head from the rear. Her hair, he realized with a shock, was the same brown as Beverly's—wanting to turn gray but frozen in youth, as his wife's hair was.

The squeaking wheels of the metal stand came to a halt, and the woman swayed a little. Horace backtracked quickly, put a hand under her elbow, and asked her where she wanted to go. "Oncology unit," she said. There was deep fatigue in her voice. He shuffled slowly up the hall with her and had to ask directions when he came to the intersection of the administration and patient wings. Oncology was two floors up. "You got blown way off course," he said.

"I had to prove to myself I could do this."

"You're doing fine," he said.

She nodded. The strength of her will coursed through his hand. The elbow he held felt surprisingly sturdy, even though the gown and bandages all said *fragile*.

They were standing at the elevator now, waiting. The doors opened, and he helped her in, feeling rattled and inadequate. He was frightened he'd hurt her if he had to catch her. How did the nurses do it, caring for people every day who might live or die, they never knew which?

They arrived at her floor, and she hung onto his arm, using it to carry her. He wondered who was waiting for this woman back home. He hoped it was someone who'd be good to her. She was trembling now with the effort of walking the last steps onto the unit.

"Can I get you a chair?" he asked.

"No," she said, as she sank softly to the floor. She leaned against the wall, holding her arm up where it was attached to the drip.

"I'll get a nurse," Horace said, getting to his feet.

He thought she might be crying, but she was gathering her

breath to say, "Wait a moment, don't worry. What happened to me isn't a bad thing."

"What isn't bad?"

"Come closer so I don't have to talk so loud . . . I'm not afraid. It's like being in a new country. Do you understand?"

He believed her. She looked as though nothing more could harm her. What came out of his mouth surprised him. "I'm often afraid . . . "

"Of what?"

A nurse stood over them. "We need to get you back to bed," she said. "What are you doing down there?" She helped her patient to her feet and smoothed her gown at the back.

As the nurse was leading her away, the woman turned to Horace and told him good luck. He wanted to take her hand but was prevented by the nurse on one side and the tubes on the other. He said, "I'll pray for you." He never prayed, but that was what he meant, more or less. He wanted her troubles to be behind her, and for something or someone bigger than all of them to make it so.

She looked steadier now, as she walked away from him, her hand holding the nurse's elbow. Horace stumbled away, down the stairs and back up the hallway to the administration wing. He *had* been afraid. He'd worn clanking armor everywhere he went, trying to protect himself. From what danger, he wasn't even sure.

As Horace waited in the anteroom, Nikki, the president's secretary, worked at her computer. He'd never been able to crack her glacier, and he didn't try again now. Harry emerged and led the way into his office. "Please," he said, gesturing to a couch. "How are you? How's Beverly?"

"Fine, thanks." Horace sat down and waited while his superior took a seat on a deep blue velvet wingback, crossed one knee over the other, then uncrossed it.

11

"This is not easy news to deliver," Harry said, "but the hospital can no longer afford your services."

"I don't understand," said Horace.

"We're reorganizing the Legal Services department," said Harry. "I'm sorry to say your job is being phased out, effective a month from today."

"You're getting rid of my position?"

"That's right."

"Why wasn't I consulted?"

"Because the reorganization involved you, and you couldn't have been expected to maintain a neutral stance."

"Will anyone else be affected?"

"No."

"You're firing me, in other words."

"We're not firing you. We've reorganized the department."

"You're covering yourself. It's the Drummond case, isn't it?"

Harry's eyes shifted left. "I learned from Nolty late this morning that she's planning to sue."

"I assume this didn't come as any surprise. She's got an excellent case."

"I imagine you helped her see that," said Harry.

"If she were your daughter, you'd want her to fight this."

"She's not my daughter. If she were my daughter, what happened wouldn't have happened. It was your job to see that she didn't sue. Your job was to represent the interests of the hospital."

The past tense wasn't lost on Horace. "This isn't something we're going to reach an agreement about."

"Apparently not."

"So what are my choices?"

"You can resign with a good severance agreement, or we can drag this thing out."

"I know how to fight when I've a mind to."

Harry waited while Horace considered.

"But I don't believe I really have a mind to." He thought of the woman with the nut brown eye, her bravery. "You know what I really think? I don't believe you ever gave any particular thought to Nancy Drummond or what it might have meant to her to have a doctor pawing her at two in the morning without her consent. Why wouldn't she eventually explode? No, she didn't vent in an appropriate manner. But all anyone can think about at the William T. Stover Memorial Hospital is whether something's appropriate or not, not whether something's right or wrong. This institution has lost its way. When was the last time you looked into the face of a woman with a bandaged head? That's what it's all about."

"So you'll resign?"

"Did you hear any of what I just said?"

"I heard it. I don't wish to respond."

"That's exactly what I'm talking about." He felt his chest shaking with rage. "All you want to know is whether I'll resign or not. Yes, I'll resign. I'm done."

It moved quickly from there to the severance package. Horace heard none of the details. The quicker he was out of there, the better. As he got up off the couch, the president thanked him for all his efforts over the years and held out his hand. Horace took it, but he wished he hadn't. It felt cool, untouchable. Glacier Woman looked up briefly as though she'd known all along—last year, the year before—that the ax would fall on him eventually.

It can't be true, his head said, as he made his way back to his office. He climbed the stairs to the third floor, closed the door to his office, and sat down on his swivel chair. He was aware of the pigeons cooing on the windowsill and his secretary moving about in the other office. They'd worked it out, had probably been planning it for weeks while he'd trudged to work, unaware, every day going through his daily rounds.

He was mortified. If he'd missed something this big brewing around the edges of his life, what else had he missed? He placed his hands on the desk and clasped them together. He felt like a dull creature with too few axons and dendrites. There was a stain on the sleeve of his gray sports jacket. He covered it with one hand. No doubt Harry had seen the stain in the act of firing him. He'd have registered it and said to himself, *Horace is a loser. I don't need to feel bad.* Not that he'd given any indication that he had.

Horace telephoned Madeline, in the next room, to hold his calls. He couldn't face her, especially not her, the way she believed in him without reservation. He could hardly face the pigeons. He wondered now whether he should have fought the thing. But he didn't feel like it.

He'd spoken the truth in Harry's office—at least part of it. The truth was he hadn't wanted to be here, doing this work, for years now. Habit had kept him driving here day after day, mounting the stairs, attending the required meetings. He hadn't allowed himself to think of any other life, even though he now recalled Beverly urging him to imagine something else. "We have enough money," she said. "We could do anything." As he sat there, he felt a glimmer, some wildness seize him: permission to take off the stupid sports jacket, ball it up, throw it in a corner of the closet, and never look at it again. *I'm not afraid,* the woman with the bandages had said. *It's like being in a new country.*

Finally, he heard Madeline pack up her things and put on her coat; he waited a few minutes, picked up his briefcase, and left.

Driving home, he turned off the radio and rolled down the window a crack. The sky was filled with deep charcoal clouds, blown about by wind. When he thought about it, he was unhappier with the way he'd been fired than over the fact of losing his job. There was something dishonest about the whole business. Reorganization, my foot. Why not just fire me? Harry was covering his ass, that's why. There ought to have been more shouting and mayhem, bloodshed even. What had he, Horace, said? Something about how no one thought about anything except whether it was inappropriate or appropriate. (He hated the word appropriate.) That no one thought about right or wrong anymore, that the institution had gone to pot. (Had he really said 'gone to pot'?)

The thing that seemed to bother Harry the most was the question Horace had asked, something about when was the last time you looked into the face of a woman with a bandaged head? That seemed to hit a nerve. Not that he, Horace, had any real right to lecture anyone on that subject. He'd not understood anything himself until this morning. He saw the woman's hair sticking up like winter grass through a patch of snow. He couldn't remember ever seeing anyone so gallant: after all she'd been through, she still wanted to get out of bed and walk.

I've been fired. He imagined saying it to Beverly. Another two years, and he'd have made it to sixty-five, a crushingly undistinguished career behind him. He tried to remember what had drawn him to law in the first place. Perhaps a sense that the world is balanced between right and wrong and he'd wanted to be one of the good guys. More likely, it was: I have to do something. I can't teach, I faint at the sight of blood. Law.

He looked in the rearview mirror, in time to see a truck closing in on him, and changed lanes. *I've never been fired before,* he said to himself. It was interesting to observe himself: his back felt better. It was as though he'd been asleep and someone had shaken him roughly by the shoulder—*Horace, you moron, wake up!*—and he had.

The day had started like most days. He remembered scraping his cheeks clean with a razor. He remembered turning away from the mirror and walking down the stairs, holding onto the banister. Beverly was already sitting at the kitchen table in her furry robe and beige slippers. She hadn't put on her glasses yet, and her eyes had a fresh, undisturbed look. In front of her was a glass of water and a piece of dry bread—dungeon food, she called her breakfasts. It's how she liked to start the day. The table was strewn with unopened mail, Bob's dog dish on top of the pile. Horace got down his shredded wheat from the cupboard as he did every morning, opened the box, took a biscuit out of its paper wrapping, and crumbled it into a bowl. "I've got a meeting with Nolty today," he'd told Beverly. Nolty was the vice president for administrative affairs, Horace's immediate boss.

"What does he want now?" she'd asked.

"I have no idea."

He turned off the exit toward home and stopped at a light. He started up, turned right, and turned right again. On his street, the snow had turned to liquid dirt; and at the end of his and Beverly's driveway, a spindly forsythia seemed to say, "Make me bloom, I dare you." It had been a long winter, and he felt like running the thing down; he'd always thought a forsythia was a poor excuse for a flower.

Bob, who was waiting for him in the yard, leapt around and banged his tail against Horace's leg. "I've been fired," he told Bob. He climbed the stairs into the house, calling, "Beverly? Where are you?" He found her upstairs in her studio working on a painting. Her back was toward him. "I've been fired," he said.

She held a wide paintbrush in her hand, dipped in deep blue. "What do you mean?"

"Just that."

"Let's go downstairs," she said as she poured turpentine into a glass jar and set the brush in it. In the kitchen, she opened a bag of chips and set it on the table while he began to tell her what had happened that morning in Bradford Nolty's office.

"Are you listening?" Nolty had asked suddenly, swiveling toward Horace. Horace hadn't been. "I said I've been disappointed in your handling of the Drummond case. If I didn't know you better, I'd think you didn't care."

The case: late one night at the nurse's station of the urology unit, a doctor had found Nancy Drummond alone and fondled her against her will. She hadn't said anything to anyone, exploded at her head nurse a few months later in a staff meeting, and was fired for insubordination. She was in the process of suing for wrongful discharge.

"How do you think I should have been handling the case?" Horace had asked Nolty, while a glass dolphin tried to leap from a crystal on the desk.

"You're the expert. Your job was to see that she didn't sue. Now that she's taking this further, your job is to win the case."

Horace made a cathedral of his hands. He always thought more clearly with his fingertips connected. Like a circuit. He laid out the case for Nolty in about three paragraphs and summed it up: "She didn't deserve to be fired."

"Is that what you think?" asked Nolty.

Horace looked at him.

"Well then, I have to say I no longer trust you to do what's in the best interests of the hospital."

"What's that supposed to mean?"

Nolty wouldn't meet his eye. "I'm meeting with Harry later this morning to come up with some recommendations. Do you have anything else to say?"

"No." Horace gathered up his papers and left.

When he finished telling Beverly, she said, "You did the right thing all around." They ate the chips in silence.

"Do you think so?"

"Absolutely."

"I wonder what my life's been lived for," Horace said.

"Plenty of things."

"Like what?"

"That's the kind of question people ask who end up blowing their brains out."

"I'm not going to do that," said Horace. "I don't even have a gun." He picked a burr off Bob's rump. "But I should never have been a lawyer."

She ate another chip and pushed the bag toward Horace. "Take this away before I eat any more . . . "

"I'd have done better as a bricklayer. Or something." He ate a chip absentmindedly. "Do you think I'm obtuse?"

"Of course you're obtuse."

"No, I mean, do you think I should have seen this coming?"

"I don't know. I love you just the same."

"I'm embarrassed."

"You never belonged there. It was too awful. There's so much suffering in a hospital. Even if you didn't see it, it was there."

"I did see it. Today."

"Come here," she said, standing up. She led him down the back stairs and out the door, where the climbing rose was just beginning to show green at the tips. To the left was a small patio made from slabs of dark gray slate, one of the improvements they'd put in since they'd bought the house twenty years ago. Above the mossy stones, a huge black walnut tree spread its limbs.

"Look," she said. Knobby-brown sheaths at the end of each twig gave way to a cluster of baby leaves, which opened into small, wet perfect things. Every year, he found himself disbelieving that such a thing could happen. Under the tree were two canvas-slung director's chairs and a wobbly wooden table that Beverly had found at a yard sale. For the first night since the onset of winter, a little warmth was in the air. They sat down.

"They'll schedule a farewell tea for me," he said. "I suppose

I'll have to go."

"You don't have to."

"I don't feel like being difficult. It's expected . . . I'm sorry to have made a mess, darling, to have caused you trouble." He looked into the tree.

"You didn't make a mess. I'm relieved."

"You are?"

"And I bet you anything they'll regret it when you're gone. They'll say, 'You remember that Horace Woodruff? Why didn't we pay more attention to him when he was here? He was a good egg.'"

Horace snorted.

2

Beverly sat down at the piano and opened the Gilbert and Sullivan book. *Poor wand'ring one!* she began. *Tho' thou hast surely strayed, / Take heart of grace / Thy steps retrace, / Poor wandr'ing one!* Horace had asked her not to come to the tea, but she would have liked to have been there all the same. He'd be under a lot of strain—all those people wishing him well; Madeline, his secretary, close to tears.

Beverly was just coming to the grand finale—*Ah, ah!* she sang; *Ah, ah, ah!* reaching for that impossible G, where her voice was sure to crack—when she thought she heard the doorbell and then decided she hadn't. But then it rang again, and Bob barked. She missed the high G, and her voice broke into a hundred tuneless shards. "Stop it, Bob!" She got up and went through the kitchen and opened the door. "U.S. Forest Service," said a man in a sage green uniform. "We've got the trees."

"Which are those?"

"The ones that were ordered."

It must have been something Horace knew about. "Wait a moment while I clear a space in the garage." She pushed a few boxes to one side, left the garage door open, gestured vaguely to the man, and went back to the piano.

Loudly let the trumpet bray
Tantantara, tantantara!

Bob groaned and put his head on her foot, so that each time she used the damper pedal, she had to raise his head along with her foot. She stopped and looked under the piano. "What's the matter with you?" His eyes shifted back and forth, and finally he went barking out of the room. She looked up from the music and saw a man's head go by the window, a different man from the one before. He seemed to be carrying something, but when she got up to look, he was gone.

She thought nothing more about it as she went upstairs to work. She opened the window and had a look at what she'd done yesterday. She was experimenting with the combination of oil paint and aluminum. The color of the paint was almost black, the color she imagined the ocean floor to be, although she knew in her brain that it was plunged in darkness, black black, but that's not how she thought of it, and that wasn't how she painted it. It was an indigo that glowed from inside itself, the way water is alive with tiny phosphorescent animals. The aluminum paint gleamed from deep blue. She pulled apart strips of steel wool, shaped them into ropes, and laid them vertically on thick paint. She liked how the dull gleam of steel increased the intensity of color and added weight. She stepped back to have a look. Tomorrow, another layer or two of paint, and she'd call it done. You could fuss with something forever, but then you never went on to anything new. Over time she'd had to learn to stop her tinkering, and begin again, full of new questions and decisions and neurotic twitches.

She set the canvas aside and brought out a blank one. It helped her to see this blankness, to let it into her head. She remembered pictures she'd seen of the ocean floor. Mountain ranges rising from miles down, rift valleys and deep ocean trenches. Beyond the continental shelf was the abyss. If you mapped the ocean, you had an entirely different map of the world. And if you drew closer to it, to a place like the hot springs in the Galapagos Rift, there was such an abundance of strange, otherworldly life: giant clams and tube worms, green vegetation with waving, sucking arms. One of this series would be blues and bright chromium greens. She saw the colors before the form; the colors always came to her suddenly, unbidden. But the form was trickier and caused her no end of trouble before she stood on solid ground. Once that took shape, the struggle was over, and she had freedom. Until then, the dark abyss.

She'd done four paintings in the series, this last one the fifth. There were at least two more in her head. A month and a half from now, she'd be showing seven or eight in a joint show with Kenneth Osheroff, another painter.

Out of the corner of her eye, she saw a streak of gold and turned to the window to see the sun low in the sky. She'd meant to make a special dinner for Horace on his last day, but now it was too late. She wiped the excess paint off the brush with a cloth and swirled the brush in turpentine. Pouring the thinner into an old maple syrup can, she poured fresh turpentine, wiped again, and kept at it until there was no color left. The last time she'd seen Gerald, one of her artist friends, he'd told her to switch to acrylics. "You'll fry your brain," he said. But she'd used oils as a student at the Chicago Art Institute way back when, and she liked them still. They didn't rush you, and if you made a blunder, no problem, just go over the top. She banged the window shut and ran downstairs to the kitchen.

There was nothing to eat but canned tuna. Ah, so be it. Tuna sandwiches, leftover green beans. That bastard Nolty. She'd never trusted that man from the moment she met him. Horace was twice the person he was.

Custard, she could at least make him custard. She broke four eggs into a metal measuring container and threw the shells in the wastebasket. *Clang, clang* went the fork on the sides. She poured milk into the container and took out the baking cups, stirred in sugar and vanilla. An odd quiet lay over the outdoors, something she couldn't place, like something listening with many ears.

Horace would have liked his well-wishers to go away and leave him in peace, but they all stood around staring at him, as though he might say something memorable. His secretary, Madeline, had secured the hospital's silver-plated tea urn for the farewell tea, a rococo bit of bedizenment he'd always liked. Gladys from Food Services, who always called him "Honey" when he went through the cafeteria line, presided over the urn. He wouldn't miss the food she slapped on the plate at lunch hour, but he'd miss her big-hearted, wisecracking approach to life that could get a person through five earthquakes back to back; looking at her, he'd imagined she'd done something close to that. And there was high-waisted Richard from Computer Services, the most patient man on earth, who'd taught him how to use a computer. And Evelyn Prato, the vice president of Nursing Services, who shook his hand nervously, as though leaving was a disease you could catch. And here came Bradford Nolty, looking a little guilty, and damn it all, Horace wasn't going to make it easy for him, even though it turned out he was happy enough to be going, when it came right down to it.

Someone said, "Twenty-seven years—imagine," and he heard his own voice say, "It can't have been that long."

And then Nolty said a little grimly, "It was," and Horace thought of saying something like, "Nuts to you," but let it go. Madeline brought him a cup of tea and a plate of vegetables, which he appreciated but didn't want, and she stood next to him, protecting him, as she'd done twenty out of the twenty-seven years he'd been here. They'd never been to each other's houses and now they never would, and of all the things he felt that day, the saddest was that Madeline had never seen his living room. To have accepted her support over and over, and to know so little about her, to have given so little back.

He loaded the boxes into his car and turned to take one last look at the old brick building. On the ledge outside his office window, he thought he could just make out the straggly nest where the pigeons were raising their young. The weeping cherry was in full bloom beneath them. As he turned to go, he thought he'd probably miss the pigeons more than anything else. Never would he have imagined spending twenty-seven years anywhere. *We Care* was the hospital motto. He hadn't really cared. What had he been thinking all those years?

He drove home, his hands on the wheel at ten and two o'clock. The city was not a happy sight at six. He clung to the right lane except for one section—cars dodging around each other to get in and out of exits—and came into the middle lane. A car followed right on his tail, trapped by a bus on one side and a truck on the other and Horace in front. Horace was going nine miles above the speed limit, but it wasn't enough for this man, with three inches to spare between his car and Horace's back bumper.

As he approached his exit, he reached his hand to his face and felt the day's stubble. The pretense of normalcy, the outer garments, comforted a man. He took his foot off the accelerator and put on his blinker. A bus bore down on him, and Horace gave the accelerator a little gas as he exited.

Surely he could come up with something meaningful for the next ten to twenty years, however long he had. He didn't mind being a nobody, but he didn't want to be a nothing. He might learn to cook. In fact, Beverly deserved a break from that kitchen miasma. It had been unforgivable how he'd used his upbringing to his advantage, milking his ignorance for all it was worth. And in return, she'd learned how to burn food—it was only fair.

He could do anything he wanted. He could write mysteries. He could write trash. He could become a piano tuner. They were always in modest demand. He could become a ham radio operator with squealing apparatus in the basement that beamed in Moscow, Khartoum. He could be the first man to, to what? A man in India had ground up a bicycle and eaten it a spoonful at a time. He felt interest in his life, for the first time in a long time, maybe ever. He'd never go back to the William T. Stover Memorial Hospital again, not for anything in the world, not even for a brain tumor.

When he rounded the corner onto his street, he saw the magnolia tree in front of his and Beverly's house, really saw it for the first time that spring. A few white flowers had already opened wide. Mostly, the tree was still in bud. As he turned into the driveway he thought of a magnolia tree he used to lie under in college, when he ought to have been studying for exams. Its smell was so heavy and sweet, that anything other than obedience to that tree felt like sacrilege. How many lifetimes ago was that?

But something felt amiss. He pulled up on the emergency brake and sat still for a moment, his heart racing abnormally. He felt for his pulse. Was this how people died? He closed his eyes and took three deep breaths, but he didn't feel any different when he opened them again. *You're not dying,* a voice said. *Don't be ridiculous.*

He got out of the car and slammed the door on his legal boxes. It wasn't until he was standing in the driveway that he saw it: There were splashes of green all over the ground. Dozens of little potted plants lined either side of the asphalt driveway and crowded in front of the privet hedge that hid the back garden.

It was the strangest thing.

He walked through the opening in the hedge and into the back garden and cried out in astonishment. Everywhere, every square inch of yard was jammed with green plants in pots. Someone had stacked the director's chairs on top of each other and shoved them against the trunk of the black walnut. The terrace had disappeared under pots of green.

He got down on his hands and knees. The plants appeared to be small trees, about six to eight inches tall, squat, grayish-bluish green. The black plastic pots stood in rectangular trays, each with a plastic tag that said, USDA FOREST SERVICE, BLACK SPRUCE (*PICEA MARIANA*). Horace rubbed a branch between his thumb and forefinger and smelled. They didn't smell piney, or like much of anything. The trees crowded into the flower beds with Beverly's narcissus and daffodils; they flowed like lava around the corner of the garage toward Bill Yardley's fence.

Still on his knees, he drank in the hush of green. Happiness overcame him. He peered at one of the trees nearest him. It was tiny, perfect, beautiful beyond words. It seemed to Horace that it offered him something he'd longed for his whole life. He didn't have words for what he felt, but if he had, he would have said he'd fallen in love with a yard full of trees.

3

He got his coat from the car and went into the house. "Beverly! Have you been outside?"

"What?" she asked, coming out of the kitchen.

"I can't believe it!"

"Sweetheart, what are you talking about?"

"Trees! Tons of them!"

"Some men delivered them this afternoon," she said. "I told them to put them in the garage. Were you planning on doing some landscaping?"

"I thought they were from you."

"They're not something you ordered?" she asked.

"No, no—you haven't seen them?"

"I was just making you custard to celebrate your last day."

"You haven't been outside?"

"You just asked me that. I did go as far as the garage. They're blocking the car. You hadn't forgotten, had you? I'm going to visit my sister in the morning."

"You have to see." He took her hand and pulled her down the hall and through the door overlooking the back garden. They stood on the top step.

"My God!" She put her hand over her mouth.

"Come see them up close." They stepped out together, and

he got down on his hands and knees and motioned for her to join him.

She leaned over and touched a tiny branch. "What are they doing here?"

"Aren't they beautiful?"

"But we can't even sit down in our own yard."

"Look at the color."

"We'll have to tell whoever to come get them."

"What do you mean?"

"What do you think I mean? They don't belong to us."

"They do now." His voice shook with emotion.

"Horace, you can't be thinking of keeping them. There's been a mistake. They belong to someone else." She got up and walked toward the steps.

"Something's happened," said Horace, following her. "Don't you understand?"

"I'm going to finish the custard," she said.

The black walnut tree made a huge umbrella over the potted trees. The sky was going from pink to gray by the second. He went into the house, took off his tie for the last time, and threw it over a chair. He turned to Beverly and opened his mouth, but nothing came out.

"Dear, you look all wild," she said, putting her arms around him. "Turn around." He put his hands flat on the wall while she kneaded his shoulders. "It's all done," she said. "You never have to go back to that job again." She came around to one side and looked at him. "You know, they were darn lucky to have you."

He suddenly thought again about the trees, the yard growing dark, and his heart lurched.

"How was the tea?" she asked.

"I got through it. Just. They were all very kind."

"I've made you custard."

He loved custard, but he hardly heard her. The ground seemed to shake under his feet.

Horace got up at six the next morning to move trees out of the garage. An hour later, Beverly came out to check on him. "I've had to put them out front," he said, out of breath.

"I've seen. There's not an inch of space, Horace. The grass will die. They have to go. Monday, I'll try to track down who brought them."

"You didn't hear me yesterday."

"I *did* hear you. What do you want with all these trees?"

"It's not what I want with them. It's what they want with me." He knew he wasn't making any sense.

"They'll die in their pots. If we plant them, they'll just grow bigger and bigger, the house will be shrouded in darkness . . . "

"Damn it, I know that. Give me time to think."

"Why don't you come with me?"

"I've already said no. I don't enjoy piano recitals. I don't like party dresses and patent leather shoes, the way little girls click in them." Lois's granddaughter, Angela, was playing "Dance of the Elves." "And even if I wanted to come, which I don't, I can't leave the trees." His voice softened. "I'll miss you, though. When will you be back?"

"Sunday."

"I *will* miss you," he said.

"You won't overdo, will you?"

"No."

"You have that look in your eye. There's food in the freezer," she said.

"I'll find something. You're going now?"

He followed her inside and brought her bag downstairs while she washed out her cereal bowl. She patted Bob good-bye, and

31

Horace watched as she got into her car and pulled onto the street. She often forgot things, and he hadn't counted to ten before she'd backed down the street and driven back in the driveway—it was the wet clothes in the washing machine. She kissed him once more. Suddenly he wanted to tell her, Don't go.

"You can change your mind," she said, as though she'd heard him.

"No."

She beeped the horn and waved. As he watched her round the corner, he was overcome with emotion. The magnolia buds had opened overnight; the air was filled with their sweetness, making him want to sink beneath the tree.

Potted plants surrounded him. How many? Ten trees in each black plastic tray.

He went into the backyard and began to count the trays. Fifty-six by the time he skirted the paving stones, seventy-eight by the time he'd gone around the daffodils, ninety-nine by the time he'd finished. He thought he might have miscounted and began again, this time going backwards from the privet hedge. By the time he'd reached the climbing roses, he was up to one hundred and one. He counted one last time and reached one hundred trays.

One thousand trees! *Picea mariana*. He said it aloud. *Picea mariana*.

In the basement, he stacked up the lawn chairs against the oil tank while spiders scuttled away. He moved Beverly's flower pots and soil mix and kept on digging until he reached the hose. Bob trailed him into the kitchen as he poured himself more coffee, added half-and-half, and sat down at the table. He had a sip of coffee, stood up again, and went out the back door.

Down on all fours, he had a closer look: the green needles were firm and a little unyielding, the tree bushy and broad like a fat little wrestler.

"What's happening?" Horace's heart sank when he heard the voice. The Reverend Hockness leaned over the fence. He was a feverish man in charge of a dwindling Presbyterian congregation in West Avon.

"I haven't made up my mind where they're going to go yet," said Horace.

"You've sure got your work cut out for you. Where'd you get them?"

"They just turned up."

"Fell from the sky, huh? Well, you're gonna be busier than a one-eyed cat watching two mouse holes, ha ha."

Horace chuckled. "Yes. Well. Take care of yourself. I was just about to head into town. I'll see you soon."

"Don't be a stranger."

"Yes, all right."

"What do you want with all these trees anyway?" Horace thought he heard behind him as he raced away.

The local library sat in an island of nineteenth-century inno-cence next to a shopping plaza. Sometimes Horace liked going there just to sit at the large oak table and to hear Marjorie, the librarian, glide about on her crepe-soled shoes. Today, it was Mar-jorie who led him to the reference section and *Trees of North America,* where he found Black Spruce (*Picea mariana*):

> *Needles are rigid but not prickly, dark green, plump to four-sided in cross section and 0.3 to 0.5 of an inch long. Numerous short, brown hairs are typical on new growth of the twigs. The ovoid cones, 0.5 to 1 inch long, have brittle scales, rough along the outer margin. They often hang on branches for many years. The outer bark is reddish brown; the inner bark is olive green when freshly exposed. Black Spruce is a sturdy tree and grows in extremely inhospitable environ-ments, seeming even to prefer them, particularly boggy situations, where it becomes 30 to 40 feet tall and a foot in diameter.*

He wrote down the last sentence in his spiral-bound note-book. Bogs. He'd never been partial to bogs. You never knew what would be winding itself around your ankle in a bog. Marjorie drifted by and nodded to him. "Are you finding everything you want, Mr. Woodruff?"

"Yes, excellent," he said, and she glided away. He went back to the reference section and found another tree book, which said that black spruce trees were often the last surviving trees as forests degraded into the treeless environments of northern Canada. In other books, he found photos of black spruce growing in ragged stands, many of them tall, scrappy-looking survivors. Some of the pictures showed trees that had battled wind on one side and had grown twisted and strong-rooted. A picture of tall spruces in mist, with a dark hill behind, made him think of the beginning of the world.

He replaced the book on the shelf and went back to the table. He made a cathedral of his hands, but nothing came to him. Closing his eyes, he pictured the backyard full of green, and a great hush fell over his mind. He remembered a day when his father had taken him out in the *Woodruff Tree Service* truck. His father parked the truck and got to work high overhead. Horace had looked up from inside the cab of the truck and had seen a tiny figure swinging in the air from the end of a line, moving through giant limbs, the saw tucked in his leather holster. His father was short and compact and sure-footed as a squirrel. If he'd lived, Horace mused, he'd have taught his son something useful, something real, unlike medical law. It grieved him still, all these years later, to have lost him; not enough to make him morbid or bitter, but he recognized something hung up in him, the way plastic bags snag on branches, impossible to dislodge unless a gale blows like the dickens.

Horace left the library and went out to the car with something taking shape in his mind as he drove home. When he reached his driveway, he sat for a moment looking out the wind-shield at the changes wrought in the yard overnight. Getting out, he screwed the end of the hose into the outlet by the basement window and began to spray. The more he watered, the more he loved the trees. Water hung in their tiny needles. The smell of loam grew ripe in the air. Bob, who sat on his haunches and watched, seemed perplexed by what was unfolding in front of him.

It came to Horace all of a sudden. "You and I are going on an adventure," he said to Bob. "To a bog. We need to get ourselves outfitted." Bob wagged his tail noncommittally. "You and me. I mean it."

4

An oversized American flag snapped above the roof of a showroom while, out in the lot, the windshields of hundreds of cars and trucks glinted in the sun. Horace stepped out of his car and slammed the door. His stomach was roiling with excitement even though he wasn't planning to buy anything. A salesman with a broad Slavic face, whose nameplate said JURG, stuck out his hand.

"I need a truck," Horace said. "I'm going to be hauling trees."

"Trees?"

He didn't want to explain. "Where are your trucks?"

"Right through here, sir."

He followed him into the lot where they paused in front of a royal blue Ford.

"Sharp," said Jurg.

"Yes," Horace said. "Very good." He looked it over. "It's not big enough."

"Yes, I understand. Over here, please." Jurg led the way to a group of medium-sized trucks, picked out a red one, and opened the door for Horace.

It didn't feel right, he couldn't say why. "I don't think so."

"What are you looking for, sir?"

"I don't know exactly."

They walked a little further, and Jurg opened the door of a yellow truck. "Go on. Get in," he said. "Two years old. Top condition. Only 26,000 miles."

Horace put his foot up, and a hand pushed him up from behind.

"Go ahead, turn it on," said Jurg, handing him the key.

"I don't know anything about four-wheel drive."

"No problem. You just drive. Don't worry."

Horace turned on the key, and the thing roared to life. He was sitting up very high. He tried out the windshield wipers, looked out, and Jurg waved him on. Go on, go on. *Okay, I'm going, hold your horses.* He put it in first and drove out of the parking space. He tried the brakes, stopped suddenly, and jerked forward again. He put on the blinker, rolled out of the lot and into the street. Second gear. It was surprisingly easy to drive. He accelerated and put it into third, and then fourth. Beverly's face flashed before him, her eyes quizzical, then incredulous. He should wait. But what if someone bought it later this afternoon? He liked everything about it. They'd given him a larger severance package than he'd expected. He stopped at a light, and turned left. Accelerating past Wal-Mart and Shop-Rite, he turned left, and left again into the lot.

Jurg was waiting for him, his hand visored against the sun. "Yes?" he said. "What do you say?"

"I like it." He wasn't supposed to say that. "I'm concerned about the shimmy," said Horace.

"Shimmy?"

Horace wobbled his hand.

"Oh, that you will find." Jurg waved his hand dismissively.

"The color," he said. "It may lower the resale value."

"This is the last truck for this year. You want a new truck?"

"No. How much would you give me for my car?"

"You talk to the manager. Okay, I'll show you to him . . . You like this truck. Yes?"

"Yes, I do," said Horace. He wasn't supposed to say that.

The manager explained to Horace that already the price tag was rock bottom and he couldn't consider cutting the price further. Horace went back and forth without much energy—he'd never liked bickering about money. Finally, he watched himself agree, saw himself hand over his car keys and take the keys to the yellow truck. Why not? he kept telling himself.

On his way home, he drove slowly, downshifting, shifting up, trying out the windshield wipers, locating the variable wiper-speed wand. He went over his negotiation moves and found nothing he'd change. The manager had knocked $200 off the price because of the color and thrown in some free floor mats. He'd forgotten to ask anyone to explain four-wheel drive, but how hard could it be?

Horace slept poorly. He was hot, and his pillow felt like a pile of shoes in a pillowcase. The moon shone brightly, and he went to the window and looked out. When he saw the small trees down there in the yard, he was suddenly frightened for them. Anything could happen. A hail storm could wipe out every one. He imagined himself racing into the kitchen with load after load, his head pocked with pellets of ice. Bob scratched and knocked his foot against the bare floor and came up to the bed and whined until Horace let him up.

When he finally got to sleep, he found himself in a bog, thick with undergrowth, while a rasping, dry-wet sound like a great tongue followed him down a path. He ran from it and fell and picked himself up and ran again in a bumbling, disorganized terror, and for a moment he thought he could see a clearing ahead, but darkness fell. Vegetation clung to his face, and he woke and turned on the light and there was Bob licking him. "For godsakes," he said. It was four o'clock. Horace changed out of his sweaty pajama top and lay awake for a long time. At some point the moon went down beneath the horizon, and the birds began, first the mourning dove, then the crows and a blue jay. In the middle of the uproar came five pure notes. For a moment, it seemed that the other birds listened, so beautiful and true was the song. He'd have to remember to ask Beverly what it was.

He got up, made himself coffee, and took it to the living room. He'd had so little sleep that the room shimmered in a thin haze. A map lay across the floor where he'd left it the night before. He sat down in his grandfather's chair and studied northern Vermont and New Hampshire, looking for tracts of wilderness bogs. On the Vermont-Canadian border was a large body of water, Lake Memphremagog, close to Route 91, but there were too many towns dotted around. Close by, in northern New Hampshire, a string of lakes connected the Coaticook River on the west and the Dead Diamond River to the east. And then Lake Francis, and something called the First Connecticut Lake and Second Lake. A town nearby was called Happy Corner, but he didn't like the look of it, and the name gave him the creeps.

He flipped the map over and there was Maine. His eyes found Casco Bay, and he saw himself, a plump adolescent on a sailboat with his grandfather. His mother's father had been a superior being, filled with beef and fighting force, a high-wattage gentleman who died young. Horace remembered the day they went out together, with a torrid sun behind fog, the way his teenage limbs had been filled with weakness, how he couldn't understand the words spoken to him, how he'd broken the face of his grandfather's brass compass through his clumsiness.

He took off his glasses, and Bob was suddenly all over him. It took a lot of effort for Horace to reach the floor, but he finally did by going down on his knees and jack-levering himself to a sitting position, where he put his arms around Bob, the closest thing to a son he'd ever have. A path of wet drool grazed his cheek and proceeded across his chin. He got back up on the chair and let his eye wander up the state of Maine. There, north of a huge patch of green, he found where he was going.

5

Late that afternoon Beverly came home, and she hadn't even stepped all the way into the kitchen before she said, "What would you think about buying out Lois's share of the house on Vinalhaven?"

"Whoa, take off your coat first." It was pouring, and her hair streamed with rain, just running from the car to the house. She unbuttoned her coat and hung it, dripping, over a door.

"I don't know," said Horace. "Just stop a minute, would you? I'll make you some tea." He filled the kettle. He'd been to Vinalhaven only a few times while Beverly's mother was still alive. The island was peaceful, claustrophobic, friendly. He remembered the sound of gulls, a rowboat that went in circles, a bean supper at the grange. Main Street with a handful of stores, teenagers with nothing to do, grizzled men in old boots and plaid shirts, something called a galamander across from the island library that had once been used for transporting slabs of granite out of the quarry and onto barges and to municipal buildings up and down the Eastern Seaboard. Vinalhaven, Maine, was proud of its granite. He remembered the historical society, the strange old tools, the black-and-white photos of elementary school classrooms, bright faces that had never been off the island.

"Whose truck is that in the driveway anyway?" she asked. "And where's your car?"

He rattled around in the cupboard. "Green or black?"

"Black. Tell me."

He took down the box of tea bags and put a bag in each cup. "I got rid of the car. I'm going to plant the trees up north, and I needed something to transport them in." He poured the boiling water in to steep. "Do you like it?"

"You sold the car? I haven't been gone two days, and everything's turned upside down."

"Do you want to come with me?"

"To do what?"

"Plant trees. Dig holes. Live in a tent. Cook over a campfire."

She laughed.

He poured milk into her teacup and stirred in a spoonful of honey, took out the tea bag, and gave it to her. He shoved a pile of unopened mail nearer the wall to make space, and they sat down at the table.

"Are you serious?" she asked.

"Connecticut's no place for these trees. I went to the library. They like bogs."

"Bogs? You're mad. What happened to your cheek?"

"I ran into the truck mirror."

She looked directly at him. "You've gone nuts."

"I haven't."

"You're not making any sense."

"I'm going to Grand Lake Matagamon." He took off into the living room for the map and brought it back to her. He traced his finger for her up Route 95, past Bangor, Maine, to Millinocket, the last town in bold. He pointed to an upright rectangle of green, Baxter State Park, and then a large lake, shaped like a dog stretching out its paws. There were rivers all around, and many small lakes and swamps.

"It's too far away," she said, looking at him appraisingly. "There aren't any towns."

"You've never seen the outdoorsy side of me."

She laughed. "True."

"Maybe I'll surprise us both."

"You're actually intending to drive up there on your own, live in a tent, and plant trees?"

"Bob will be with me."

"How are you going to get there?"

"In the new truck."

"Where exactly on this lake?"

"There's an established campsite over here." He pointed on the map. "I called the Maine State Park system. And if that one's taken, I'll find somewhere else."

"Darling. It's across the lake . . . "

"I'll have to rent a canoe."

"And paddle it by yourself?"

"Don't forget I went to a summer camp once. We had a whole summer on water safety."

"What? Fifty years ago?" She took a sip of tea. "If you're restless, darling, we could—I don't know—we might travel to Tuscany. Lots of people seem to like it there. I don't have a need to go, but if you wanted to get out of town, I'd rather do that than have you live in a bog. Honestly, Horace."

"I don't *want* to go to Italy," he said. "What would we do that for?"

"Do you know what I was thinking on the way back?"

"What?"

"That, at most, you and I have twenty years left. If we're lucky." Her voice shook a little. "Do you ever think about that?"

He swallowed. "Yes."

"What do you think about it?"

"I hope we'll have more than that," he said. "I imagine we won't."

"So we'd better make the best of it."

"I need to plant these trees. They'll die . . . "

One of her eyebrows went up.

"They *will*."

"Why do they matter so much? What do they mean to you?"

"What do they mean?" He stopped. "Everything. They mean everything. I can't explain." He never thought about God anymore, but it occurred to him that when he was sitting in the Episcopal church of his youth, supposed to be finding Him, longing to be outdoors, God, the jokester, was in the tangled ravine behind his house, sitting in the tossing trees. He'd known it all along, even as a kid. His father knew it. Why else would he have doctored trees for a living?

"I don't know what to say."

"I'm sorry."

"You're not really."

"I'm sorry to worry you . . . "

She finished her tea and stood up.

"By the way, do you know what this is?" He whistled the five-note birdsong for her.

"It's familiar but I don't know the name . . . Horace, you're not going to kill yourself, are you?"

"No. How was your sister? How was the recital?"

"All right. Angela had a memory lapse, and outdoors, she fell down in her patent leather shoes and skinned her knees. Recitals are dreadful things to do to children."

"What about the island?"

"Lois doesn't want the house anymore."

"We don't want it either," he said. "Do we?"

"I don't know what's wrong with me. I can't bring myself to let it go. It's silly."

"There's nothing silly about it."

6

Horace was outdoors, and Beverly on her way upstairs to add paint to Number Five in the series when the phone rang. She thought of ignoring it, but got it on the fourth ring. It was a woman named Chris, a friend of a friend, who worked as head of the education department at one of the Connecticut prisons. Not someone she ever expected to hear from.

"Your name came to me like a lightning bolt," said Chris, after reminding Beverly who she was. "Please don't say no right away. You'd be perfect for this."

"For what?"

"A teacher who promised to teach a drawing class starting next week just called to say his wife's got appendicitis. I was hoping you'd teach the class."

"You've got to be kidding. That's the last thing on God's earth I'd ever do."

"It's only six sessions."

"I'd be terrified. I wouldn't be able to breathe."

"You'd be good at it."

"You've got me mixed me up with someone else."

"You'd be a natural. Most of these men have served a number of years; we don't get the real young troublemakers, not in the classes. They're geared toward making something of their lives."

"Drawing's the last thing they need . . . No, I'm not cut out for social work."

"I've heard teachers say these are the best classes they've ever taught. We've already got fifteen people signed up—you won't believe how many people draw here. Listen, take a day to think it over and call me tomorrow. We'd need to get you into an orientation pronto, but that's not a problem. Here's my number. I wouldn't have called if I didn't think you'd be terrific."

"I don't even like art classes."

"This'll be different, you'll see."

It wasn't lost on Beverly that Chris had switched to future tense, a bad sign. She didn't know how to say "no" any more definitely than she already had. "Okay, I'll call you." She put down the phone, got a drink of water, and went upstairs, troubled in her mind by even the thought of teaching in a place like that.

Number Five was finished, she saw right away. Something had happened overnight, as though it had gathered itself. Odd. She'd noticed that sometimes. Tomorrow she might come back and see that it was unsettled again, that something had moved, and it wasn't finished. For now, though, it was.

She opened the window and put the blank canvas up where she could take its measure. You'd think all blanknesses would be the same, but they seemed to carry something with them, some suggestion separate from what she brought to it. She was surprised to get a sense of a shape before she saw the color, an unequal grid of four quadrants, with the heart of the thing in the lower right. She drew graphite lines on the surface, a 24- x 30-inch piece of stretched linen, which felt open and prairie-like after the 18 x 24 she'd just finished. Right away, she saw the colors laid thick on it: a warm, dark, living brown—and a sapphire blue, a blue that absorbed light, pulled darkness into color. The whole thing surprised her. She unscrewed a tube of raw sienna and squeezed some out, added a dab of black, a smaller dab of vermilion.

She worked for a couple of hours, not hearing Horace going in and out the back door, only coming back to the world when she heard Bob barking at the mail carrier. She looked at what she'd done. The canvas had a brooding, human look to it. Something subterranean like an ocean floor, only more urban, less elemental. She set her brushes in turpentine, and went downstairs.

How lucky can you get? was something she thought to herself at regular intervals, and it came to her again going downstairs. To be able to spend days working like this when most people were scrabbling through life. Sometimes, she felt as though she should give something to someone. But there was no one, really. Her friends had what they needed. Lois's grandchildren were well cared for. Some people are born with a grace for good deeds, but the few times she'd worked in a soup kitchen, she'd felt embarrassed. In fact, she'd dropped a plate of spaghetti on the floor her last time there, undermining a semblance of goodness, which wasn't really goodness at all: she was a fraud and knew it, playing at something that her heart wasn't in at all.

She took a few crackers out of a box in the kitchen cupboard and ate one. Horace was eating toast at the table. "A woman named Chris called me this morning," she said to him. "She works at the Enfield Correctional Center and wants me to teach a drawing course."

"In a prison?"

"I told her it was the last thing I'd ever do." She munched thoughtfully. "But I've changed my mind. I'm going to say yes. What have I really given the world in all this time, except a handful of paintings? That's all right as far as it goes, but there's something else." She heard the words coming out of her mouth.

"What sort of prison is it?"

"She said Level Three, whatever that means."

"There'll be a lot of very rough characters there is what it means."

"Well, I don't know anything about it, really."

"Is it men or women?"

"She said there were something like seven hundred men there. Fifteen people are signed up for the course. The person who was teaching it can't do it after all. I'll only be teaching six sessions . . . Don't look at me like that."

"What about the gallery opening?"

"I've still got plenty of time." She ate another cracker and smiled at him. It was crazy; she was terror-stricken. But it wasn't social work, it was teaching. Teaching she could do.

7

From a distance, a long distance, it might have been an airport. Three flags flying, an elevated lookout tower like the ones that air traffic controllers sit in. She'd taken I-91 north to Enfield and gotten off on Route 220. A right onto Elm and then a mile to the fork, where she took a left. Chris had said not to go to the first prison—called the Willard-Cybalewski . . . Cybusky or something Correctional—but to come to the second, Enfield Correctional. She found the signs, blue with gold letters, and parked the car. Fumbly and nervous, she signed in at a low brick building, surrendered her car keys, and slid her materials across the counter for the security officer to check.

"You can't take this in," he said. His hair was cut into a triangle that hung down over his brow. He held up a photocopy of a pen and ink by Rubens.

"It's for a drawing class. I just wanted them to see it."

"No nudity in the facility." He laid the picture to one side. "Count the ballpoints when you give them out, make sure you get them all back."

"Yes, all right."

"Don't give them anything, or receive anything."

"No." She'd learned this already in orientation. Nothing in, nothing out. They'll try and manipulate you, she was told, they'll

51

take you for everything they can get. The guard lifted her bag beyond the checkpoint and called for an escort. Chris was at an all-day meeting, and it was five or ten minutes before Leon, a teacher in the education department, turned up. He looked torqued up on coffee, or something else. She passed through the metal detector, and the first door opened for the two of them.

"It's one of those days," Leon said. He took her bag for her. "I can't find you a classroom. Anger Management's in two, Steer Straight's in three. Four's been taken over by the Substance Abuse people. By the way, two more people have signed on to your group. Don't worry, they won't all come." Her stomach turned over. The class was already big enough.

They stopped at a cage in the wall, where Leon pressed a metal button in the wall. A tray slid out from a darkened room where two guards watched black-and-white TV images of long corridors and checkpoints. Finally one of them turned around. "Your driver's license," he said. She put it in the tray; it disappeared, and out slid an orange clip-on visitor badge.

At the end of the corridor, after Leon had pushed another metal button, they waited for a door to open. At the end of that corridor was another door; beyond that, another, and another, opening onto a long, open, concrete walkway. Men walked up and down in blue jeans and white T-shirts, baggy sweatshirts, drug-worn faces that had seen better days, young punks on top of their game, muscles, black guys with shaved heads, hooded eyes, a few stringy ponytails, lost men, shame dogging them, a splash of Spanish, street talk, white-guy banter. She felt their eyes on her. Leon spoke to this one and that one, in a hurry, ricocheting off one man and another, and they crossed a large open courtyard into the education building. But first through the gym area, which felt the saddest of all—if hope lived anywhere, it lived in muscles.

"I'm going to have to put you in One," said Leon. "It's small and kind of off by itself, but you'll be okay, right?"

She nodded. He handed back her bag and showed her the room. "You can move the furniture any way you want. The guys can help. Ten minutes to count." And he left.

The table would fit ten people around it in a pinch. The rest would have to draw on their knees in the corners of the room.

The first two men to arrive were in their late forties or fifties: Charlie and Mike, who looked as though they'd come from two different sides of the tracks before ending up here. They helped her move tables and chairs, and then the others came in a wave. Clinton, wisecracking, on edge. Wendell, a young black man. His white buddy, Chuck. Sanford, hungry, narrow, rural-poor face. Oz, big head, big shoulders, six-three, six-four, young, something calm about him, scar under one eye. And the others.

They bantered among themselves, tested her. "Fucking A . . . sorry, I forgot there was a lady present."

She'd brought pastels, three boxes of them, and decent paper—cold press from an artist's supply store. She'd cut it into generous pieces at home, all the same size. She figured that would matter here. She talked briefly about what they'd do and apologized for the lack of space. She saw the radiator would do as a table for three people, moved a few chairs, and took off one of her shoes—a brown leather oxford—and put it on the table. "They wouldn't let me bring in fruit . . . " She laughed. "Charlie, would you mind?" She asked him to take off a shoe— "Where're the gas masks?" someone said—and he added it to the table. One of the radiator guys took off a basketball sneaker and put it on a desk. Out of the corner of her eye, she saw a guard drift by outside the glass. "You can either draw a shoe, or something from your imagination. It can be real, or just shapes and colors."

She set out the paper and pens and pastels, and their jaws went slack with concentration; for an hour, the room was quiet except for the sound of hands traveling over paper. Beverly drew a shoe asleep on a couch, another shoe lolloping over a field with its tongue hanging out. She'd never liked drawing classes, the way people grow solemn and effete in the face of Art, but this felt different. She was completely happy drawing here, free. She felt them freed too, temporarily suspended from themselves, from their pasts, floating in the simple present.

An inmate named Kurt turned out to be a consummate draftsman, every line of the shoe accurate, every shadow delineated. Chuck, the young white guy, created a forest world in miniature, full of tiny houses and creatures, a fire reddening the sky, menace on the horizon. Oz, the big, calm guy, drew a raven over and over. About twenty poses spread across the page, finely drawn with pen: one with a clear bird eye looking straight at you, another soaring over a field, another back to, black feathers sleeked down. A quiet bird looking over one shoulder, a tough, predatory beak, a profile with a beard of feathers, a beak half-open, about to say something. "You know these birds, don't you?" she said stopping beside him.

"I used to spend a lot of time in the woods," he said. "But I forgot if the feathers shag down over the legs or the legs are smooth."

"I don't know; I could send you a photocopy."

"You'd do that?"

She was suddenly aware of others listening. She didn't think she was supposed to send them things. "Why not?" she said. It was five minutes to count. The guard looked in through the window. "Okay," she mouthed through the glass. She gathered up the pens and pastels and extra paper, and the men shuffled out. As Oz was leaving, she said, "By the way, do you know birdsongs?"

"Some."

She whistled the five notes Horace had whistled for her. "What's this?"

"White-throated sparrow," he said. "*Zonotrichia albicollis.*" He looked almost embarrassed.

What a waste, she thought, watching his back disappear down the hall. She moved some furniture, picked up her bag and what was left of the paper, and went to find Leon.

On the way out, he asked how it went.

"There's a lot of talent in the group," she said.

"Who are you thinking of?"

She didn't want to single anyone out, but she mentioned a few names.

"I'm surprised about Kurt," he said.

"Why?"

"He's in here for—maybe you don't want to hear this—for raping a five-year-old girl."

She lowered her head. It was true, she didn't want to know. It felt as though Leon had told her so she wouldn't get too starry-eyed about the men she was dealing with. But Kurt. To look at him, you'd say he was uptight, upright, breakable. Not a terrible man.

"Clinton's in here for a series of rapes in Alabama," continued Leon. "He's been in prison a long time. Wendell—he's the kid who got sixty years . . . "

"Stop," she said. "I know it's bad if they gave him sixty years."

"Most of them are in for drugs." He punched a metal button in the wall for the control room to open a door. "Makes no sense to lock a man up for that," he said under his breath. She wondered how he stood it day after day, all this sadness. She gave up her visitor's pass and picked up her license, and Leon left her at the front desk. She unloaded the locker, said good-bye to the security guard, and took back her car keys.

Driving away, she remembered. The guard hadn't given back the Rubens. It pleased her, the thought of that hard-faced guy with the nude in some drawer. She was exhausted, as though she'd been holding her breath for two hours. But they couldn't have been more generous to her. Chivalrous, really. After the hour of drawing was up, she'd asked the group to spend a couple of minutes saying what they liked about each person's drawing, one by one. There was only one rule: no slamming each other's work. Only Sanford passed. "Maybe next time," she said to him. Now that it was over, she saw their faces one by one. *The waste,* she thought, *the dreadful waste.* All those men, their lives beginning with every good intention, hundreds more like them. Not for one moment had she felt unsafe with them.

On the way home, she stopped at the library, photocopied a raven, and wrote a note on a small scrap of paper. "Shaggy legs, it turns out. All the best, Beverly." She went to the post office, bought an envelope, and dropped it in a mail slot.

"It was a white-throated sparrow," she said to Horace when she walked in the door. "That bird you were wondering about. One of the men knew about birds."

"How was it?" he asked, hugging her.

She didn't know how to tell him. She was touched by something she hadn't named to herself yet. Not the sadness or loss, although that was there in spades. "People talk about criminals. But I don't know how to explain . . . They were vulnerable, frightened, I don't know—unsophisticated really. They thought this class would somehow help them. There was a lot of hope there. It feels like a big responsibility. An honor almost. This probably makes no sense to you."

That night, a dream: People milled about the streets of a foreign town, pushing and shoving in panic. A man had gone on a rampage and murdered four little girls. Women on granite rocks wailed for them. She woke next to Horace, thinking of Kurt. Outside, rain fell hard. Kurt didn't look capable of what he'd done. But you could see by the hunger in his face that he was missing something, some connection to something outside himself—she wouldn't call it God, because lots of people didn't believe in God and still lived without a hole in their hearts. Something had to matter, though; something had to move through you. What caused it to go missing? What made people do unspeakable things?

8

Oz sat with his back to the wall.

"It hurts, you know," said Clyde.

"How much?"

"Have you ever fainted?"

"Once—when they tried to get my shoulder back in the socket during a football game. Sometimes I go light-headed when I see blood." If he were having a tattoo just for the hell of it, he figured the pain wouldn't be worth it, but for her—he slid the page of raven drawings across the table and pointed to one sitting in profile on a rock. "This one," he said.

"If Anderson's on, we'll go the next night. I only do arms," said Clyde.

Oz turned his wrist over and pointed to the underside. "I was thinking here."

Clyde nodded. He was a long-haired backwoods songwriter in for breaking a man's jaw and blinding him in one eye, but he wasn't a hothead; Oz thought the guy must have deserved what he got. "I use a brand-new guitar string, clean—you'll see me unwrap it. I learned tattooing from Rabbit. Remember him?"

Oz did. As fine a tattoo artist as he was, he wouldn't have let him come within fifty yards. Some screw loose—they sent him back to the Supermax for trying to kill someone.

"How much do you want for it?" asked Oz.

"How about drawing something for my daughter's birthday?"

"Like what?"

"I don't know."

"What does she like?"

"Animals, any kind you can think of."

Oz could already see the scene: a couple of moose, a bear with her cubs, fox, mice, raccoons, squirrels, birds in the branches of trees. He'd do it the next drawing class, tell them it was for a little girl so they wouldn't think he'd gone soft. He wouldn't say what it was in return for.

The tattoo gun was made out of a plastic ballpoint pen shaft, a rubber band, and a motor off a cassette player; the ink came from a contraband Uniball. They met in the weight room at 5:30, and Clyde set up the rig off a treadmill outlet.

Old Norton was there pumping iron, hair combed over a bald spot, getting ready for the bench-press contest. His shoulders were big as woodchucks. He'd won the contest every year for five years, and Oz thought he'd probably lie down and die if he lost. There were men lifting in every possible spot, waiting in line for machines and weights.

"Hey, man, time's up." A kid with undone shoelaces.

"It's only been five minutes."

"No fucking way."

Hot sweat, clanking metal, ceiling lights, only half of them worked. "Can you see in this light?" Oz asked, nervous.

"Yeah. You still want this?"

Suddenly he wasn't sure, but he nodded and unfolded the picture and spread it on his knee. The raven stood in profile on a rock, alert, its beak thick, its eye bright and smart. Clyde opened the guitar string, wrapped in paper, and wired it to the motor.

"Okay?" he asked. Almost tenderly.

The end of the wire bit into the underside of Oz's wrist. Clyde was like a surgeon, total focus, all business. Oz tried to breathe deep and think of Lucy. He couldn't give her much. But this he could, wire biting into flesh, pain traveling up the back of his head. *For you.* Her favorite bird.

A few guys came over and watched. When his head muzzed over and spots floated in front of his eyes, Oz gestured for Clyde to stop. "Give me a second." He swallowed, pushed a thumb into the muscle of his leg, hard. "Okay, go ahead."

Afterward, he returned to his cell, weak and wobbly. Wilson was there, lying on the upper bunk, drumming on the wall. Oz lay down and said, "Cut it out, would you?"

The drumming kept on.

"Hey man, I need some quiet."

Wilson said nothing, drummed a little harder. *Fuck you* was what he was saying. Oz thought of getting up and making something of it, but it wasn't worth it, not when he felt too shaky to defend himself. Anyway, it happened more often than not, just when your time's almost up, you get into it with someone, get slapped with another six months. Only a little over two months left, that was it. Let this asshole have his victory. What's that song? *Sharp as a razor, soft as a prayer, finish it out in good style.*

He turned over his wrist and felt sick. *For you.*

The last time he'd seen Lucy it was snowing, big flakes falling fast; she came into the visitors' room with cold cheeks and snow melting in her hair. He knew he was lucky. She was beautiful, the most unusual person he'd ever seen. She'd been born an albino: white hair, white eyelashes, white eyebrows, the whitest skin, the palest gray eyes.

He remembered a picture he'd been drawn to as a boy. A

group photograph. An old woman in the center, made from white paper. His mother said, "That was your great grandmother. An albino." He didn't know what it meant. Something magical, he thought, a good witch.

"One out of seventeen thousand are born like me," Lucy had told him.

"One out of a million," he'd said. They were in bed together. She had her legs wrapped around his waist, with him over the top. Her hair was spread on the pillow, like a cloud. She reached up and touched his face.

A lot of guys lost the people they loved. Maybe they did something so disgusting no one ever wanted to see them again. But even if what you did wasn't so bad, doing time was like a gear slipping. Every day, Lucy lived her life, and every day, he missed a day. The big machine of the world kept going, and you just kept losing ground.

When they first brought him in here, he remembered how bad it smelled. Now he was close to leaving, he could smell it again. Sweat, caged men. It wasn't so much the sweat as something sad. People think sad doesn't smell. Bullshit.

He stood up and went to the window. After Lucy, the first place he was going when he got out was that place by the river where he and Eddie went when they were kids. Used to swim right up till there were no leaves left and the skin on their arms goose-bumped in the cold. So cold that he hit that piece of sandstone under the surface and never even felt it until his shin came up bloody. No one out there but cold, lazy fish and the mud bank.

Crazy Larry yelled down the cell block, the night a nail in his palm. He'd been quiet the last few nights, but tonight he was wailing on a metal mirror with his fists. "Shut the fuck up, you fuckin' faggot!" someone yelled. Then everything went quiet. The night thickened.

Lucy'd be coming for a visit at the end of the week. He turned his wrist over. For a moment, he wondered: Should he have picked the one he did, or the one just taking off? No, this was right. Clyde did a decent job, but the wings might have been beyond him. A lot can go wrong with wings.

Up above him, Wilson let loose a fart in his sleep.

The mockingbird, *Mimus polyglottos,* was sitting at the top of a coil of razor wire, singing, a long, liquid line like a river of song. Odd to have it singing this time of night, but the lights never stopped shining out there. The song carried him into fast current, shooting along rapids and finally over the lip of the falls, feet first, tumbling in a froth of water until he hit his head on a jagged boulder that opened the doors wide into light. Every day closer to release he did harder time. Everywhere he looked, everywhere his mind went, doors swung shut, clanged metallic. He imagined he heard each door between him and freedom—nine in all— each with its buzzer and someone watching, the hard click and the sound of it opening and clanging shut behind him. There were stories, legends of men who'd escaped. One guy knocked out a guard, dressed in his uniform, and walked out the front door. But there weren't any stories of men who'd made it over the wall. He saw the mesh in front of his face and imagined the links unraveling, men running out, wading through the opening in the fence like pilgrims to Jordan. He saw them in camouflage as though returning from war, imagined them heroes rather than the rabble and scourge they were.

9

Ripley's campground was on the edge of a shallow river not far from Horace's house. He and Bob drove through the gate and stopped at a log cabin. A woman in high heels came onto the front porch. "I'm here to try my new tent," said Horace, getting out of the truck. He saw that she didn't care to know this. She had a face like someone who's been sitting in a laundromat too long, watching clothes tumble in a dryer.

"Do you have a site?" he asked.

"Take any one you want. You're the only one."

The only one. The hair on the back of his neck stood up. He imagined sounds at night, thumpings in the woods, down by the river, frogs as big as your head. The day was fading. "Do you have a flashlight? I'm afraid I've forgotten mine."

She went into the cabin and came back out. "Five dollars," she said, holding up an aqua one with a cracked sleeve.

"Is there a map I could look at?"

"Down there," she said. "I already told you, take any one."

"Do you want me to pay now?"

Her look said, *You don't think I'd trust you for it.*

How did you end up here? He wanted to ask. This wasn't where your life was going when it started out. It took a wrong turn somewhere. Her high heels were covered with dust.

She looked at him.

He paid her and walked out to his truck, hoisting himself back into the cab while Bob slammed his tail back and forth against the seat. They bumped down the dirt road to a fork, and Horace took the way toward the river. He stopped the car in front of one site and almost got out, but a dirty newspaper blew around, whappety-sad, and he moved two sites down where beech and birch trees spread their shade over a root-bound square of earth. Balls of tinfoil littered a fire pit. Below was a river, dribbling over a muddy bank.

He took the new tent from the truck. An hour and a half later, with the sun low in the sky on the far bank of the river, Horace just about had it up. He hammered in the last two tent pegs with a rock, dragged his new sleeping bag out of the truck, filled Bob's bowls with water and dog food, and set them on the ground.

Finally, he sat himself on a log overlooking the river and let the quiet seep into his bones. But even in the quiet, the chatter went on in his head. Words, words. He always had too many words kicking around, like a room crowded with furniture. He could blame it on his legal training—you had to make sure you covered your back. But it wasn't the training. That cluttered, Latinate, multisyllabic language came naturally to him. Did other people have this many words in their heads, because if they did . . . *Shut up,* he told himself, *just shut up for once, why don't you?*

The evening star came out, and the wind dropped. Bob sat down next to Horace and looked out to where the sun had set. His back was wet as an otter's. Mosquitoes circled their heads. A rustling started up behind them. There was the turn of a wing overhead, a darting through leaves.

He and Bob climbed into the tent, and Horace kneeled to close the zipper. Something was wrong. He held up the flashlight, and found the zipper was off the track. It was typical. If you want something done right—"Goddammit. No, Bob, get away." In the light of the flashlight, he saw two or three mosquitoes slip through the opening. "I said, get away, Bob!" He pulled the two sides of the tent together as best he could and lay on his back on top of the sleeping bag. Mosquitoes gathered one by one until he got into the sleeping bag and pulled it over his head.

A mosquito landed on his forehead. He swatted and felt the bug smear in his palm. He pulled the bag back around his face and found himself in a nervous state of expectancy, waiting; it felt as though his mind would shatter with suspense. Something landed on his cheek, and he struck blindly. After a moment's pause, the high humming began again, coming from three or four directions. He held his breath and waited for the next one. He didn't feel the legs on the outer edge of his eye, only the pierce and poison. The humming intensified, coming from everywhere now. He drew the bag closer around his face until just his nostrils were sticking out; he closed his eyes and focused on his breathing. The sleeping bag was a sweat lodge. He had a retrospective flash of sympathy for Beverly, who'd told him during a hot flash not long ago that she'd wanted to climb into the vegetable drawer of the refrigerator and never come out. Sweat crawled sideways along his legs and dribbled around the barrel of his belly toward his back. He'd mislaid the light. He imagined the mosquitoes inside the bag like leeches, latched on to his flesh, and he shot out of his bag. "Ah, ah!"

Stuffing his sleeping bag in the sack, he groped around for his glasses and put them on his nose. The bag of dog food split. He pulled up tent pegs, flapped the tent down until it collapsed on itself. Stuffed it into the truck still attached to the pegs, his shoes somewhere in it. He climbed into the truck in his stocking feet, and the engine roared to life. "Come on, Bob, get a move on!"

The headlights lit up green leaves, tree trunks, ferns. At the main road, Horace stopped the truck, reached into the glove compartment, and took out a brown bag. Lifting out an oatmeal cookie, he took a bite and drove until he came to a lighted sign by the side of the road. DAVE'S MOTEL. NO PETS. Within minutes, he had a key and had smuggled Bob into Room 4.

10

"It's all wrong," said Beverly. She wasn't looking at him straight on, more out of the corner of her eye.

"That's what the test run was for."

"Your eye is swollen shut."

"I don't need that information." They were sitting at the kitchen table, and he moved the salt shaker to one side and back.

"Don't get surly with me."

"I didn't sleep well."

"What if you'd had a heart attack out there?"

"There's nothing wrong with my heart." His eye opened to a small slit.

"It'll be even worse when you go up north. God knows the trouble you'll get yourself into."

"You only live once."

Beverly walked over to him and sat down on his lap, something she hadn't done in maybe ten years. She touched her head to his. "You know, you can do whatever you want."

He patted her rear end nervously. "Are you being ironic?"

"No. It's no good telling you to be careful. 'Be careful,' what good does that do anyone?"

He patted her once more. "I ate the cookies you got me," he said.

"Why didn't you come home last night instead of holing up in that motel?"

"I didn't want to scare you. Bob and I bedded down at midnight, but you won't believe this—I turned out the light and heard a mosquito. I was so mad I put a hole in the wall . . . "

"You didn't."

"With a Gideon Bible. I offered them twenty bucks to fix it. They said don't worry about it, it happens all the time."

"What kind of a rat hole were you in?"

"I couldn't really see it."

She laughed and stood up. "You want a cup of tea?"

"I'm going outside," he said. "What are you doing today?"

"Working on the show."

"I'll stay out of your way. Probably take a nap before long. And maybe take the tent back."

He found a couple of his trees turning brown by the Yardleys' fence, moved them into the shade, and hosed them down. "Bob," Horace said. Bob was under the porch. "Some adventure, huh? You want to come for a ride?" No response. He opened the side door and called out from the kitchen. "Beverly? I'm off in the truck. Bob's outside . . . Beverly?"

"What?"

"Did you hear me?"

"Yes." She sounded annoyed. He'd never get used to it. If she couldn't make out what he said, she yelled *What?* But she never answered if she heard. He'd never met anyone who did such a thing. He backed out the driveway and headed toward the mall, where that young man, who'd probably climbed every peak over 5,000 feet in North America, had sold him the tent. Opening the tailgate of his truck, he took out the tent with its poles sticking up every which way. An hour later, he was on the way home with a new green tent in a nylon stuff sack.

11

The spring geese returned to the prison, barking like seals in the sky, urging each other on. The place came alive with their smell and voices. They settled on the hillside and ate grass and shat; they came out of the air, a thousand wings bringing news of wind. One of Oz's buddies who worked outside said the crew'd been ordered to douse the grass with some chemical called methyl anthranilate to get rid of them. It felt as though the birds were on death row and didn't know it. Oz wrote a letter to the warden, the first time he'd stuck his neck out here, to plead the birds' case. Days went by before he heard anything, and the geese thinned out. The guards must have been removing the bodies at night. Finally the warden's secretary sent for him and said that methyl anthranilate was made from the bitter part of concord grapes; it didn't kill them, just drove them off. By the day of Lucy's visit, their voices were gone.

He went through the strip-search routine, opened his mouth, spread his buttocks. How the guards stood it. What kind of a man would ask another man to do that for him? Peer in. He'd never told Lucy what he had to do to see her, never would as long as he lived. It took enough courage for her to come. To visit him today, she'd have to take a bus to Hartford, then another bus, get off and walk in the long road. Sometimes, he wanted to say, *Don't come, I don't want you seeing me here.* At the end of each visit when she said good-bye, he said, *I'm going to write and tell her not to come.* But he couldn't do it. Too much of a selfish bastard, he thought, to save her from that.

Standing in front of her closet trying on clothes, a pile of discards mounted up on the mattress. Lucy took off a red sweater and threw it down. She dug in a drawer under the bed and pulled out a black tank top with spaghetti straps. She was already late for the bus; she put on the tank top, grabbed a sweater, slung a purse over her shoulder, and slammed the door behind her. She'd fought with her roommate about Oz last night and was glad she wasn't here. Gina said Oz was a low-life, and how could someone so smart and beautiful be dating someone like that.

"You've never met him; you have no idea what you're talking about."

"I don't need to meet him. I know what he's done, I know where he is."

"You *don't* know—he earned a cooking certificate—he cooks for hundreds of people. He can cook anything."

"Whoa," said Gina in mock admiration.

Lucy felt like punching her in the mouth. No way would she have chosen Gina for a freshman roommate, but only a month to go before she'd never have to speak to her again.

She ran down the stairs and out the door into a cold day, spitting rain. There was no going back. She pulled the sleeves of her sweater down over her hands and walked to the bus stop. When the bus finally came, there were no seats. It lurched over bad streets, and the passengers who were standing swayed like one tired body. At the bus station, she hurried in for a ticket with only three minutes to spare. There was a seat in the far rear of the bus, next to the bathroom. Everything looked smudgy: the window, the mother with her small son across the aisle, her own hands in her lap.

She thought of her father alone out in Denver, the way he'd taken off on a bus like this. She hadn't seen him in a year and a half, hadn't heard from him in three or four months. She saw his face so clearly, etched in the rain on the window: square on top, rounder below, brown hair semi-parted near the middle, clear plastic frames on round glasses. Behind them, serious eyes, blue-gray, lit with intelligence, a short moustache and beard framing a full mouth. He was wearing a black T-shirt the last time she'd seen him. He sold antique maps on the Internet, traveled all over the place to find them.

What she remembered: a map of the Western Hemisphere, drawn by Giovanni Battista Ramusio in Venice in 1565. North America squashed inward where Northwest Canada should be. South America, labeled *El Peru*, without its graceful curving tip. *Polo Artico* and *Polo Antartico* without shape, the top and bottom of a balloon. A woodblock of Cyprus and Western Turkey, drawn in 1525. A map of the East Coast from Labrador to Florida, *Tierra Nueva America,* by another Italian, she forgot his name, in the fifteen hundreds. From her father's maps, she'd learned a little Italian, and then Latin. The Latin stuck, as did his love of old things. There was something that happened to her when she held an old map in her hands. She imagined it might have happened to her father too. The world grew bigger; it vibrated with the life of all those people who came before, who tried to make sense of the lands they'd stood on, the oceans that lapped at shores.

Rain pounded the window. Her father and mother had never belonged together. You could see that, just looking at them. They'd held it together for more years than was good for them; probably for her, even while she wished they wouldn't. There was no violence, just searing loneliness, more obvious in her father because he didn't go in for friends. Their marriage—her mother working in retail and her father in his room of antique maps—was like two people stranded on either end of a time capsule.

An hour and a half and two buses later, she got off at a traffic circle and walked in a long secondary road past a vacant brick house surrounded by old apple trees. Over a rise, the razor wire surrounding the Supermax came into sight; the place smelled evil. She quickened her steps toward the medium-security prison administrative building a quarter of a mile away. She signed in, put her purse in a locker, and a security guard gave her a visitor badge. "You been here before?" He stared at her.

"Yeah."

"Then you know where to go . . . What's someone like you doing in a place like this?" He said it disapprovingly, on the edge of flirtation.

"I don't know." She turned to go.

"Do you *dye* your hair that color?"

"No." Usually there were two men on, but today there was just this one—cocky, unpredictable. She didn't answer. He had the power to keep her from seeing Oz—might even revel in it. *Don't say a word; just leave quickly.*

It was still drizzling, and she went into a large brick building where a group of women and children were gathered—two-year-olds with bottles and potbellies, girlfriends in shimmy skirts and jean jackets. In the corner of the room was a wood lectern, handmade, with a cross burned into the wood; a bulletin board announced AA meetings and prayer groups. She felt nervous. There'd be no time to just be with each other, no way to really talk or touch, no time to walk away and come back; even talking ninety miles an hour, she'd walk down the hill with a head full of things she wished she'd said.

12

By the time Oz came into the visitors' room, she was already there.

"Hey," she said, kissing him. He felt people staring at her. People always stared at her. "You look beautiful," he said.

"How're *you* doing?"

"Pretty good." He found it hard to know what he felt, whether it was him or this place. Depression was like Legionnaires' disease here—it clung to walls, swept through heating ducts. "I've been drawing. They're offering a new course."

"What course is that?"

"Drawing." He smiled.

"Duh," she said. "I knew that."

"I made you these," he said, giving her the page of raven drawings. In one corner, he'd written, *For Lucy. All my love, Oz.* And beside his signature, a nest. Rough sticks around the edges, soft feathers inside, four speckled eggs in the center. She looked at the sketches one by one. "They're beautiful." She peered into his face. "*Ab uno disce omnes . . .*"

He touched her across the table. The only Latin he knew was the names of birds; but she spoke it at random, not to show off— she loved it for reasons he didn't really understand. Once he'd asked her, *Why do you speak a dead language?*

It's not dead. If enough people speak it, it won't be.

Sometimes you make me feel stupid.

You're nothing like stupid.

Her collarbones stuck out like oars. "You look like you've lost weight," he said. He picked up her hand across the table.

"I've got exams. When I'm nervous, I don't eat." She shrugged and looked into the distance, to the wall behind his head with the bulletin board.

"What about a pepperoni pizza on your way home?"

She made a face.

"A Big Mac," he said, naming another version of heaven. "Lucy," he said, his face suddenly stricken. He didn't know what he wanted to say. She squeezed his hand.

"We beat Holy Cross in soccer yesterday," she said.

"What else?" He gulped her down.

"I'm writing a final paper for Greek Mythology," she said. "It's about Cinyras, the King of Cyprus, and his daughter. It's a pretty good story . . . Aphrodite, the goddess of love, got mad at Cinyras because she overheard him saying that his daughter, Myrrha, was more beautiful than she was. To get even, Aphrodite fooled Cinyras into committing incest with Myrrha. When he found out she was pregnant with his child, he tried to kill her. Aphrodite, the bitch, finally took pity on Myrrha and turned her into a tree. But then Cinyras found the tree and split it down the middle with an axe, and out came Adonis. He turned out to be so handsome that Persephone and Aphrodite got into a fight over him. Then Persephone's lover got jealous, and he turned himself into a boar and killed Adonis. All because of a little innocent bragging."

He didn't know what to say. She'd dropped in from the moon. He had nothing to tell her that mattered: the chili con carne he cooked for lunch, the latest dumb thing Wilson did. He squeezed her hand.

"Do you remember," she asked, "that time we went out to the lake and there was a huge storm with big balls of hail?"

He laughed. "And we got under a picnic table, and you said we were going to die."

"And you said there was no one you'd rather die with. But you didn't believe that the storm was going to kill us."

"No. But I'd want to be with you if it did . . . I'm going before the parole board next month, did I tell you?"

"What does that mean?"

"They'll figure out when they're going to let me out. *If* they let me out."

She squeezed his hand. Next to them, a little boy sitting on his mother's lap slipped and banged his head on the table. His mother tried to shush him, but the boy cried and cried. Visiting time would be over in five, six minutes. He and Lucy had only just begun to talk, and he could feel the sadness waiting for him. *Time's up.*

Without thinking, he turned over his wrist to check it, the way he did a hundred times a day. And turned it back quickly when he remembered.

"What happened to you?" she asked.

"Nothing."

"Someone hurt you." She took the hand covering his wrist and moved it out of the way.

"It's not healed up yet. It's a raven. For you—I was going to show you next time." He saw something pass over her face, and all at once he knew he'd done something she didn't respect and that he loved her more than she loved him.

"I don't want you brutalizing yourself for me," she said.

"I didn't."

"God knows what kind of needle they used on you, what kind of disease you'll get from it."

"It was clean."

"That's what they all say."

The anger rose up his neck. "Why don't you just go," he said.

"We still have a couple minutes."

"We don't. It's over."

She picked up the drawing and stood up. She was beginning to cry. "*Honey*," he said under his breath as she walked through the doorway, disappearing with four minutes on the clock. He saw Anderson, the guard, check out her ass on the way out. Anderson, his dirty eyes.

They made her wait in the hall until visiting hour was over. She couldn't bear to think of him alone, sitting at that table waiting to go back to his cell. She saw the bird on his wrist, inflamed and fiery. *For you.* It was awful.

In the visitors' room, chairs scraped the floor, and a sea of crying women and children spilled into the hall. There was a boy with a thin neck and dark hair cut straight across his forehead, big teeth. An old woman with gray, over-permed hair, balding at the crown, big ears, sagging cheeks. A black woman with a round face, large hands. Here they all were, people like her who loved someone locked in a cage.

When she'd arrived, everything had been good. And now everything was fucked up. It amazed her how fast it had happened. Like the Greeks. Even though their love was a little odd, Cinyras and Myrrha loved each other and were happy; but before you knew it, Myrrha was a tree and her father had split her with an ax, and then their beautiful son was dead.

She unrolled the drawings he'd given her. One after another, those strong, dark birds. A crabby one with its beak open, another with its neck hunkered into its neck. A joyful one—she could almost hear it calling from a tree. A nest. She knew why he'd drawn that, and she rolled the paper up again before she began to cry. She didn't want to lose it in this place. Tears would prove her roommate right. They'd flood this miserable room with more misery than the walls could bear. How could he have risked some horrible disease for her? *I never asked for that.* It felt as though he was too desperate for love.

They checked her out and told her she could go. She took off out of the building and walked down the road past the Supermax. A small herd of cows stood in the field near the abandoned brick house—she hadn't seen them before. One ambled up to the fence and snuffled its nose through. She picked some new grass on her side and held it through the slats. A rough tongue wound around the grass and pulled it from her hand. She picked some more and held it out, and the cow took it from her. White whiskers hung from the cow's square jaw; she chewed happily, her lips soft and fleshy. Lucy touched the fur of the cow's nose near the big nostrils, damp from rain, and looked into the brown eyes, and before she knew it, she was crying. It felt as though something had broken, and then she knew she'd never see him again in her whole life, never hold him or feel his arms around her, and she wailed on the edge of the field as the cars passed her, one by one, and the cow breathed hot air out of its nostrils onto her hand.

13

Standing behind the steam table, Oz waited to dish up macaroni and cheese. An hour ago, with shaking hands, he'd opened a letter from Lucy. He knew she'd never tell him they were finished to his face, not when he lit up like a fucking Christmas tree every time he saw her. She told him she was sorry. She said, *Don't get in touch with me. It's hard enough as it is.* He heard a song in his head. *And when you go I'll remember . . . I never really loved you anyway, no I didn't love you anyway, I never really loved you anyway, I'm so glad you moved away.* Who was he trying to kid? He adored her. He always would.

He could pretend he was sick today and get out of his job, but then he'd be stuck in his cell. It didn't really matter where he was. He heard footsteps on the concrete stairs, men ravenous, heading for the pit. The sound of their feet said, *Life goes on. Life goes on.* Here came that poor bastard, Mark, with his big head and bruised eyes, in here for helping a girlfriend suffocate a baby; the papers said they stuffed a sock in a little boy's mouth because he wouldn't stop crying. When he came to prison, they gang-raped him in the first holding tank. Someone told Oz you could hear him screaming all the way over in Building A. Every time he tried to speak now, someone would say, "Stuff a sock in it, ass-hole." Honor among thieves: Hurting a kid was the lowest of the low, and after that, hurting a woman.

He'd hurt Lucy. He remembered one time, they were still in high school, he was high scorer in a basketball game. Thirty-six points. All pumped up and full of himself. A girl named Danielle, who'd been after him for weeks, came up and put her hand on his wrist and invited him to a party at her house. He and Lucy were already going out, and when Lucy turned up, he told her he was tired and wanted to go home. Something in him was embarrassed to be seen with her. She'd lost a contact lens and was wearing her old glasses, and her eyes were jittering back and forth the way they did sometimes when she was stressed. He hated himself later. She found out about the party and wouldn't speak to him for weeks. That wasn't the only time he'd hurt her: every time he got arrested, he told her, *Uh-uh, never again. Trust me, baby.*

Rocky stepped up next in line, long hair, potbelly. He'd told Oz about a vein of semiprecious stone he'd found in a cave in New Hampshire. He'd be a rich man when he got out if no one else got there first. He looked the part, a little crazed around the eyes, but most of these guys, you see them on the street and you wouldn't look twice. Except for the prison pallor, the pasty look from the food and lack of sun; after a while, even that looked normal. But a lot of people got fat here: Come in fit and trim, go out five years later with a pot they'd never lose.

The men thundered through and sat at tables, some of them in groups, a few alone.

I'll always care about you, her letter said. He turned over his wrist, and the raven peered at him, hunkered down, round-shouldered.

"Hey, Oz," said Clyde, "how about seconds?"

"I'm not supposed to . . . " He looked around, stretched out his hand for the plate, and spooned on another serving.

"Did you cook this?"

"Yeah, why."

"Reminds me of my grandmother's. Hey, the bird's healing up pretty good."

"You did a decent job." He'd never tell him the raven was the end of him and Lucy.

"Hey, my kid loved what you did. She put it on her wall."

"Yeah?"

He wanted to get high so bad it hurt. He remembered telling his drug counselor that he needed it to see things he couldn't see any other way.

"Cut the crap," she'd said. "You're too smart for your own good. That's nothing but a rationalization to keep you doing the same old shit. There are other ways to get there."

"Like how?"

She didn't say. "You have to find out for yourself. Like everyone else."

Lunch was over, the place emptied out, the big garbage can at the end of the room full of macaroni. Mike, the head cook, told Oz to get himself something to eat. He scooped macaroni onto a plate, gave himself a mound of cooked carrots, and headed over to a table. He liked sitting next to the far wall, the only time in twenty-four hours he could count on being alone. He speared lengths of macaroni onto his fork and ate without tasting. Lucy told him back in high school he'd end up in prison if he kept doing what he was doing. They were lying in the bed on her porch, blowing smoke with their cold breath. The whole world was sleeping. She leaned forward and tucked the quilt around his back. She said the odds would get worse every time he broke into someone's house. But something bigger than him was running the show back then. He still couldn't put a name to it—like a hungry wolf.

The first time he broke into a house, he told his mother he was off to see a friend. Her imagination didn't stretch far enough: my son, a burglar, a cocaine addict. When it got dark he smeared his face black with a tube from his stepsister Maggie's Halloween costume face-mask kit and waited in a garden for the moon to set and the house to settle. One light shone inside, up next to the bathroom. He heard the flush of a toilet, the sound of a shower. It was late fall, the night cold. He wanted to go home, but he needed the money. He could picture Dennis Fahooty waiting for him, saying, "You got it?"

He sees Fahooty pulling out the sandwich bag and him taking it and giving him the money and going up on top of Moherty's hill and the leaves already gone and the whole fucking world so quiet you think you've fallen off, and saying, *Come on, come on, baby,* like what's in the bag is a lover. Like he can't wait to get her clothes off, only what he's taking off is the top of his head, the wind comes into his mouth and nose like a bird slow at first, then buzzing upward into his skull, lifting it off until his hair's sitting in the branches of a tree laughing and his brain is wide open, anything can happen, fucking anything can drop in and amaze him.

Anyway. He waits for the shower in the house to stop, and finally it does, and then he hears a woman's voice answer the man. "In the medicine cabinet." He can picture her breasts just under the top of the blankets, the nipples growing hard. A violent shiver takes him.

The big light goes out, and there's just a glow in the window and after a few minutes, they start up. The headboard must have been right next to the wall. Wouldn't you think if the headboard banged the wall every time you banged your wife, you'd do something about it? But he's not really thinking about that. He climbs up onto the windowsill and tries to open the window, but it won't budge. He zigs his flashlight over the casing, tries again. He thinks of kicking in the glass, but if he does that, some guy in his underwear will be running around the garden with a shotgun like in a bad movie.

After a while he gives up, but not before he carries their birdbath down the street and smashes it on the road. After that, he heads down to the wharf. He climbs down toward the dark water where a few wooden slats are nailed into a pylon and holds on with one hand; with the other, he scoops seawater onto his face. It's cold, and the lights of the far shore shine on the hulls of boats. He rubs his face until he can't feel the greasepaint anymore and his hand smells like fish and fighting gulls and motor oil and rusty undersides of sad old boats.

When he comes up the ladder, he nearly shits his pants—there's a pair of eyes staring at him. He gets up onto the dock and the cat rubs against his legs, and he reaches down for it, his body full of the terror, and he picks it up and hurls it as far as he can into the water. There's a long cry of surprise from her throat and a splash and then quiet and he stands there looking out at nothing.

He fishes for the flashlight and points it out in the direction of the splash. He strips off his shirt, unzips his pants, and finds the footholds on the scraps of wood and lets himself in. The cold knocks the breath out of him. He keeps the flashlight over his head and swims out to where he thinks she might be, all the time saying to himself, *You stupid fuck.*

The water is full of shadows. *Here, kitty,* he calls. He can't feel the hand holding the flashlight anymore. He swims toward a dark spot, and it changes into a wave, and he swims toward another. He feels something brush up against his leg underwater, and he swims away from it as fast as he can. A voice in his head says, *You could swim all the way to Fisher's Island and never find her, you stupid fuck. You stupid fuck, you stupid fuck,* and his arms pull him back toward shore. When he climbs out of the water, he half expects to see her eyes, but there's only his shirt and pants and his father's black shoes in a heap thrown over the thick loops of filthy fishing line, and the shivers come from somewhere deeper than his belly, shaking his insides, shaking what innocence is in him out onto those rotten planks.

He finished the last few carrots on his plate and thought how the fear of entering a house never went away. They say that happens with actors. Every new night, the shakes are back. He'd like to think that cat made it, but he didn't want to fool himself.

Maybe Lucy was afraid of him getting out. It was okay to be seeing him as long as he was behind bars. He didn't want to believe she'd feel that. They'd talked about a life together. About living in a farmhouse out in the country someday. Peach trees. A dog. She wanted a golden retriever. He'd have preferred something with more hound in it, more get-up-and-go, but what did it matter now?

He reached for the letter from Lucy and found the other one that had come in the same mail. He knew the writing even though there was no return address. His Uncle Walt never revealed himself on the outside of an envelope to the prison. Some drug addict, he'd told Oz once, might steal his identity. Uncle Walt worked for Mutual of Omaha. Why anyone would want to steal that life . . .

He turned over Lucy's letter, thought to open it again, thought better of it. He'd be reading it dozens of times. He stuffed both letters back in his shirt pocket and headed back to his room. Wilson wasn't there, and he lay down on the bottom bunk. He thought of how Lucy had looked the last time he'd seen her walking away from him, the cock of her hip, how it met the proud, sad slope of her shoulders somewhere in the middle of her back.

He took Uncle Walt's letter out of his pocket. *Dear Oswald,* he read. *If you're a Catholic, you can always come home. What I've discovered in recent years . . .* He stopped reading. Last year, he was prevented from being a coffin bearer at his father's funeral by Uncle

Walt. Even the prison had seen fit to let him out for it, but his uncle, his own flesh and blood, had said no convict would carry his brother on his last journey, he didn't care who it was.

Oz thought of a logger friend who'd once told him about a time he'd come into a clearing and found a lone crow sitting on the end of a limb. Little by little, crows flew from every direction and perched in the trees, and then the head crow made a *crawk* sound. As though accepting his fate, the loner bowed his head and flew to the ground. One crow came down and pecked at him, and then another and another, until all that remained was a pile of bloody black feathers in the dirt.

Uncle Walt, his father's brother, knew nothing about crows, or men with cinder blocks around their hearts. He'd never imagined what it felt like to be unanchored by his God, by his fucking certainty, by his wife Marilyn. He didn't mind passing judgment on the rest of the world so long as he was safe in his little house, ordering that poor son of his around and telling him and everyone else what kind of God to believe in. Oz lay there getting madder and madder until he ripped up Uncle Walt's letter and threw the scraps on the floor.

Lucy had been a white crow her whole life. It was part of what he loved in her. And now, he'd have to say it didn't really matter whether he got out. You want to get out because there's something beside yourself and your own pathetic little life waiting for you. He'd told Lucy he'd get a job cooking. Some guys got out with an electrician's license. Not him; he liked food. He would have cooked for her, her whole life.

14

Beverly found Horace in his study staring into the computer screen. "Listen to this," he said. " 'A typical to-do list should include the following: Two to three weeks before setting out, check the condition of the tent, with particular attention to pegs, loops and zips.' There's where I went wrong. It's all here. 'Clean and test-light the gas stove and lamp if they are to be used. Ensure that the stove burns well, and if going on an extended trip, consider taking spare gas jets.' The South African Caravan and Camping Association. They say in summary, 'Camping, like most other things in life, can be simple and pleasurable or complicated and unpleasant.' "

"Can't argue with that," said Beverly.

"How'd it go?" he asked her, looking up.

"Pretty well. Not brilliant." She'd just come back from her third class. Before it started, Leon told her that someone had been stabbed in one of the dorms the day before. The whole place felt jittery. It was spring, but it wasn't. Everything was coming to life, but it wasn't. Oz didn't draw anything, just kind of doodled unhappily. Wendell, the young black man, didn't turn up. Sanford had a toothache, and a nurse called him out in the middle of class to have it pulled. A couple other men were sick. At the end of the class, she asked the group if things were okay. Nobody met her eyes, but Mike said, yes, everything was fine, they were glad she came. It didn't feel like a lie. It just didn't feel exactly true.

It was healthy, she supposed, to have her idealism flung back in her face now and then. It takes more than a few sheets of paper and a box of pastels to change things. Most lives don't change at all.

Tomorrow Horace and Bob would be leaving for Grand Lake Matagamon. She hardly knew him anymore. He'd pitched the new tent on the front lawn for practice and already selected the fifty trees that would be going with him. Mr. Outdoors. Over breakfast, she'd mentioned beaver traps, how trappers slide them into bogs, how Horace needed to be careful where he put his feet. Her eyes misted up when he crumbled his shredded wheat into his bowl, as though this were the last time they'd ever have breakfast together.

"It's not as though I'm going away forever," he said. "I'll be back in a week."

"You don't suppose the wild animals up there have rabies ..."

"I'll just take it as it comes," he said.

"Let me buy you a cell phone."

"I'm not going to stand in the middle of a bog with a phone up to my ear."

"Kaopectate," she said. "You need to take Kaopectate in case you get the runs."

"That's enough; I'm not going to die." He turned off the computer. "Can we run through this watering drill one last time?"

She already knew how to water those little stupids, but she went outside with him anyway.

"These over here," he touched a branch, "see how they're getting brown around the edges? In a few days, if you could rotate them to the front of the house. And when you water, they should be damp, but not so damp the water's streaming out. They need plant food next Wednesday if I'm not back by then. Ten pellets to a tree."

"You'll be back by then, won't you?"

"Just in case is all I'm saying. I might be held up. I still need to pack Cutter's lotion," he said. "The digging spade and axe. Extra tent poles. Long underwear. A woolen sweater, a line of rope for hanging wet clothes."

"Kaopectate," she said.

By six o'clock in the morning, he was ready. And by seven, he was on the road, with the memory of Beverly standing in the driveway next to the forsythia bush trying not to cry. By noon, he was on the outer rim of Boston. By six o'clock he was on the edge of the end of the world, calling Beverly one last time from a phone at Gram's Place in Millinocket.

By mid-morning of the next day, he and Bob were bouncing along a dirt road that led to the northern rim of Baxter State Park, a rental canoe strapped to the top of the truck; and by two o'clock that afternoon, Horace was standing on the edge of Grand Lake Matagamon, studying the map. The air was cold, more like March in Connecticut, the sky gray and socked in. He had on his wooly socks and sneakers, the red moose sweater that Beverly had found in a secondhand store, and a windbreaker over the top. His old brown woolen hat on his head.

Bob sat beside him looking out onto the water, nose raised delicately. The weather report had mentioned the possibility of mixed precipitation. Horace looked across the lake in the direction of the campsite where they were headed, three miles away; he reckoned they could make it by six. Four or five, more likely. He untied the canoe and slid it off the back of the truck, turned it over, and dragged it to the edge of the lake. His hands throbbed with cold. He pulled the rubberized bags out of the truck one by one and packed the canoe for extra stability so he'd be sitting in the bow facing backwards. Tent, clothes, food. Back and forth. Sturdy army surplus metal box filled with crackers and cheese. Axe. Spade. Trees. And finally, a medium-sized paper bag holding his last civilized meal, fresh from Gram's Place. Fried chicken, coleslaw, French fries, and a piece of lemon meringue pie.

Turning 360 degrees before sitting down, Bob crammed himself into a small space between the bags. As Horace paddled out onto the lake, a cold breeze blew in his face, a tinge of winter in it. The lake was huge and tranquil. Ahead of them swam a raft of twelve loons, their beaks parallel to the water, black and white plumage like lake shadows. One dived, and another. Horace couldn't really make out the details of the far shore where they were headed. Dark evergreen and brown blurred together. He'd never paddled a canoe alone, and it was a challenge to keep it pointing in the direction he wanted to go. Long-unused muscles woke up.

He thought of Beverly—it pained him to worry her. In the past when he'd heard people talk about callings, it had always sounded overwrought and grandiose. But he understood now that it was like falling in love, a kind of mental stampede toward one thing. A calling wasn't a subtle, delicate thing any more than love was. Poets put a good face on love, but it was a rout. Anyway, Beverly's work at the prison was far more dangerous than what she called his "adventure." Inmates could hold her hostage. They could track her down after they were released. He laid his canoe paddle over the gunwale and reached for a cracker. Popping one in his mouth, he thought he heard an odd sound. The air was too cold for thunder, but that's what it sounded like. Before he had time to think, the light on the water went yellowish and eerie, and the wind gathered force.

Get off, a voice in his head said.

He put the top back on the army box and secured the lid. All at once, the sky turned charcoal gray. He steered between dozens of dead stumps poking out of the water as the wind kicked up the water; drops of rain fell on his arm and quickly became pellets of ice collecting in the creases of the rubberized bags. Thunder exploded behind him, and the wind blew the canoe sideways.

His grandfather had always said the number-one rule when you were in a boat was, get the hell off the water in a thunderstorm. Many people lost their lives every year, he said, too stupid to find cover.

Only a second or two passed between the flash and the thunder. *Crackk!* Bob cowered and whined. A wave came up over the side and splashed in. Another flash of lightning and another crack of thunder, and the lake erupted into a high chop of white, churning and seething. Horace thought, *I'm going to die.* It was futile to paddle, but he kept it up, and to his surprise, washed up on the shore of a small island. Bob leapt from the boat, and they both ducked under a half-dead spruce as another flash sliced the sky. The wind blew and blew, and sheets of water curtained the lake. When it seemed it couldn't blow any harder, it did.

And then, miraculously, the interval between flash and thunder lengthened, and the storm turned to wet snow and then a steady drizzle. A tiny clearing in the sky gave way to another layer of brighter clouds. At last, thunder rumbled at a distance. Bob looked up from his station under the tree, and his tail thumped on the wet ground.

"Get up, Bob." Horace felt like whooping and hollering. His windbreaker clung to him, his brown wool hat was stuck to his head. Bob climbed back into the canoe, and Horace paddled in and out of a gallery of headless, dead trees. The loons had disappeared, and Horace thought if he could only find them, he still wouldn't know where he was, but he'd be comforted. He fumbled his way into a bag, his fingers too cold to work right, wiggled out the map, and had a look. He untied his shoelaces, took off his shoes, and laid his wet socks over one of the bags.

His toes were blue. He laid a tarpaulin over the tops of his feet, and when he looked at the map again, things began to make sense. He estimated that they were about a third of the way across. A patch of clear sky showed ahead, and suddenly he felt as happy as he'd ever felt in his life. He opened his mouth and sang: *Oh, the wayward wind is a restless wind!*

They arrived just before sunset. Horace put his wet socks and shoes back on and got the tent up. He stretched a clothesline between two trees and hung two rubberized food bags from the line so bears wouldn't get them. Lighting the Coleman lantern to see better, he got out a dry sweater, poured Bob's food into his dog dish, and brought their dinners into the tent. It felt like winter. The tent had a double door with no-see-um netting, and with the outer storm door unzipped, he could see perfectly to the lake; the sight stirred his soul, pine trees creaking in the wind, water lapping onto sand. He unwrapped his fried chicken and French fries and took the top off his little container of coleslaw and sat in front of the door, looking ahead to the lemon meringue pie packed in the bottom of the bag. *Oh, the wayward wind is a restless wind* . . . the best fried chicken he'd ever eaten. Bob lay in the tent, his fur steaming. Horace thumped his wet back. "We did it, Bob, you and me."

The clouds were mostly gone, and from the horizon up was dark pink, lighter pink, greenish yellow, blue and gray. Two contrails penciled across the sky. Bob suddenly sat up, looked out in the direction where the moon was rising, raised his chin, and howled. *A-woowoo wooooo.* Horace looked at him. "What are you doing?" Bob stopped as though he didn't know either. "Good dog." He patted him on the head and opened the container of pie, and just then he heard it. A throaty growl, a shuffling sound from behind the tent. "Shhh!" The shuffling moved around to the side. *Baboom baboom* went something beating on Horace's ribs from the inside out while his head grew large with terror. Without thinking, he unzipped the tent and threw the pie toward the lake. The footsteps stopped and started up again, and then he saw the bear a few feet in front of the tent, moving like a huge wooly dog. Shaggy baggy rear end, hulked up, matted with pine needles. He had only three legs. The bear reached the pie, opened the styrofoam container, and with one swipe of his tongue, finished it off. He stepped into the water and looked out toward the horizon, big burly bum, turned and walked up the shore.

I've seen a bear, thought Horace, *me, Horace, in the wild.* As a child, he'd had nightmares about bears, meeting them outdoors in the wild, running until his lungs exploded, yelling. His mother would come, shake him awake, tell him, *Don't worry, there aren't any bears.* But it wasn't true—they came back night after night. Horace slid down into his sleeping bag, not bothering to undress, and fell asleep at once.

The clouds rolled in again, the temperature went below freezing; Orion, the archer, moved across the sky, and it was morning. Horace stood on his sleeping bag in his bare feet and pulled on his soggy pants. Blowing on his hands, he stepped outside and noticed a little snow had fallen in the night and collected in low spots between the roots of trees. He also saw that the bear had knocked over the small plastic garbage can and helped himself to half the tub of dog food. Greasy, three-legged footprints led away from the campsite, back to the woods. Bad luck, Bob.

15

Crystals of ice clung to the shore of the lake that morning, like small bells. The search for black spruce began: where *Picea mariana* grows, other *Picea mariana* will grow. Horace found white spruce, birch, maple, oak, red pine, white pine—everything but black spruce. All day, he looked, returning to the campsite only as the light began to fade.

He built a large fire to keep the wildness away and heated water in an aluminum coffeepot; when it was boiling, he added it to a freeze-dried pouch, labeled LOUISIANA BEANS AND RICE. His mind turned toward Beverly, who'd be puttering about the brightly lit kitchen. He stood up, circled the perimeter of the campsite, and sat down again in front of the fire. He'd never known such stillness, although when he listened, it wasn't really still. Bob scratched a flea. A deep glottal sound came from the direction of the woods behind the tent—*garump, garump*—with a kind of loud swallowing before the *garump*, like a membrane moving clear of a throat. Bats skimmed through the dark trees, and the tamarack over his left shoulder whispered to itself. The sun sank into a bank of black clouds.

Horace got up and found his jacket in the tent. If it hadn't been for the bear, he'd have been at peace. A three-legged bear felt more dangerous to him than a four-legged one. Captain Hook. The lingering effects of trauma.

The trouble with fires was the way the shins got too hot and the back stayed cold. He felt something creep up his spine like the wing of a bat. Darkness fell behind him for miles upon miles until the hair on the back of his neck was too tired to stand up and he had to give in to it, the dark wild. In his mind's ear, his mother's favorite hymn came to him. *Now all the woods are sleeping, through fields the shadows creeping, while cities pause to rest . . .*

He pictured the exit he used to take from the hospital, the one he always had trouble getting off, semis trying to nudge him back onto open road when all he wanted was home. Was there such a world, where huge trucks hurtled down roads at eighty miles an hour? He could hardly believe it. The evening star came out, and he heard the call of a loon nearby, and then an answering loon—*Ah-wooooo*—to the left, and then stillness again.

He could have been the last man in the Western world. What would it be like to be responsible for passing on all of Western civilization, its history, literature, art, music? Whatever you couldn't remember would be consigned to the dust heap forever. He could hum a few tunes, describe Botticelli's *Birth of Venus*, Van Gogh's *Starry Night*, Picasso's *Guernica*, Brancusi's *The Kiss*. Recite a little Shakespeare.

> *I told you, sir, they were red-hot with drinking;*
> *So full of valour that they smote the air*
> *For breathing in their faces; beat the ground*
> *For kissing of their feet; yet always bending*
> *Towards their project. Then I beat my tabor;*
> *At which, like unback'd colts, they prick'd their ears,*
> *Advanc'd their eyelids, lifted up their noses*
> *As they smelt music . . .*

He still knew the whole speech. It amazed him. And the song he'd had to sing when he'd played Ariel in sixth grade. *Where the bee sucks, there suck I. In a cowslip's bell I lie . . . On a bat's back will I fly.* He'd been sent to a private school in Hartford for just one year until the money ran out, an all-boys' school with green lawns and brick buildings. He and his friends were horsing around in English class one day when Mr. Fletcher said, "We're going to put on a Shakespeare play," and the boys looked at him in disbelief, those sows' ears tumbling around. *The Tempest?*

Mr. Fletcher imported a girl from a neighboring school to play the part of Miranda. Cynthia was her name. Horace had desperately wanted to play Ferdinand opposite those beautiful shiny eyes, but Tony Spitelli got the part. Horace's second choice was Prospero, but Terrence Alexander, who always followed the rules, got that part. Horace was given Ariel against his will, and he'd had to wear a flimsy raiment around the shoulders that would make—Mr. Fletcher said—his footsteps into air.

A horrible boy named Brian got Caliban, which no one wanted. Brian looked perfectly at ease in the drunken scenes, and meanwhile Horace was meant to sing in a piping voice, *Where the bee sucks, there suck I. In a cowslip's bell I lie. There I couch when owls do cry.* It wasn't owls that scared Horace. It was Brian; and being laughed at, which he knew would happen on the night of the performance, and did.

They painted stumps of brown trees and the green of leaves on old General Electric washer and dryer boxes folded flat. The audience was lit from the stage lights, and during his cowslip bell song, Horace looked out and saw his own mother smiling, and then a great wave of laughter seemed to come from her throat and travel through the audience, and all at once he realized that his gossamer material had caught on the edge of the dryer box, and that was why he'd been unable to cross the stage. He wanted a bat to swoop down and take him far away on its back to the other side of the world where no one could ever find him again.

In front of him, a log cracked softly at first and then thumped down, jagged and fiery; as it did, sparks exploded into the air, crackling and glowing, like Ariel when he was finally released by his master and flew upward and could see for the first time beyond the tiny island he'd called home. Horace poked the burning pieces of log with a stick to make a heap of coals and thought of his own home so far away and what Beverly would be doing—maybe brushing her teeth with her purple toothbrush, or with one of her knees on the bed, ready to climb in, or already asleep, dreaming.

16

It stunned Beverly how sentimental she'd become. Horace had been gone only five days, and it felt almost as though he'd died. She'd been working all day and into the night on frames. Not her favorite thing, and not something she'd have done after supper if he'd been around. Before she went up to bed, she caught herself picking up a pair of his gloves and burying her nose in the leather palm. She didn't smell Horace, only the lingering smell of a hoofy animal, but it was the right smell, she thought, for what he'd become.

She picked up a stack of books she'd bought in a secondhand store that afternoon and carried them upstairs. Levering the heel of one shoe off with the toe of the other, she left both shoes under the chair, lying on their sides. She took off her clothes and flung them over a chair, pulled on a nightshirt, and went into the bathroom to brush her teeth. Normally, Bob would have followed her in, their last little ritual of the day, his toenails click-clicking across the tiles. She'd squeeze a little peppermint toothpaste out of the tube and offer it to him, and he'd lick it off her finger and make an odd face, and the following night, he'd be there next to the sink, wagging his tail again.

She climbed into their queen-sized bed, the end result of various bed phases she and Horace had weathered, starting with a double bed, evolving into two single beds in separate rooms because Horace thrashed and rumbled and ground his teeth. But one day while he was at work, she'd bought a queen-sized bed and had it delivered because it was too lonely without him in the same bed.

A number of years had passed since they'd made love. Desire had faded like the color of her hair—rich brown, and then by degrees, less shiny and dark. Their bodies were a comfort to each other, but nothing more. Of course, some people kept it up into their seventies and eighties, but not the two of them. *Okay*, she said out loud, *okay*. If someone had asked her what was okay, she wouldn't have known. She spoke the word to fill the absence of Horace's hand reaching out from his book and smoothing the hairs of her arm closest to him.

Leaning over, she picked up *The Bog People* by a man named Glob. She'd bought it, of course, because of the title, and she was only going to read a couple of pages, but the more she read, the more she couldn't stop. In the Middle Ages, men and women had drowned in bogs all over Europe: stumbling into them, drunk or stupid, or thrown there for their sins or as offerings to gods. The first picture in the book was of the Tollund Man, who wore a tidy little peaked cap of leather, sewn with eight seams. His face was beautiful and gentle, tanned, like a piece of leather. His eyes were lightly closed, laugh lines at the outer edge of each, the eyelashes perfectly preserved. There was a vein at his temple, and his forehead was wrinkled, as though he'd been puzzling through something as he died. She studied his curved nose, the sweetness of his mouth—his lips pursed a little. He'd been naked. She loved the way his feet were curled like a boy's, his ankle bones, his toes. She imagined how he might have tucked his feet under him at night as he sat in front of a fire. Everything was gentle, serene, until her eyes traveled down to the leather noose about his neck.

Connecticut was experiencing an unseasonable warm spell,

and she had just the sheet over her. Her hands sweated as she stared at the noose, and she wondered what he'd done that they'd done this to him. Her mind turned to a few of the men in the prison group. In another age, they might have met a similar fate, dragged naked from their beds of straw and drowned in a bog.

How would they have come for him? Would he have been surprised, or was he expecting something in his black dreams? The house creaked in the wind, and she had to turn the page. It was the acid in the water, Mr. Glob said, that preserved the bodies. Sometimes the water was so acidic it pulled the calcium right out of the bones so all that was left was skin, flat as a rug. After they found him in the bog, they took the Tollund Man to a museum in Copenhagen where people stared at him in a glass case. It seemed unfair, naked and vulnerable as he was. She wouldn't want anyone to see her when she was dead. It was meant to be private, like being in the bathroom. In Copenhagen, Danish schoolchildren would stare into the glass, their reflections mingling with his face. They'd go home and drink milk and have nightmares about him. None of them would see the sweetness of his mouth in the face of that shuddery, satisfying, gruesome thing that he'd become.

She turned another page and came to a picture of a young girl from Windeby, England, who'd been pulled from a different bog. She was holding a long stick, and over her shoulder was a bag that looked like a wing. One arm was drawn back, and her legs were parted as though she'd been flying when she sank.

The book reminded her of a picture in her fourth-grade geography book of an Egyptian mummy. She remembered the bandages that went round and round the Thing inside. That mummy—it was worse than dead, a kind of mega-dead that traveled forward into a future where it shouldn't have been. She couldn't have said back then what drew her to it. Death was part of it certainly. How people die, how they decompose, what happens to skin, to brains, to lips, to eyes. She was no different from any other gawker. How do we die? What happens then? And then? And then?

She slept. And in the morning, rose to go to the prison feeling hungover. The bog book, the heat, but especially the thought of going in there, behind those horrible metal doors, sickened her. She rehearsed their names. Clinton, Mike, Charlie . . . She went downstairs but didn't feel like eating. She went out and watered the front-yard trees and got on the highway.

Oz was waiting for her in the classroom, his bulk taking up the space of two men. "How are you doing?" she asked.

He looked at his feet. "My girlfriend dumped me."

"I'm sorry, Oz."

"Yeah, thanks."

"If I can do anything for you . . ."

"I'm getting out soon."

"When?"

But Leon came around the corner. "I've got that tape player you asked for," he said, handing it to her. "Hey, Oz." Oz wandered off. Men filed in. Wendell—she was surprised to see him back. Kurt, Sanford, Mike. The sun was shining outdoors, and you could feel spring breaking in. Clinton set down a vanilla layer cake he'd made in the kitchen. He was a large, bald man, clumsy in body and mind, with thick, taped glasses that took up half his face. He'd brought paper plates and plastic forks, but the others told him they didn't want any. It tore at her, reminded her of kids in her elementary school no one would sit next to because they had lice. She made herself take a piece. *Rapist*, she thought, with the first bite of bone-dry cake. How to square that with Clinton, the man, lonely, maybe sorry for all the people he'd hurt.

She gave them photocopies of ancient trees out of a picture book—a different tree for each person. "You can render this photograph in a drawing, change it in some way," she said, "or use it as a basis for something else. Or simply see where your hand wants to go.

"Think about your paper as the frame of a camera. Experiment with that edge." She picked up a piece of chalk and drew half of a squirrel on the edge of the blackboard. She laughed. "I've never been any good at squirrels." They looked at her. She felt suddenly awkward. "I brought some music to get us going." She put a tape in the tape player, but the machine didn't work. She messed around with it, and gave up on it. Kurt tried and couldn't get it going either. "Forget it," she said.

The men helped themselves to paper, and she looked out in the hall, thinking she'd seen Oz lumbering toward the classroom, but it wasn't him after all. She picked up a piece of paper and pen and a couple of pastels and began to draw. What emerged was a sea of spring green, with the color of fire bang up against it. It gave her a kind of a sick feeling; she didn't know why. She felt bad for Oz, wished he was here to let his own hand lead him out. After a couple of years inside, she had no idea how you'd even begin to find your way out.

17

A state car drove him down the long entry road to the main road, and the officer opened the door and wished him good luck. Oz was wearing prison-regulation blue jeans and a T-shirt—he had no idea what happened to his own clothes. He didn't remember anything about the night they brought him in. He walked out to the traffic circle and stuck out his thumb. The traffic was steady, but no one stopped. He kept walking out to a straight stretch and stuck out his thumb again, and finally someone in a pickup pulled over. Oz looked into his face and saw a drooping mouth and disappointed eyes.

"Where you headed?" he asked.

"New London."

"Jump in."

Oz hesitated. "I just got out of prison."

"If you want a ride, get in."

Oz jumped in and slammed the door.

"Drugs?" the guy asked.

"Yeah."

"I have a buddy's in down state for that."

He told Oz he was a day laborer, hoping to learn welding and maybe land an indoor job for the winter. He had three kids—a teenage daughter and two younger boys. The youngest had a hearing problem, and he and his wife couldn't get the school to give him the help he needed. His eyes smoldered. "Fucking bureaucrats. That's all they are."

When Oz got where he was going, the guy reached in his wallet and took out a $20 bill.

"I'm okay," said Oz.

"C'mon, take it; pass it on to someone else when you get on your feet."

Jesus. His own father had never given him a present like that. "Thanks," he mumbled. "I appreciate it. I really do." The guy roared off as though his heart embarrassed him, and Oz watched the back of the truck disappear around a corner. He walked to Eddie's apartment and sat on the steps and watched cars go by, waiting for his friend to come home. Dandelions grew on the lawn, and the grass was already a few inches high. A weird, sad feeling crept up the back of his knees, up his backbone. People could go wherever they wanted out here. *Bad lives and a broken heart*, went a Tom Waite song. *Meet you at the bottom of a bottle of scotch. Name your prison.*

He waited an hour or two until Eddie finally roared in the driveway. "Fucking hell," he said, getting out of a rusted wreck. "I missed you, you fucker." They went inside, and Eddie fixed him a cup of coffee, as though he'd never been away. The wastebasket smelled like something had died in there.

"What about that girl you used to be with?" said Eddie.

"It's over."

"The bitch."

"No, you've got it wrong. What about you? You seeing anyone?"

"Nah."

"So what's happening?"

"I'm thinking of heading south—you wanna come?"

"I don't know."

"I'm going down to the Keys. I heard you could make three thousand a month waiting tables. Good Mexican dope, cheap. Everything's supposed to be cheap."

"I don't know. Maybe." He'd watched a TV program in prison about people diving off Key West and thought he might be a diver when he got out. Suit himself up in rubber, kick his feet down down into a world that few humans were lucky enough to see. He recalled the clouds of bright blue fish, the fingers of coral.

"I've got Peruvian," said Eddie. "Want some?"

"Sure."

When it hit, they went up a hill behind Eddie's place. As the ego floats away, the mind sharpens. Clean burn. Eddie went on ahead. The hill was covered with tin cans that turned to moons, moons to stumble over, and they laughed and the sky was blue black but not one solid color, streaks of it like it was boiling the color out of the top of the hill in watery ribbons, and after, he didn't remember what he said or what Eddie said, but he remembered when they got to the top, swear to God, a brown horse was standing there, his muzzle whitened with age, big sad eyes looking at them coming toward him, kicking past those moons. He looked into the face of the horse and heard a song coming out of the eyes: his father's voice.

He slept at Eddie's that night; when he woke late morning, he felt like crap, stale, cabbage-headed, right back where he'd been before prison. He found Eddie drinking a Bud in the kitchen, and he slipped out after telling him he wasn't coming south. Diving didn't seem practical. You'd need money for equipment and a course, and besides, he didn't want to be with Eddie doing the same old shit, just transported south.

He hitched downtown, bought a bagel with the twenty in his pocket, and ate it on a park bench. The pigeons gathered at his feet, shiny new with their iridescent neck feathers and smart beaks. He took out a piece of paper and drew one that stood a little apart from the rest of the flock. As he was leaving, he emptied sesame seeds and bits of garlic out of the bagel bag and turned back to see the small flock eating what he'd left. As an afterthought, he took the drawing out of his pocket, put it on the park bench, and anchored it with a couple of stones.

A man walked down a path from another direction, his face tattooed like a jaguar, black and yellow. He passed, and Oz turned around. The man looked normal walking away from him. He'd never seen anything like that jaguar man. He turned around again, but the man had disappeared.

He headed out of the park into a seedier part of town. There was something oppressive in the muzzy sky trying to give birth to sun, in the shoes of a kid scuffling along the pavement, his life already finished. It was necessary to find something to live for: One of his buddies in prison hooked a hose up to the exhaust of his car the winter he got out. Another was stabbed outside a bar in Boston and died in an emergency room. Mostly, though, they just came back to prison—one day they were gone, and then one day, there they were again.

He thought if he could find his way to the river . . . he and Eddie used to hitch up Mohegan Avenue and then cut west. Another lifetime it was.

He stuck out his thumb, and a kid picked him up. He got out when the road turned north, walked to another road, and got picked up by an older woman. It surprised him that she'd stopped—she had a hat with a black rim and white polka dots, and under it, dyed black hair and a pouchy face. A drinker. She told Oz she was going to the wedding of her nephew. Looked as though she'd seen trouble but knew how to float above it. It felt good just being around her, like sometimes you're walking along in the cold, and across your path comes a warm patch of air.

The road looked familiar even though he wasn't sure where

he was, and about ten miles up, he thanked her and got out. He stood by the side of the road and watched the low blue car draw away. A robin sang in a clearing. He tried to get his bearings, walked a little further, and turned down a dirt road. The path was torn up from four-wheelers, but it looked right. And there, around a bend and down a steep hill, was the place he'd pictured all these months. He could hardly believe it was here, real, in front of him, the current moving lazy near the shore, fast out in the middle. In the mud at his feet was the footprint of a raccoon. And a green leaf floating upside down in the water, curled a little and turning around and around, like it was saying, *Where am I?*

"What's Happening Here?" Wynton Marsalis played that tune. It was the first cassette he ever got—from his mom for his birthday. He played it over and over until the tape unraveled onto the floor. Every now and then, there'd be a throaty edge come out of the trumpet when it rose higher, but mostly it was low, the way a voice sounds just before it speaks its last words at night, husky, the fight gone out of it, when all you want to say is, *Who cares, just be quiet.* What he wouldn't give to play a trumpet like that.

He picked up a stick and doodled in the mud. It was smooth as paper, and he drew a hand, then Lucy's face. She wasn't smiling.

Caw, caw, went a crow in a tree.

Caw, caw, he answered.

Silence. And then with a scrawk and a screaming through air, it came toward him, midnight on wings, and beyond, more crows gathered in the air and cried. The bird made one more pass over Oz's head, and then he and the other crows were gone. From a nearby pine came a drowsy-tender crow sound, like a mother with a cigarette cough tending a baby. Over beyond, a few leaves were still lit. He took his shirt off, one sock off, other sock off, smooth mud. Pants off. That wind out of nowhere, ease down the bank. Just go, water over the knees, over thighs, crotch, waist, don't think. He lurched off one foot, fell backward and swam underneath, the breath knocked out of him by water cold as mile-high sky.

18

The cart that Lucy pushed around the New London library three days a week had a squeak. Wherever she went down the aisles, she announced herself. And whenever she heard herself coming, she saw herself pushing a cart down the aisles. She could never get into her own thoughts and away from the picture of her doing this job, her hands on the handle of the cart, the Dewey decimals lying spine up, her eyes trying to make out the numbers, reaching and kneeling, reaching and kneeling. Every now and then, she passed Gwen, her friend, pushing another cart. They'd met on the job. Gwen was twenty-two and hoping to teach science in an American school in Bulgaria in the fall. "Take me with you," said Lucy.

Mrs. Mavarones, the librarian, was a Mormon with a downturned mouth. When she typed on her computer, she went so fast you couldn't see her fingers; she never made a mistake on the keyboard, or anywhere else. Lucy made all sorts of mistakes— shelving mistakes, mistakes with library patrons, pointing them toward the 300's when they wanted the 900's. *I hate my job,* said Lucy under her breath, squeaking down the aisle toward the cookbooks. She held a book up under the light and turned her head to get a better look at the numbers. Mrs. Mavarones ate the same thing for lunch every day: sardines out of a can on two slices of pumpernickel bread, with a piece of fruit for dessert. After lunch, she smelled like a fish for the rest of the day. She had nervous, thin hands and a mole on her cheek that sprouted four dark whiskers. In the interview for the job, Mrs. Mavarones had asked her whether she'd ever worked in a library before, and Lucy had lied and said yes, even though she'd disliked Mrs. Mavarones from the moment she'd met her, but it was exactly as her mother had said—when you drop out of college, you have to take what you can get. Anyway, she hadn't exactly dropped out. She'd finished the first year and wasn't going back next year. What happened after that was an open question. And this job still beat what her mother did—stocking shelves with perfumed chickadee candles.

Once, she'd said to her mother, "You could do more with your life, Mom. You're smart. I don't know anyone who knows as many languages as you do."

"That doesn't mean anything," her mother had said. "It doesn't take intelligence to learn languages. It's just a knack I have. I only learned them because your grandfather was in the service and we moved all over Europe."

"You're not hearing what I'm saying, Mom."

"You're embarrassed by me, by what I do."

"Stop it, that's not it. You could be a translator. You could live in Spain or Greece or Italy and teach languages, do interesting things."

"I don't want to."

"Why not?"

"Maybe I'll do something different when Rusty dies."

Rusty was an old dog with molt on his haunches. The last time Lucy heard from her mother, she'd gotten a new puppy to keep Rusty company. Now it would never happen. Her life would be a monument to Rusty, and now to Waffles, or Wuffles, or whatever that new dog was called.

She replaced the book on the cart and squeaked down the aisle to Birds, where she wedged *Companion Parrot Handbook* onto a tight shelf. Not that she was doing anything with her life, but that was different. She was still young and screwed up the way you're allowed to be until twenty-five or so. She *would* do something, though. She damn well would.

In the World War II section, she replaced *Ghosts of the Skies*. All at once, *The Long Walk: The True Story of a Trek to Freedom* jumped out at her. Its cover was in shades of gray, crisscrossed with barbed wire. Rawicz, the author, had been arrested in 1939, taken prisoner in a Soviet camp, and with the help of the camp commander's wife, escaped with five other men. Turning the pages, she could hardly believe what they'd endured—crossed the Gobi desert without a container to hold water, ate thick black snakes to survive.

She kept *The Long Walk* open and squeaked over to the 380's to shelve *Legendary Lighthouses, Volume II*. She'd learned that when the wheels of the cart stopped turning for more than a couple of minutes, Mrs. Mavarones would be all over her; if she wanted to read anything, Lucy kept to the less-traveled parts of the library and wheeled forward and backward while turning the pages. She was in Mathematics and Natural Science now, where few people came. She passed through Celestial Mechanics into Mathematical Geography as she read about the six men in *The Long Walk*— wait, they'd picked up a girl on their way, and now she was sick in the desert. Lucy skipped ahead a few pages. The girl was dying, and then she was dead.

She passed Gwen with the squeaking cart, through Solid Mechanics, and on into Sound & Vibrations, and stopped. The men fled through the Himalayas, far higher than people can usually go without oxygen. Lucy dropped to the floor with the book and sat cross-legged beside the cart. She skipped ahead again. They made it to India, three thousand miles from where they'd set out, emaciated, covered with lice, and villagers greeted them and cared for them and brought them back to life. She imagined Oz escaping, arriving in her apartment, a broken leg from a leap into a river. She'd nurse him back to health, he'd change his name, they'd move to Montana and have a baby.

He was trouble, her mother said. She'd got that right. But you can't be alive, the kind of life that surges right out of your skin, without being trouble. Nothing boxed in, held back, smothered and strapped down. When she looked around, she saw people who were half alive, like lumps of mud. Oz reminded her to live all the way; he was a hard rain, a plow in rocky ground, a car on the outside curve. She saw him with a plate of food, leaning forward to smell what was there, a look on his face. *Ah, good. Yum.*

She remembered a time when she was in high school, Oz slipped up the back stairs onto the sleeping porch where she had her bed, while her mother slept. "Lucy?" she heard in the darkness. "Are you awake?"

"You're cold," he said, taking off his jeans, but it wasn't cold—she was shaking with something else. He slipped under the quilts. He was the first person who ever thought she was beautiful.

He called it radiance; she told him she was afraid.

"Shhh," he said, kissing her on the lips. "There's nothing to be afraid of. I love you, baby." The flame began slowly, her arms and legs around him. She had her period, but she couldn't wait for anything. He pressed a hand, warm, hard, against her hip. Oh. She didn't think at all. I want you. Hurry.

It was quick, not what she expected. Thinking back, she couldn't remember what she'd felt. Fear. Shyness. Relief. Was that all? The thing she remembered best was what happened afterward. She'd left the tampon in and needed to get it out. She crept to the bathroom, past her mother's room, while he waited out in the bed on the screened porch. Everything was slick with love;

she couldn't get hold of the string. She got scared and went back to the porch and climbed back into bed beside him. "I'll have to go the hospital!" she cried.

"What? What are you talking about?"

"The tampon I was wearing. The string. It's gone." It was the first emergency they'd ever faced together, and she still loved him for what he did next: laughed. And put his hands inside her hair and brought her head close to his chest, and suddenly it was all right. She went back to the bathroom and got a hold of the string, washed herself. What did she know?

Her mother called it young love. Yes, she was young then, but that didn't mean she couldn't be in love. They'd lain out on the sleeping porch, the ice settling onto the trees. They burrowed under the quilts and warmed themselves on sparks.

Lucy smelled fish, raised her head, and found Mrs. Mavarones standing over her. "What are you doing?" she heard.

"Taking my fifteen-minute break," said Lucy.

"You've already had your afternoon break," said Mrs. Mavarones.

"That was my lunch break."

"No, you went outdoors. In fact, you were five minutes late coming back."

Lucy closed *The Long Walk*. *I hate you*, she thought, *you big sardine*.

Two hours later, she was out the door and on her way home, walking with Gwen, who lived in her neighborhood. Gwen was telling her about how she'd driven her parents' Chevy onto a raised road divider in the middle of the night, scraping off the muffler. She'd almost saved up $250 for Bulgaria, but now she had to start again.

"Is that what mufflers cost?" asked Lucy.

"More than that. It really wasn't my fault either. The sign looked like it was pointing right at the divider."

"That's too bad."

"What about *you?*"

"Okay." It often went this way. They'd talk about Gwen on the way home, and ten feet from where they said good-bye, Gwen would ask her how she was. Dimly, Lucy was aware that it wasn't meant to be like this, but today, she didn't really give a damn.

"See you," said Lucy, heading toward the river. She'd moved from her old apartment finally, away from the landlord who spied on her, who looked up albinism on the web and told her what he'd found, as though she didn't know. It was creepy to hear him talking about her as though she were a chloroformed frog.

Stopping in at a neighborhood store, she bought RyKrisp, cheese, and a green apple. When she came out, swinging her bag, the sun was low in the sky, with golden light gilding the seedy tenement buildings. Today, she missed Oz, missed him the way Ceres longed for Persephone in the underworld: so sad, the crops failed, and the earth withered and blistered in the sun.

19

Horace sat up in his sleeping bag and saw his breath at first light, while out behind his tent, the birds went crazy. *Peewee peewee. Chewy, chewy. Wa-wa-wa-wa-waaaa.* And then out of a silence, clear and true, came the five notes of the white-throated sparrow. There it went again, the clear notes thrown into the new day like a question. The lake looked forlorn, stretching cold and misty to the end of time. He unzipped the tent, put on his shoes, and stepped out, rubbing his hands together for warmth. The water he'd left in a coffee mug on a stump had turned to ice. Bob muscled past him and peed against a tree.

The day before, he'd planted his first nine trees, but he didn't feel good about it. His idea had been to find other black spruces and tuck his trees between the others. In the absence of black spruces, he'd found a boggy place behind the tent surrounding a fetid-looking pond and thought they'd be happy there—but would they?

Horace sat down on a log to eat his cereal. He had a bite and another bite, and he worried about whether he'd made a poor decision. *Forget it,* he kept telling himself. *You did the best you could.* But perhaps he'd been lazy. Perhaps he hadn't explored enough, hadn't wanted to face going home without having planted any. Wasn't this pretty much what he'd done his whole life? The line of least resistance? *Stop it,* the voice said. And then the face of Timothy Edward Stearns flashed before him, and he thought, uh-oh.

Years before, Horace and Beverly had meant to have a child, but it turned out there was a problem with Horace's sperm. They tried for several years, and one day Beverly said it was no one's fault, and they could have a perfectly good life without children. "Look at Cleopatra," she'd said.

"What does she have to do with it?" Horace asked.

"She had a rich, full life without children."

"I'm not Anthony, and you're not Cleopatra."

"I'm trying to tell you it's all right, darling. I think we should forget it."

But then a minister told one of Beverly's friends that a sixteen-year-old girl was looking for parents for her baby. When Horace came home from work one day, Beverly had made pot roast and mashed potatoes and green beans and a lemon pudding. She hadn't burned anything, as though to say, "See? I'm as competent as anyone." Over dessert, she mentioned the baby in an offhand way. Her eyes went soft under her glasses. *There's this baby*, she said, as though she was telling a story that had nothing to do with her. Horace had seconds and thirds of pudding. But it didn't register until too late that she'd been saying they might be parents.

Michael and Rosalie Stearns ended up with the baby, and Timothy Edward Stearns grew up the next town over, went to Bucknell, and became a landscape architect in Minneapolis. Horace was a judge at a science fair when he met the boy, who was then nine years old. His coloring was high and healthy, and his entry had to do with sand dunes.

Horace remembered a snatch from the Episcopalian prayer book of his youth, something the whole congregation had intoned, getting slower and slower like a great wheel grinding through a field—*We have done those things which we ought not to have done, and we have left undone those things which we ought to have done, and there is no health in us.* When he'd been young, it was the things he'd done that were worst—broken windows, India ink on a white tablecloth—but as he'd aged, it was the other way around. If he could turn the clock back to that moment when he had his face in his third helping of pudding . . . *Sweet, sweet peabody peabody peabody,* went the white-throated sparrow.

Maybe it was just as well—he might have been a lousy father. But then again, that was an easy way to let himself off the hook. He had a last swallow of coffee, threw the dregs over his shoulder, and stood up. It wasn't something he and Beverly ever talked about.

Dipping his camping saucepan into the lake, he brought water to the remaining trees. The wind was picking up. Across the lake was Mount Katahdin, snow still covering its summit and shoulders. He sat down on a stump and spread the geological survey map out on his lap, his hands fumble-fingered with cold, and decided to proceed westward.

He loaded the day pack with the map and compass, a bottle of water, nuts, peanut-butter crackers, and dog chewies, whistled up Bob, and started along the shore. At first, the going was easy, but further on, the scrubby bushes crowded in next to the water. Horace wore his heavy moose sweater, long johns under his pants, and his brown wooly hat. As they walked, the ground grew wetter until he found a stream leading to the right, and beside it a path—hardly a path, more like a depression—with the print of deer here and there. Bob plunged down it, nose skimming the ground while Horace followed, stopping at a tamarack fallen across the path. When he looked up, he saw at a distance what he thought might be a stand of black spruce.

His heart quickened at the sight of the tall trees at the edge of an open area, with untidy dead branches halfway up their trunks. They had bottle-brush tufts of gray green on top and reminded him of the pictures he'd seen in the library. Not exactly majestic, but he found himself strangely affected by them: you looked into their high, blasted branches and were reminded of Don Quixote, with his rackety bones and weathered face. *Survivors.* The eccentrics of the forest.

Near him, young evergreens grew. Were they related to the tall ones? He examined the needles: short and stiff, blue-green, four-sided in cross section. Cones: oval, half an inch to an inch long. Bark: thin, scaly. He let out a whoop and did a small, hoppy dance. "I've found them, I've found them!"

Bob, exploring down the path at a distance, barked and ran back to see what was going on. He found his master staring into a small tree. The tree stood about four feet tall, growing in a perfect cone shape. Behind it was a smaller one, with a bird's nest in its branches. "Little beauties," he said, husky-throated. The trees stood there shoulder to shoulder, a few shorter, a few taller, like companions to each other.

For a few moments, he was Neil Armstrong on the moon, he was Roald Amundsen at the South Pole, Tenzing Norgay at the summit of Everest with Sir Edmund Hillary. His was a small achievement, he knew. The name, Horace Woodruff, wouldn't be appearing in the Academy of Achievement anytime soon. But he'd done this himself, crossed an unknown lake, survived thunder and lightning and bear and biting insects, and found what he'd set out to find. He couldn't recall a single moment in his life when he'd achieved something like this, unless it was asking Beverly to marry him and hearing her say yes.

He looked toward the large spruces in the distance. Even if he left this place today and never came back, he'd feel them swaying, somewhere in him.

Under his feet were deep tracks of moose leading down the stream. They ran along straight and suddenly plunged off in a different direction, hundreds of pounds shifting weight and turning toward the high black spruces.

He hadn't brought his spade or any trees along, but as he explored the little clearing, he thought it could take at least a dozen trees spaced out. He crouched down to look at the ground covering—thick sphagnum moss, and under that, roots. It was getting colder by the minute, and out of the air, something fell in front of his eyes. At first he didn't recognize it, and then . . . God almighty, snow. He retraced his steps with Bob, the wind and snow in his face, and when they returned to the campsite, he made for the tent, took off his wet boots, and crawled into the sleeping bag. The birds had grown quiet. It was a lonely place with the wind rising and the snow turning everything to its will. He imagined them finding him here several years from now, bones in a bag—Woodruff's last expedition.

It snowed the rest of the day and into the night, and by next morning, the air snapped with cold. The sky was clear, the lake calm and quiet. "Let's get out of here," he said to Bob. He put on his boots, unzipped the tent, and stood outside, snow above his ankles. Bob goofballed around upside down, legs in the air, tunneling his nose forward under the snow. Horace packed forty-one trees back into the canoe. *Not what I expected, not what I expected,* the reptilian part of his brain said.

All the way to the other shore, paddling in his leather driving gloves, he thought of Beverly; with every stroke closer, his regret deepened. He imagined starting over, making it up to her somehow, but he didn't have the faintest idea how one did that. He could hear her voice—*Silly old thing.* Bob sat in the bow, his head looking forward. *If you were a dog,* thought Horace, *you'd always be starting over.* As soon as you forgot something, you started over.

Several hours later, arms aching, he pulled the canoe out of the water onto the snowy bank. He'd packed warm gloves, but he hadn't seen them the whole trip. His driving gloves had a leak in them where cold and water had poured through, and one finger had lost all feeling. He unpacked the boat and slid the trees into the covered back of the truck. Next, all the gear. Turning the canoe over, he got under and walked with little steps, unable to see, feeling with his shoes for rocks, set the stern upright on the ground behind the truck, and pushed the canoe up. The first time he'd tried this, he could barely get it up. It still wasn't pretty, the way his arms shook.

The truck heater went full bore as he and Bob bounced down the dirt access road, and the feeling in his finger returned. He dropped the canoe off at the rental place, thinking it was time to spring for his own canoe—with four more trips, he'd have paid for the price in rental fees. He stopped at Gram's Place on the way south and ordered fish chowder, a toasted cheese sandwich, and lemon meringue pie. He felt sleepy and bilious as he climbed into the cab of the truck next to Bob. By Ellsworth, Horace needed a nap by the side of the road. *Nine trees,* a voice in his head said as he nodded off, *you'll have to do better than that.*

"You're home!" Beverly cried as Horace dragged in the door. All he could think about was sleep.

"I'm sorry," he said.

"What're you talking about?"

"I can't explain." *Timothy Edward Stearns.* He was too tired; things were suddenly less clear, his culpability fuzzed into affection.

"Bob!" she said. "Come here!" She scratched him behind his ears and turned back to Horace. "Look at you. You're a mess."

"It snowed yesterday. I only planted nine trees in all."

They unpacked the truck, and he sank into a bath. Who was that person who canoed across the lake in a thunderstorm, set up a tent, dug nine holes and tucked trees into them, cooked packets of dried food with labels like LOUISIANA BEANS AND RICE and HEARTY STEW WITH BEEF over a campfire, explored the environs, slept while snow blanketed the tent? *Someone else,* he thought, looking at his pale, slack tummy rounded over the bathwater.

Beverly paced outside the bathroom, called through the door, and finally came in and sat on the toilet seat. She looked at Horace, his brown, furry eyebrows giving way hair by hair to gray. *You can't hold onto things,* her mother said when she was a girl, that spring when the ocean took away the rock in the high bank that held the nest where the three baby gulls sat with their mouths open.

Horace had soaped up his balding head, and now he was holding his breath and going under. And then he was back out again, water streaming from his shoulders. They were rosy and young-looking from the warm water. He opened his eyes, turned and looked toward her, as though he was expecting her to say something.

"What?" she asked.

"Nothing. You're a sight for sore eyes."

The Tollund Man came into her head. Probably someone had loved him too. A wife or daughter had sewn his little peaked hat for him, had missed him when he was gone.

20

"It makes no sense," said Beverly.

"I'm going to wait for the weather to warm," said Horace.

"No sense no matter *when* you go back. How many left?"

"991 . . . no, 989. Two died."

"Let's send them back, sweetheart."

They were sitting on the front steps, the sky darkening with an oncoming shower. Horace turned his whole body toward her. A drop of rain pinged off the end of his nose.

"Well, I'm coming with you then," she said.

"If you want to."

"I don't."

"All right then."

"Why not hire some high school students to help you?"

He thought about it a moment. "I don't know anything about teenagers. They frighten me. It gives me a stomachache just thinking about it. They'd tip over the canoe, they'd stumble over the trees and break off branches, they'd scream and jump in the lake and waste food."

"If you wanted to, you *could* find someone."

"I don't want to find anyone. You're the only person whose company I can stand. Anyway, I don't need to rush. One tree at a time."

It was raining steadily now, and still they sat on the steps. "When are you going back?"

"The snow will be gone by mid-May."

"Promise me you'll get a weather radio and not set out across the lake if there's a storm coming." Her voice grew passionate. "Horace! You'll have at least one hot meal a day?"

"Yes, all right."

That night, he ground his teeth in bed, and in the morning, he went out and counted trees. He made a five-column chart of their condition, rated on a scale from poor to excellent; day by day, the "poor" column grew as the "excellent" shrank. He called nurseries for advice, experimented with plant food, snipped off brown tips. One night, his grinding was so bad Beverly had to move down to the couch. The next night, his feet began to vibrate.

While he was out watering trees one afternoon, Beverly dragged a single bed mattress into their bedroom and made it up on the floor.

"*I'm* sleeping there," he said that night.

"You're sleeping in a real bed while you're here."

"I'm used to the ground."

"Well get *un*used to it." She took her pillow and moved to the mattress and looked out at the calm night. From where she lay, she could see a few stars, faded in suburban lights. Above her, Horace's foot jiggled the bed. He'd cooked scrambled eggs for dinner, a first. He was trying hard. He was here, but his feet were already walking north.

A week later, he was back in the truck with Bob, fifty trees neatly loaded behind the cab.

21

Bog, verb. To fill with water and sink, as in bogged down. 2)
Bog, noun. An herbaceous area where land and water meet. 3) Bog fever.
A border of the mind where sanity and madness meet. He'd heard
about blackflies but had never encountered them. They went for
the corners of his eyes and the back of his neck and up his pant
leg, crawled under his clothing, and hacked out pieces of flesh.
They ripped and gouged and traveled in packs like a gang of
chain-saw massacre-ists. Everything they touched turned to raw
meat.

It was an early spring day without wind, on the muggy side.
He slid off his knapsack and got out the bug dope. He slathered
it over his neck, rubbed some around Bob's collar, and the two
of them left the campsite and pushed off onto the lake, carrying
a couple of trays of trees. Around the corner, the boat startled a
great blue heron; it took off with a sweep of outstretched wings,
circled the end of the lake, and came back to the starting point.
He imagined a camera panning away from them like a helicop-
ter rising, until he and Bob grew smaller and smaller, tiny specks
in a wilderness of white spruce and hardwood forests and marsh-
land and open water and sky.

He and Bob headed for the place he'd discovered on their
last trip, just before it started to snow. They canoed westward

along the shore and turned in where the stream led to the right. He located the fallen tamarack, and beyond, the group of black spruces. All morning, flies climbed into his shirt and swarmed around his eyes, and he understood for the first time how men went mad in the woods. If he'd had a cannon, he would have fired it off in all directions. He wanted to take more care over the trees, but he dug as fast as he could dig, threw in compost, got the tree in the ground, went on to the next. By two in the afternoon, he was covered with welts and had planted fourteen trees and used up all the available open space in the clearing.

The next morning, with another load of trees, he turned up the same tributary and paddled between the narrow banks past the area where he'd planted the day before. At a beaver dam, the stream gave way to a marshy heath. He and Bob forded a clattery heap of beaver-chewed sticks while blackflies circled their heads. While he tied the canoe to the bough of a tree, Bob bounded toward a small pond; all at once, Horace noticed that he was stepping oddly: the land was moving like the back of a whale. "Bob, get over here!"

Bob kept going, his nose to the ground, and Horace crept closer. He put one foot on the vegetation and felt it roll—it looked like land and moved like water.

Near his boot, a fly buzzed in the throat of a pitcher plant. Horace peered down the trap and saw a bug drowning in sticky liquid. Heat, collected in the water and moss, rose up his ankles and swirled up his pant legs. He jounced up and down, and the earth under him moved; he stepped out a little further and jounced again. Down on his hands and knees, he pushed his hand down through matted greenery, trying to find water, but all he reached were tangled roots. Small shrubs and pitcher plants grew, and something that looked like miniature orchids. Before him stretched the pond, a stagnant emerald eye.

Ankle deep in sphagnum moss, water up to his ankles, he realized that small *Picea mariana* were growing all around him. He backtracked toward the stream and carried the spade and an armload of trees toward the whale's back. He tried digging a hole or two with his spade, but the roots and moss held fast. He considered for a moment, knelt down, and made the beginnings of a hole with his hands, pushing roots aside, working until the tangle would take one of the small trees. He dug as fistfuls of flies flew up and sweat ran down his neck. His face was stained with tea-colored water. All day, he counted off the trees he'd planted, seventeen, eighteen, nineteen, until he looked up and saw that the sun was sinking. The blackflies had quit, and the mosquitoes were coming alive. After the flies, they seemed almost dainty, flying in singly with their neat little punctures. He was beyond caring. He planted the twentieth tree, called to Bob, and headed back to the mouth of the stream where the canoe waited.

They arrived back at the campsite close to dark, and Horace started a fire and put water on to boil. He riffled through the dried packets: BEEF BURGUNDY, he read in the light of a flashlight. *Tasty chunks of carrots and potatoes and meat, rich brown gravy.* He poured boiling water into the pouch and peered in. Sticking in his plastic fork, he had a bite: chewy cardboard flavored with gray gravy. He ate it mechanically, and when he'd finished half, mixed the rest with Bob's dog food and set it on the ground.

Night unraveled its dark spool around him, and he felt eyes in the woods belonging to creatures that would later creep forward and sniff around the edges of the fire pit. He was aware of leaves opening overhead, life bursting at the seams. He looked into the white center of the fire. The day he met Timothy Edward Stearns, the boy was holding a round fish tank, half-filled with sand, to demonstrate how sand dunes formed. He'd hardly looked at Horace.

You could go overboard with remorse. *Enough.* He separated the fire, poured a little water over it, and retired with Bob to the tent. He heard his mother's voice putting him to bed. *Good night, sleep tight, don't let the bedbugs bite. Pleasant dreams and sweet repose, slam the door on the doctor's nose! Tickets in your nightcap.* It was the best thing between them, the way she said, *Tickets in your nightcap* with a spark of gaiety each night.

In the morning, Horace discovered three-legged bear prints; they came in from the stagnant pond to the rear of the site, circled the tent, and disappeared into the lake. With eighteen trees to plant before heading back home, he wanted a hearty breakfast, and he started a fire for coffee and eggs and oatmeal. He added bigger sticks to the twigs, another log, and replaced the grate. While he was waiting for the fire to mature, he loaded the canoe with his paddle, the spade, a plastic container filled with lake water, a bag of compost, and the trees. He was dragging today, his head poisoned with bug repellent. Some burden of lonesomeness had him in its grip. Eating his oatmeal on a stump, washing his bowl in the lake, he felt like bogman, forgotten by the world. "Last day," he said to Bob, "and then we'll be heading home. I'm ready—how about you?" Bob wagged his tail tentatively, trying to catch the drift. "I smell bad," said Horace.

In the canoe, Bob sat solemnly in the bow, his tawny back forming the long side of an isosceles triangle. His tail wagged gently. *You've come a long way, Bob,* thought Horace. *Do you remember when we met? You were one of those hind-tit pups, the kind your mother would have sat on. You'd be surprised how fast a life can change, Bob. One minute I was standing out there with a hose watering the grass, respectable job, yellow house, black shutters; the next minute, Bam.*

He paddled up the stream, overhung with trees. The water reflected sky and clouds caught in the reeds like fish. They landed with a bump, and Bob jumped out. Horace clambered forward, stepping over tools and trees, pulled the canoe up on land, and carried the first load of trees to an open area. Five hours later, he'd planted eleven out of the remaining eighteen trees. He was going about half speed. He calculated: 937 trees left. Finish the rest tomorrow, get an early start, plant, break camp, paddle across the lake. He began the hole for the last tree of the day. It was too close to the other trees, and he moved over a foot or two and started digging again. As the light slanted earthwards, the mosquitoes appeared, and he stopped and slathered on lotion. "Bob?" he called. "Where are you?" He spaded out a few more shovelfuls of dirt. "Bob?! Bob!" His voice echoed back to him and got lost in the small animal trails gouged in sphagnum moss. "Bob! Dinner!" Silence.

Horace was so tired he could just lift his arms. The last tree was bent and brown, and he wanted to dig deep and give it a chance, but he didn't have it in him. He threw in some compost, mumbled a few words over it, popped it in the ground, and watered it. He picked up his spade and water container and dragged himself toward the canoe, stumbling over roots and shrubs. "Bob!" he called. The knees of his pants were covered with dirt, his boots and face and hands splattered with mud. The middle finger of his right hand was partly crushed where he'd tried to dislodge a rock from a hole.

With a splintering of underbrush, Bob popped out of the shrubbery, dragging dinner. It was an unrecognizable brown animal, reeking of death. Horace had just been about to say, "Why don't you stick a little closer?" when he found himself running from Bob. "Stay away! Drop it!" Bob wagged his tail, his teeth firmly clenched around the animal. It had probably been a woodchuck at one time, but its fur had chunked off, and its hindquarters were missing. Horace hoped it wasn't Bob who'd eaten it. "Put it down!" he said from a distance. "Good boy, drop it." But Bob said with his eyes, *No way.*

"Dinner," said Horace, climbing into the canoe. "We're going back for dinner." Bob wagged his tail. "It's not coming in the boat. Drop it." Horace went a little closer. "Home. Time to go home." Bob waved his tail continuously and growled.

Horace paddled to the beaver dam with Bob trotting next to the canoe, forded it, and came out onto the lake. In the distance, Mount Katahdin stood out in the late afternoon light, deep blue. He paddled slowly down the lake, while Bob splashed along shore with the thing. All the while, Horace talked to him, told him dinner was coming, he'd make himself sick.

They rounded the corner of the lake. "But what's that? What's that smoke, Bob? What's happening behind those trees? Bob, Bob, look lively. Our woods, Bob. Don't wag your tail at me. I've set the woods on fire. Oh, Bob, look what I've done."

22

Beverly finished up the sixth painting in the series and began on the seventh. It was giving her trouble. She wanted to capture what she imagined of the blue-green plant life of the Galapagos Rift, but what came out looked like curly cabbage. It needed to be darker, more abstract, and she was fed up with herself, her confidence tired and low. She painted, not because she thought it would save the world or anything like it, but because she couldn't *not* paint. With all the stuff that came into her head every day—words, images, claptrap—she had to make sense of it in some way or she'd implode. But today, nothing made sense, or even close to it.

She couldn't have said what took her to the library that afternoon. Loneliness maybe, a need to get away from all that underwater life, to see other humans. She opened the door and went in. Around the computer card catalog, high school kids pushed each other with their elbows and cracked gum. An old man sat on a chair reading a newspaper, a soiled knapsack beside him. Beverly found a seat at one of the big oak tables and looked around. The light streamed in the high horizontal windows into the top of the old room, where it picked up motes of dust and fell like rain onto the tables below. She opened her sketch pad, and the back of a young man's head caught her eye. She liked drawing the backs of people's heads: you were in a better position to see the world through their eyes somehow. She drew quickly. The hair, cut short, was mowed every which way like a kid's. The head was large and calm—but from the back, he looked hurt somehow. The neck was short, the shoulders and back large, square and muscular. The man turned, and she stopped drawing. He picked up his baseball cap and jammed it on backwards, a style that Horace particularly disliked. *I don't care who it is,* he said. *It makes them look like morons.* This young man, however, didn't look like a moron. He stood up, and she saw the scar under one eye. Not a long, thin scar, more like something . . . Oz. For godsakes.

She went to him.

"Beverly!"

"How *are* you?" she asked.

He shrugged. "I've been out a week."

"What're you doing?"

"Trying to figure things out."

She held up the picture of his head, ripped it out of the pad and gave it to him.

"Hey, I look pretty decent from behind."

"I liked you even before I knew it was you." Suddenly, she didn't know what else to say, and they stood there looking at each other.

"It's hot out there," he said. "Nice and cool in here."

"Are you living nearby?"

"No. I don't have a place yet."

"Are you staying with friends?"

"Not really."

"Oh." She felt as though she wanted to offer him something. "You know, if you ever need a reference . . ." She thought of writing down her address and phone number, but something told her not to. "The prison has my address if you ever need it," she added quickly. They'd never give it to him even if he asked. *So why did you say it?*

"Yeah. Well, I guess I'll be heading along," he said. "Good to see you."

"Are you drawing?" she asked.

"Not at the moment, no."

She watched as he lumbered toward the front door. He pushed it open and disappeared onto the street. She walked back to the table, sat down, and opened her sketch pad. *You talk a good game,* she said to herself. *Your heart went out to him as long as he was behind bars, but as soon as he's out . . .* Suddenly, she couldn't stay inside her own skin a second longer. Without thinking, she hurried from the room, past the circulation desk, and out the front door.

The heat hit her solid. She walked fast a couple of blocks in one direction, trying to catch a glimpse of him, and finally stopped. Turning around, she walked a couple of blocks and looked around. His big, slow head was just disappearing down a side street. "Oz!" she yelled. She stepped into traffic and dodged her way across.

He turned, and she caught up with him. Swiping at her forehead with two fingers to catch a trickle of perspiration, she hadn't thought about what to say, just started talking. "Where did you stay last night?"

"In the park."

"You don't have any money, do you?"

"No."

"Want to come over to my house for a cup of coffee?"

He paused for a second. "Sure."

"My car's in the parking garage."

They drove through suburban neighborhoods with the windows down. She looked at the streets through his eyes, the snipped shrubs and shorn lawns, houses too big for the people inside them, quiet, wide sidewalks. He seemed nervous, out of his element, and she tried to make conversation until it became too much of an effort. The lights were against them all the way, and they'd just stopped at another when all of a sudden he said, "Don't move!"

It was the kind of thing that happened in the movies. For a second she wasn't scared, and then she was. She glanced in the rearview mirror, hoping other cars would come up behind her, but the street was deserted. She waited for him to pull out a weapon, thought of trying to get out to make a run for it. She was about to say, *Take my car, my purse, whatever you want,* when he said, "You've got a bee in your hair." He leaned toward her, cupped his hands around it, and put it out the window.

She looked at him in disbelief and laughed. "How stupid of me."

"It wasn't your fault; it could happen to anyone."

The light turned green. She stepped on the accelerator harder than she meant to, and they shot forward. She was so dumb, she could hardly believe it. Beverly Woodruff. IQ 70. She didn't need a baseball cap turned backwards. She thought of confessing, but no. "It didn't sting you, did it?" she asked.

"No."

"Thank goodness." She was so ashamed of herself.

She turned onto her street. "This is it, where we live," she said. "My husband's name is Horace." She pulled in the driveway, pressed the garage door opener, and drove into the garage.

"How long have you lived here?" he asked.

"Twenty-five years—maybe even longer."

"I've never lived anywhere longer than four years," he said.

"Horace and I are old stick-in-the-muds. He's up north at the moment. Anyway, we don't have to sit in the garage all day. Come in, I'll make you something."

They went in the side door, and he followed her down the

hall toward the kitchen. She saw him touch the gilded edge of a small oil painting as he went by, a picture of a lonely rural road with a house in the distance.

She carried a tray of peanut-butter toast and bananas and cookies toward the back garden. Oz opened the door and stood in astonishment as though he'd come to a roaring waterfall. "What's all this?"

"The trees came from the Forest Service," she said. "They delivered them by mistake, and Horace is planting them." She offered him his pick from the tray and sat on the steps. "It's really not at all like him. I don't know why he's doing it."

"Sometimes," he said, peeling a banana, "you don't understand why you do certain things." He pulled back each strip of the peel carefully, a kind of tenderness, and then ate the whole thing faster than it took her to say, "It must take a lot of food to keep you going. You're very large." After that, he ate a piece of peanut-butter toast and three cookies and another banana, and then he stopped.

"I was in prison for selling cocaine," he said. "I thought you might be wondering. They gave me three years—I was in for B&E when I was younger, but this was the first drug offense."

"It doesn't make any sense you got locked up all that time for that. I can see the sense if you hurt someone."

"I didn't."

"You don't even look twenty."

"I'm twenty-four."

"Add forty years."

"For what?"

"To get to sixty-four."

"You don't look that old."

"This is what sixty-four looks like . . . Listen," she said, "You're welcome to stay for a few days until you find a job. I know it won't take you long."

An edge came into his voice. "I didn't come to sponge off you."

"I'm sure Horace would say the same . . . you're more than welcome."

"I don't know—maybe if it rains."

"Don't be silly. What if it rains in the middle of the night? And how will you look in a job interview with mud in your hair?" She stood up. "Come on, I'll show you a room you can sleep in if you want it. You can put on the sheets, how's that? I hate changing beds."

He asked if he might cook dinner in return.

"You cook?"

"I earned my culinary certificate in prison."

"You're kidding."

He laughed. "Nothing fancy. Lasagna. Shit on a shingle, that kind of thing."

"What's that?"

"Ground hamburger on toast, in a brown sauce . . . I made a Black Forest wedding cake for one of my friends who was married last year in prison. That was the hardest thing I ever made, but it worked out."

"What about pie? Horace loves pie."

"Yeah, I make a pretty good pie. What's his favorite?"

"He likes all of them. If he had to pick—I don't know—it would probably come down to strawberry rhubarb."

A robin was still singing even though it was almost dark, a long, liquid line with a small chirp at the end of it. As he listened, his eyebrow went up with each chirp, and an indentation at the corner of his mouth released something like joy.

23

The window was made of glass, something that would take him a while to get used to. He didn't belong between these fancy white sheets. Today, he'd look for a job. If it weren't for money, he'd probably hitch to the Southwest and start over. He heard Beverly moving around down in the kitchen; he pulled on his pants and went downstairs.

"Toast?" She peered at him. She didn't have her glasses on. "Coffee? Orange juice? Cereal? Help yourself."

After breakfast she got him feeding and watering trees. "Horace said each tree gets ten pellets of food, no more. I don't really think you need to be that exact. And then for water, he told me to be sure I got them good and damp but not too wet." She sprayed one with the hose. "Kind of like that." She went back inside, and he went down on his hands and knees and looked at a tag. USDA FOREST SERVICE, BLACK SPRUCE (PICEA MARIANA). He rubbed a branch but couldn't smell anything. With the bag of plant food and a teaspoon, he began. Ten pellets each. It took him over an hour to parcel out the food, and then he went over to the outdoor faucet and turned it on. He began with the trees under the magnolia. Brown petals blanketed the ground and stuck in the branches of the little trees.

The sound of the hose was amazingly normal. He watched

the water pour out onto the tiny trees and felt happy. How long since his life had been normal? He turned the hose toward the trees by the side of the garage. Had his life ever been normal? He pictured his father at the kitchen table in an old gray T-shirt, his mother standing at the counter making grilled cheese sandwiches. He remembered the refrigerator door opening, closing, bells ringing in the church across the way. His mother leaned out the window, over the red-brick linoleum counter, trying to see the bride coming out of the church. She put the sandwiches in the oven and turned on the broiler, and the bells stopped.

Who would have known that several years later his parents would no longer be together, that a couple years after that, when he was twelve, his mother's boyfriend, Mike, would move in? That he and Oz's mother would have a baby named Maggie? That his mother would go back to school and become a legal secretary working for Gleeson, Grande and LeCage? That when Maggie was four, Oz would be caught stealing, serve time, get out? That a year later, a pile of wood at Tyson's Lumber would crush his father? Was it all written down somewhere? No one could have made it up, or would have wanted to.

In school, they called him hyperactive. His father told him that he'd had ants in his pants in school, too. The bastards, he said, were just trying to control him with their labels. He hadn't thought about his father in a while, but here he was all of a sudden, riding out of the hose on a stream of water. He remembered the day the lumberyard called his mother and said there'd been an accident. His father was dead on arrival at the Windham Memorial Hospital, one of those freak accidents that takes a person and snaps him in two before he can say, *Wait a minute, I'm not finished yet.* Oz was glad he hadn't seen him.

After his father's death, his mother called Oz "ungovernable." He stayed out all night, came home with half his clothes gone.

He took one of Mike's handsaws and a set of chisels from the basement and lost them in the woods at a camp near a lake they broke into. He started dealing. A shrink might have said it was all connected with his father's death, but that was too easy. He didn't blame the way he was on anyone but himself. He had things to figure out, whatever had happened to his father.

He watered the trees over by the fence, behind the garage, under the big tree in the back. Soon, he'd need to find a job, like within the week. Probably he'd be able to land a sous chef position in downtown Hartford if no one asked him what he'd been doing the last three years, but why start a life here if he'd rather be somewhere else? And why go somewhere else if there was a chance things could work out with Lucy?

He turned off the spigot, coiled up the hose, and started toward the house. Just as he was climbing the steps, a pickup truck pulled in. A balding man was driving, with a dog beside him. "Can I help you?" the man said, leaning out the window.

"Are you Horace?" Oz stuck his hand toward the window and introduced himself. "I used to be in Beverly's drawing class. I just got out of prison. Hope you don't mind me being here." Of course he minded. Why wouldn't he mind? He watched Horace stagger from the truck. "Want some help bringing your stuff into the house?"

"Sure," Horace said over his shoulder. He looked a hundred years old as he climbed the stairs and disappeared inside.

In the back of the truck, everything was covered with ash, like a volcano had erupted. Oz pulled the tent out of its stuff sack, hung it over the back railing, and hosed it off. He brought three big waterproof bags of food into the kitchen and put them in the corner beside a stack of magazines and newspapers. Horace and Beverly were talking in the other room. He couldn't hear the words, but Beverly sounded, *Omigod*. Oz went back outside and hosed off the spade and rinsed out the plastic water jugs and set them in the garage. He brought more bags into the house.

"Oz!" Beverly called. "Come in and have something to drink."

Horace was sitting on a blue-gray chair looking out toward the marsh, Beverly in a rocking chair. "Tea?" She poured without waiting for an answer and handed Oz a mug. "Horace planted thirty-three trees, and there was a fire in the woods."

"I started it by mistake," said Horace. "I forgot to pour water on the coals, and a clump of bushes caught fire. The only thing that saved us was the wind blowing away from the woods. I shoveled dirt and brought water up from the lake, and then we left." He paused, took a sip of tea, and set the cup back down. His hands shook.

"They say the occasional fire is good for the woods," said Beverly. "If they *had* gone up, which they didn't. And you're okay, and Bob's okay; no one was hurt. I don't know how you put it out. I can't imagine you running around with dirt and water and pulling up the tent."

"It wasn't heroic," said Horace, "I can tell you that. It was my own damn fault." He sank a little further down into the chair.

"Did Oz tell you," Beverly said, "that he just got out of prison? He was a cook." As though he'd held some important position. "He knows how to make pie." Beverly stood up. "I'm going to run you a bath with some epsom salts . . . " She disappeared upstairs.

"Who did you say you were?" asked Horace.

"I was in your wife's drawing class in prison. Oz Freeman." He took off his baseball hat and held it in his hands.

"So you're out now."

"Yes."

"That's good." Horace looked as though he might fall out of the chair. "You'll have to excuse me; I think I need a bath."

Horace tossed and muttered in his sleep all night, and now, at eight in the morning, he was still sleeping. The top of his head was sunburned, and the skin on his nose peeled; his arms were plastered with bites. Beverly pulled the sheet around his neck and tucked it in. It had taken him five days to plant thirty-three trees. He'd never get them in the ground before they died. She couldn't understand what he thought he was doing. He'd had minor obsessions with gadgets, with things he couldn't get to work right, but he always came back to himself. It was probably a thing she'd never understand, no matter how many man-against-the-odds books she read. She'd always had a fondness for that kind of reading matter, maybe because it made no sense: expeditions up Annapurna and Mount McKinley, around the world in suicidal boats.

She nudged his shoulder. "Honey?"

"Mmmrph?"

"I'm worried about you."

He turned over and opened an eye. He opened the other eye and peered at her. "The world's perishing for lack of beauty," he said. He turned away from her, and soon he was snoring and vibrating again.

Oz, she thought suddenly. She heard some movement under the bedroom, in the kitchen below. She dressed and went downstairs; as she stood at the door of the kitchen, he had his back to her, absorbed in what he was doing: flouring the counter, smoothing it with his palm, scooping dough from a bowl and laying it down, his jagged restlessness turned to grace. He patted out the dough, rounded it, and seemed to gather some calmness into himself. He picked up a rolling pin she'd only used once in

145

her life, and began. Rolling from the center, his movements were quick and deft. When he had the dough thinned out, he folded it in half, then in quarters, and placed it in a glass pie dish. He was unfolding it when something snagged his attention; he turned and saw her.

"You look as though you were born here," she said, smiling.

"This is just something I know how to do."

"It's a miracle." She saw the bowl of apples sliced, weeping with sugar and cinnamon.

"I had a thought this morning," he said. "I need a job. Horace needs help. I wouldn't mind being out in the woods a few weeks. I'm not looking for pay, I could just use some time to get my feet under me."

"Of course he'd pay you."

"That's not what I'm saying. I wouldn't take anything from either of you."

"It wouldn't be possible unless you did, I know that for a fact."

He turned back to the counter, and she watched him take the other half of the dough from the bowl and begin to round it up. If she'd been in the habit of praying, she'd have thought someone had answered.

24

*Wanted: Strong back. Cooking experience a
plus. $400/week, food and tent included.*

Oz heard the thump of Bob's tail in Horace's tent and
then a doggy groan of sleep. The beat of small wings. Creatures
after his blood, and bats after them. Horace muttered a few words
in his tent, then silence fell. Just black outside, no stars, a rustle of
leaves. Finally the loons started up. *Ah-woooo. Where are you? Ah-
woooo. I can't find you.* When they arrived on the lake three days
ago, Horace told Oz that loons had been calling like this since
the time of dinosaurs. He could believe it—a sound so old and
sad. He wanted to get out of the tent but was worried about
meeting the bear. He touched his chin, which felt like someone
else's scratchy stubble.

That afternoon, they'd planted twenty-five trees between
them. Oz dug the holes, and Horace scouted out the next site.
Horace was slaphappy tired at the end of the day. *Where are you?
Ah-woooo.*

Sometimes he still believed he and Lucy had a future. He
could see them so clearly, standing in a kitchen with a divided
light window over a sink, the sink so old the porcelain was worn
through to black in places.

Lucy's scrambling eggs for supper, and he's cutting a cauli-
flower into pieces and popping them into a steamer. He's

melting butter in a pot and stirring in flour. He adds milk and whisks it smooth, grates Swiss cheese and stirs.

He sat up in the tent and looked out the front flap. Mars was hanging red in the sky in the crown of a pine tree, and beneath it, the black lake began. He dug into his bag, rolled a joint from a small stash Eddie had given him, and lit it. He heard Mari, his drug counselor. *The brain, especially* your *brain, has an infinite capacity for arguing in defense of what it wants.* The smoke tore down his throat, ragged and burning with hope, and spread into his lungs with rough fingernails of good humor. His head hung happy, the stars went bright. He heard Lucy's voice. *If you get into that shit again, we're finished.* He didn't get into it, and they were still finished.

When he woke, everything was quiet. He thought he felt Lucy's fingertips against his face, fluttering over his eyelids, down his cheeks, to his lips. He smiled. He'd cook for her. He'd make a salad of rice and black beans, the juice of limes, a couple tea-spoons of cumin. He'd chop dark green coriander; the smell would rush into her nostrils, and he'd add Spanish olive oil and think about the trees across the ocean where the olives had grown, the hands that had picked them, the wooden press that had squeezed out their oil. He'd lay shrimp around the top of the bowl, and they'd spoon it onto leaves of lettuce, and Lucy would take a forkful and another forkful until all of it was gone and then set her fork down and smile and he'd open wide as a door. He did not believe this would ever happen.

Ah-woooo. Where are you?

The next time he woke, the loon was still calling, and he thought maybe he wouldn't be able to stand that it couldn't find its mate. He sat up and looked out at the risen moon and the mist covering the lake. All at once out of the darkness came an answering loon. Their voices wove in and out of each other across the water, near and far. Something settled in him as he imagined them diving deep and swimming toward each other's bodies. And then the rain began, falling on one leaf and another until it became a sheet of wet sound.

25

Rain pattered against the nylon roof of the tent. When he approached sleep, Horace felt a sharp drop, like a plane spinning out of control, and then something in his mind grabbed the stick and pulled up on the controls. It was more than a metaphor. He was actually falling. It had never happened to him as a child, only in recent years, and it occurred to him that he was rehearsing for the final drop. He liked to think he wasn't afraid to die. At some critical crossroad, he imagined himself standing tall and saying he was not afraid, like the woman in the hospital. But he hated the sensation of falling. Even if you died fast, you'd hurtle down some long staircase. Once he'd read in the paper about a flight attendant who'd slipped out the back door of an airplane and fallen two miles, time to see sweet earth become her death sentence.

You might get around the fear, but you'd still frighten someone else with the lump of flesh you left behind. He'd always wondered where pigeons put themselves. Pigeons, for all the garbage they ate, never seemed to become garbage themselves. He heard a loon calling and calling, and a rustling in Oz's tent. He thought of Beverly, a thought like a sudden pain. He didn't want her to leave the world before him. And he didn't want to leave before her. If he were lying next to her now, he'd touch her cheek. In her youth, the outlines of her face and body had been a little severe. But time had rumpled her like a peach, like a ticket he'd once had to the tallest building in the world.

He was just a boy when his parents took him up the Empire State Building. In the lobby, his mother gave him his own ticket. It was red, with a drawing of the Empire State Building on it. The elevator went up and up, and his ears grew hot and plugged. When they reached the top, the tallest man he'd ever seen stood on the observation platform. The man wore a ponytail, and his skin was the color of a rusted hinge. Horace stared at him so fiercely that the man's gaze left the streets below and searched out the eyes of the small boy next to him.

Afterward, Horace kept the ticket in his pocket. Every day, he'd take it out and hold it in his hand. Although it grew creased and soft over the years, it turned out the ticket wasn't magic. It was no one's fault. Perhaps he hadn't been born with sufficient fire in the belly, belly-buster damn-the-torpedoes blood in his veins.

Oz, though, was a firecracker, no fooling. Yesterday he dug twenty-five holes in three and a half hours. A hole every eight minutes, hacking through roots and what-all. You couldn't stop him. And he didn't look dragged out, just a little lonesome at the end of the day. He wasn't a musclehead. The boy was bright. A three-day's growth, dirty as a mule driver. At the end of the day, he cooked a meal to make you weep. Potato salad, deviled eggs. And then he jumped in the lake, swam a half mile, and came out grinning.

He heard a rustle beside the tent, a smallish sound, like a hand crumbling dry leaves. Horace sat up and looked out; a raccoon had dragged the bones of a fish from the water's edge and was cracking them by the fire pit. *Ah-woooo. Ah-woooo.* Soon the loon stopped, and Horace settled into sleep, slipping into a backlit cloud.

$$26$$

Oz's eyes were barely open, but he registered Horace sitting shirtless on a smooth rock, his breasts sagging, his stomach hanging. Already at seven, big, sultry wallows of mist hung over the water. "What was the deal with that loon last night?" he asked.

"Love." Horace poured more condensed milk on his oatmeal.

Oz understood. How to stand today and tomorrow and the next day, waking up every morning into a life without her. He turned his wrist over. In time the dye would seep and there'd be an old raven with black feathers bled soft. Everything felt sad today. He looked up at Horace. "You forgot to zip your fly."

"I don't give a damn," said Horace. A great blue heron flapped slowly down the curve of lake that narrowed in front of their campsite.

Oz slapped a mosquito on Horace's shoulder next to a scar that had aged into his skin over the years. "How'd you get your scar?" he asked, less out of interest and more to get away from himself.

"My friend Harvey and I used to go out in the field and shoot arrows straight up in the air and see how close we could come to getting hit without actually getting hit."

"Arrows with points on them . . . "

153

"Yes."

"You could have killed yourself."

"We knew that."

Oz looked at Horace with deepened respect. He'd been to places in himself you'd never guess looking at him. "You're lucky it wasn't the top of your head."

"That's what I thought at the time," Horace said cheerfully. "I told my mother that I'd gone fishing and got a hook caught in me. I had to have a tetanus shot. I keeled right over on the linoleum floor of the doctor's office."

Oz laughed.

"He was an old country doctor. I hated that man—he sewed me up without novocaine. He knew I'd been up to no good and was out to teach me a lesson. The fucker."

"*Listen* to you." Oz felt a twinge of happiness and took a bite of oatmeal out of his tin cup. Maybe some of him was rubbing off.

"How'd you end up in prison anyway, if you don't mind me asking?"

"They caught me breaking into a house. Unfortunately, I had a bag of crack in my jacket. I threw it under a window behind some bushes, but they found it."

Horace looked at him.

"The funny thing was, I was pretty set on quitting. I'd stopped dealing. This was my last bag. But who knows—before when I stopped, I never decided to start again. That's the cunningness of the thing. I just found myself doing it."

Sticks broke behind the tents, bushes swayed, and Bob appeared. Oz got up, poured dog food into a stainless steel bowl, added lake water, and stirred with a stick. "I don't normally like dogs," he said.

"But you like Bob?"

"He's okay."

"Why don't we call a rest day—you did the work of two yesterday."

"No way." Oz scraped his bowl and set it on the ground for Bob to lick. He saw Lucy's skin, so white it was almost blue. The hottest fire, blue. Change the subject, anything but that. "What's Bob's story anyway?"

"I got him at the pound. Huh, Bob. He was sitting at the end of a row of cages trying to make a good impression. He didn't yip or run around the cage in circles, just looked at me out of the corner of his eye. I knew he was the one right away."

"Good boy," said Oz. "Yes, you." He counted out the trees and carried them to the canoe. Bob had already settled himself in the boat. "Move it, you're sitting where these go. C'mon, move." Bob wagged his tail. Oz pictured him sitting patiently behind bars. He imagined the cage door opening. A hand hooked a leash to Bob's collar, hope sprang into his legs, Horace took hold of the leash.

They headed west, about a fifteen-minute paddle from the campsite. Bob sat in the middle of the boat, surrounded by a cloud of blackflies, while Oz and Horace, sweat pouring from them, unloaded the trees and carried them inland toward a smelly, brown pond. Mount Katahdin had disappeared in the murk.

"Fucking flies," said Oz. He had on a long-sleeved shirt and pants, but they crawled up his pant legs and down his sleeves. There wasn't a breath of wind, and his ears felt plugged, as though his head was underwater. "Where do you want the first hole?" He walked around the perimeter of the pond, a place that looked as though it had never seen human foot. How about here?" The ground shook as Oz's pick bit into earth.

"Bob! Where is he?" called Horace just as Bob plunged from the shrubbery with green manure on his teeth.

Oz bit into the second hole. When he was seven years old, he'd dug partway to China with his friend, Freddie Gongoware. It was a hot day like this one, haze beating through still air. He was digging to get away from the wolves. For a year or two, he'd dreamt about them. It wasn't a single wolf but a whole pack running behind him over the stubble of a cornfield. Each time, he'd wake from the dream and scream for his mother, but she never came—she had her own troubles. Oz raised the pickaxe over his head and let it fall. Behind him, the lake swam in heat, and in front of him, brown water leached out of moss. He reached down and threw a couple pieces of root into the stinky pond and raised the pickaxe. Over his head, again. The sun beat on the back of his neck, heavy as a rag. He went on to the next hole. Horace looked like an old man today. One foot hobbled after the other down by the lake, barely moving. Oof, oof.

When Oz dug to China, he went down six or seven feet. Freddie Gongoware got tired after half an hour and went home. Oz's mother called from the house and told him to come inside, but he kept digging. "What do you think you're doing?" she asked. He didn't answer because if it wasn't obvious, he wasn't going to tell her.

The haze moved into his head, and Horace said something he couldn't hear. He moved to another place, started with a shovel and changed to pickaxe when he found two huge roots crisscrossing the hole. Sweat ran down his cheeks, down his forehead into his eyes, filled them with salt. Was it his own head throbbing, or the heat outside it? *Baby, when I rise, Lordy, baby. You have—it's I have a misery, Berta, Wa-, in my right side, sugar.* He moved on to another hole. It looked like another hole if it wasn't the same one. All the way to China. He wasn't inside his own body. The form of him, what made him Oz, dropped away, and he became some slow-moving thing, stupid as motor oil.

Pickaxe down. *Huh.* Up. *Huh. Huh.* Bile rose into his throat.

Huh. Heat was a force now, blackflies stuck to sweat—pickaxe down, *huh*—heat and shadow rolling through him, heat and shadow tonguing through hot sizzle. A tooth through the top of his skull. *Huh.* Everything slow, slow, slower. Some odorless paste over his nose. *Huh. Huh.* Impossible to breathe.

Horace said something else, but Oz couldn't hear him, and he moved onto another hole. Pickaxe over the top of his head and brought it down. Slice into earth, spade it out. *Huh.* Slice and spade. So weak, hardly lift an arm. *Huh* . . . He turned to one side and the shadow turned with him, a heavy arm of heat whipping him.

He fell sideways. Quiet.

A hand on his shoulder, a voice. Water poured over him. A tongue licked his arm.

"Are you all right? Oz! . . . *Are you all right?*" He opened an eye onto Horace's scared face and Bob's snout, close as a wolf. His head hurt. The tongue licked him across the eye, rolled across his face. His mother never came. Dog breath. His eye slid over green leaf and gray-yellow sky, and closed. Home free. All the way to China.

A tug at his foot. A tug on the other side. His back moved over rough ground. Something cool at his feet, creeping up to knees to thighs to stomach. He opened his eyes and found himself up to his chest in the stinking pond. Horace cupped water onto his neck, his face. *Are you all right? Can you hear me?* Horace's hat over his forehead. *Can you hear me?*

"Yes." When he said the word, up came breakfast. Oatmeal puke. *Gackkkk. Gackkk.* Horace pulled him out of the puke. Bob paddled in the water, head high, working his feet. Oz smiled at him. Just the smile made him throw up again.

Horace held out a water bottle. "Drink some water if you can, cool yourself down."

He shook his head, retched again. The pond turned in slow

circles, spots in front of his eyes. Bob licked his forehead. "Enough, Bob." The water lapped at his chin. *Ah-wooooo. Where are you?* Washed up on the shore of a bog, brain bobbing about. How the fuck did I get here?

"Don't try to move," said Horace. He sloshed out of the pond, grabbed a T-shirt, came back, and swabbed Oz's face while he closed his eyes. He felt strangely at peace, an umbilical cord attached to outer space. Born again at the edge of a bog.

27

That night, the woods came alive. A saw-whet owl called at dusk. Horace saw a mouse scamper toward the edge of the lake, and then heard the heavy shuffle of bear, like a quilt turning in a dryer. He looked out of the tent and saw the brown haunches, matted at one hip and thigh, shagging down to the biggest foot in the world. His face and shoulders were scarred, and he had the kind of authority that comes from being in the thick of it and coming out the other side. Shaggy baggy shuffle of feet, he snuffled through what remained around the fire pit.

In the morning, Horace watched the sun rise over the trees behind the tent and heard Oz turn and groan in his sleeping bag. When he finally woke, Oz stumbled out into daylight and said, "The worst headache of my whole fucking life." The crash of bushes was followed by the sound of retching.

He came out.

"Okay?" asked Horace.

"I'll live."

"You're not paddling back."

"The hell I'm not."

"You're not."

"Who anointed you?"

"I have forty years on you."

"It was your beans last night. Just thinking about them makes me want to puke."

"It was you digging holes without a hat."

"You're the worst cook in the whole world," said Oz. "Why would you pour rum into a can of baked beans? Rum and *salt pork*? And what are you doing with rum out here anyway?"

"In case we got cold at night . . . By the way, did you know Bob helped pull you into that pond?"

"No shit? You saved me, big boy," he said in the direction of the canoe.

"The only thing still to pack is your tent. I'm assuming you don't want breakfast."

Oz made a sick sound and staggered off to roll up his tent. With a hazy sun hanging in a weird, phosphorescent-yellow sky, they set off for home shore. Seaman Bob looked solemn. Three strokes to port, three strokes to starboard, and Horace had to correct the course. Might as well be paddling his maternal great-grandmother and all her kith and kin across the Yangtze River for all the dead weight in the boat. They stopped a quarter of the way across, and Horace laid the paddle over the gunwales. "I need something to eat."

Oz dug around in the bags and found crackers. "They're stale." Horace munched one. He paddled a few strokes and set the paddle back down. Oz closed his eyes, and Horace did too, leaning back on the seat into a load of gear.

"I never heard you talk about your parents," said Horace, breaking the silence.

"There's not much to tell. They live north of Boston. My mother's a paralegal. My stepfather's name is Mike. My half sister Maggie's ten." He thought of a time when Maggie was a baby; he put his finger into her mouth for her to suck, and she bit down with her new teeth bright and sharp and kept biting and didn't know how to un-bite, not even when he yelled and pulled.

She looked surprised and wide-eyed but still she kept biting, and by the time he got his finger loose they were both crying. His blood smelled like rust.

"What does your stepfather do for a living?"

"Sells hospital equipment. And he spends a lot of time in the basement making furniture. Coffee tables are his specialty. He's kind of an odd duck. I have to say I never really made an effort to get to know him . . . My father died when I was nineteen."

"Too bad."

"Yeah. He ran into a pile of lumber with a forklift. The pile was about twenty feet high and came down on him."

Horace was quiet a moment. "My father died young too, falling from a tree. I was just a kid. My mother said he was working on a limb forty feet up when it gave way." Horace couldn't remember his father's face clearly, although he remembered what it was like to be around him. A gentle man, happy in himself. He asked himself what you do with someone not here. It's not a hole exactly. It's more like you become aware of another dimension, unseen, off limits. He picked up the paddle.

"Some things make no sense," said Oz. "Why should that pile of lumber fall, or that tree limb break when it did?"

"There's no sense in it."

Three hours later, Horace pulled the canoe out onto the shore and sat on a log with his feet in the mud while Oz went into the bushes. At Horace's feet was something that looked like a long flower seed, dark at the tip and light at the other end. He held it out.

"Porcupine quill," said Oz.

"How do you know?"

"Just do."

A seed of porcupine. Horace stuck it in the mud and splashed water on it with his foot. He smelled like a dirty bear. He thought of Beverly when they'd first met in that walk-in coat closet at a concert, her hair pulled back with two sparkly barrettes, one pink, and one blue. She wore navy blue shoes and stockings and shrugged into her coat, almost comically, when he held it for her. He was in love with her by the time she'd buttoned the buttons. He thought of being back in bed with her. A man seed and a woman seed. They'd let that go when they'd been unable to bring forth a child, neglected it out of unspoken sorrow. He thought of her skin, the way her foot searched for his in bed, how she tucked her hair behind her ears before she was ready to sleep. Sitting in the mud, he felt the stirring of his tired arms as though he'd planted himself, his own youth.

They loaded the truck with gear, hoisted the canoe on top, and started down the dirt road.

"I've been thinking," said Oz, sitting in the passenger's seat. He rubbed his hand back and forth across the top of his head as though what he was about to say embarrassed him. "I can't come back here right away." Horace steered around a pothole. "I had a girlfriend—Lucy. She said things are over, but I need to talk to her."

"Who's that?"

"The girl I was seeing. We met in high school." He held up his wrist. "I got this for her."

"I'd never get a tattoo," said Horace. "I'm a coward."

"She wasn't all that impressed."

"Where is she?"

"I don't know. New London, maybe."

"If I ever lost Beverly," Horace said, braking for a log in the road, driving around it, "I'd throw myself off a bridge."

"Just what I needed to hear."

"How long do you need?"

"A week. Maybe less."

Horace wanted to say he hoped Oz found her, but sometimes just saying things like that brought bad luck. As he drove around another pothole, he said it to himself, quiet enough so those fat gods who like to mess up lives couldn't hear.

28

The bus rolled into New London in the late afternoon and came to a stop behind a seedy bus station. Oz swung his knapsack over one shoulder and headed toward Lucy's apartment on Water Street; he'd only been there once before, but he remembered every street and turn. As he stood in front of the building with its bent aluminum siding, it looked more run-down than he remembered. He got up his nerve, stepped up to the door, and rang the buzzer. Silence. And then steps on the stairs, the working of the lock. Through a sheer curtain over the window, he saw white hair; his heart leapt, but when the woman opened the door, her face had at least seventy years on it.

"I'm looking for Lucy Byrd."

"She's gone," said the woman.

"Where, do you know?"

"No." The woman went to close the door, and without thinking, he stuck his foot in the way.

"All I want to know is where she went."

"Please," she said, "don't hurt me." She had light blue eyes, clouded with cataracts. "She left last month. Somewhere over by the hospital, that's all I know." He took his foot out of the way, and she closed the door and slipped the bolt.

"I wasn't going to hurt you," he said through the door. Lucy had told him about this place, the way the landlord appeared at her door at twilight for no good reason. "Get the hell out of there," was what Oz had told her. He'd hated not being able to protect her.

He went down the porch steps and wandered in the direction of the hospital, trying to feel Lucy's whereabouts. It began to rain and he crowded out everything around him, while inside, he howled. *Where are you?* He saw her cupped stomach as she lay next to him, her legs slightly apart. He rounded a corner and listened again. The rain fell steady now; he pulled the collar of his shirt up around his neck.

He walked to the end of a street and turned right. A bus went past, sweeping water up from under its wheels. *Where are you?* The light was changing in the sky, yellows turning to violets, the day ending. He thought of Lucy's hair, a sea of white froth. He used to close his eyes and stuff his hands into it. Around the side of an old brick warehouse building, a shadow moved, and he thought *fox*, but more likely it was a rat. *Where are you?* The light deepened, and still, the rain fell, pooling in dirty puddles on the sidewalk. He came to the end of a block and turned along another street that ran parallel to the water. He thought of the way she'd been in high school, fierce, solitary. She wore gypsy clothes, colors vibrating against her white skin. The kids laughed at other people, but no one laughed at her. They were probably a little scared, the way he'd been at first. Before he knew her, he didn't know why, he imagined that she lived in a crumbling apartment with a balcony that overlooked the street, the iron banister half off; he imagined that inside, the plaster fell from the walls in sheets, and the stuffing came out of a couch in the living room. About some things, he'd been right.

He wandered into a section of three-story, shabby, asbestos-sided tenements. He wanted her not to be here, but he felt her more strongly now. The neighborhood opened up into duplex houses with small yards. A few people stood out on porches looking into the rainy twilight, fast becoming night. He looked into the lighted windows and saw people moving in rooms, the flicker of televisions.

It was completely dark now, and people on the street walked differently. In a small park, water dripped from a bench onto gravel. He took off his knapsack, set it on one end of the bench, and sat beside it. He could barely hear her now. The rain stopped. He closed his eyes.

Waking with a start, it felt as though someone had shoved his shoulder. The rain was just beginning again. Putting on his knapsack, he stood up and walked toward the row of tenements. It didn't seem odd to him, or magical, or anything else, but he heard her again. He paused at the end of the block and waited. A man came out of a building with a rottweiler on a leash. Someone else went into another building. He stood there close to an hour. All at once from a window three stories up, Lucy leaned out into the darkness and left the window as quickly as she'd come into it. When she came back, he yelled, "Lucy!" She leaned out further and peered into the darkness.

"It's me. Oz," he said softer. She gave a cry and vanished.

Soon, there was a fumbling at the front door of the building, and she stepped out onto the stoop. "How'd you *get* here?" She grabbed him up in her arms and gathered him in close.

"They let me out," he said.

"How'd you know to find me?"

"Wolf nose."

"Really. How did you?"

"I went to your place, and the woman there told me you moved near the hospital. I just walked around."

She went on tiptoes and ran her palm over the top of his head. "Your hair's so short. You look like Ving Rhames."

"Who's that?"

"No one, a bald actor . . . Come on," she said, taking his hand and leading him up three flights of stairs. She opened the door to her place; bright bedspreads were draped from the ceiling, softening the square corners. She hugged him again. "You're soaked."

Suddenly it struck him as funny; the bus ride, the old woman with white hair. "I've been out in the rain." He laughed, and she started up, and they held each other and howled, and before he knew it, she was crying. "Honey, honey . . . " He lifted her chin, but she pulled her face away and buried it in his chest.

"I thought you'd never get out," she said, sobbing into his shirt. She led him to her bedroom and stripped off his shirt and pants. Lying on the bed, she wrestled out of her dress and drew him next to her. It was the first time they'd felt each other's skin in over three years.

"Turn over," he said softly. He put his hands on her back, and a great shudder went through her. He kneaded her shoulders and kissed her back. Sliding his knee between her legs, he held his hand over her throat and felt her chest rise and fall with each breath. He rubbed the back of his thumb over one nipple, and she moaned and turned over toward him.

"You're here," she whispered, nuzzling his shoulder with her chin.

He kissed her. He pressed his fingers deep into her stomach, and she arched toward him and put her legs around his waist. Lifting herself up, she lay on top of him and came down. He took her earlobe in his teeth. She moved slowly; then leaned in and bit him on the shoulder. It kicked them hard as though they were waiting for this pain. She moved faster as her hair floated over his face, and he cried out. He held her tight, his arms all the way around her, felt her breathing slow little by little.

She moved off and lay beside him. "Talk to me," she said.

"Hmmm?" He turned toward her.

"I want to hear you."

He touched her cheek with the back of a finger. "I wrote you letters every day," he told her.

"I never got them."

"I threw them away." He grinned. She, Lucy. Him, here.

She held his wrist and stroked the raven with her thumb. "It scared me."

"And now?"

"It's okay. Maybe I'll get one too."

"No."

"Oh. So *you* can, but I can't?" She stopped. "You know that letter I wrote?"

He let go of her hand; he couldn't help it.

"I wrote it because I didn't think there was any future."

"And now?"

"I don't know."

"There is." He touched his collarbone. He wanted to tell her she was the only future he had, but he thought it would scare her.

"Did I tell you I'm not going back to school next year?"

"How come?"

"I wasn't happy. I'll probably go back someday. I want to teach Latin."

"Yeah? What about now?"

"I'm working in a library, shelving books." She wrinkled her nose.

"What's the matter with it?"

"It's horrible."

"Get another job."

"It beats waitressing."

He turned, facing her. "You think that's the only thing you could get? You could do anything."

"Like what?"

"I don't know. You're the smartest person I know."

"That doesn't mean anything. My mother speaks five languages, and she's stocking shelves."

"Well *you* don't have to do that."

She shrugged.

"You could plant trees for a while. I've been helping a guy named Horace. Why don't you come?"

"I don't know."

"You'll think about it?"

"Yes." She was quiet a moment. "I love you. Do you remember the first time we ever talked?"

"Tell me." He threaded his fingers through hers.

"You asked me whether I was going to a party, and I said no. That was the first word I ever said to you. 'No.' "

He'd been watching her for weeks. He couldn't recall much about that first conversation except for her long hair, the way it hypnotized him. "I hated that school," he said.

"I couldn't stand anything except you . . . and Jane. Do you remember her?"

"Sure." He thought of Lucy walking down the hall beside her, the two of them laughing. They called themselves the Freak & Cripple Show. Jane had Perthes disease and got around on tornado-tip, titanium metal crutches. She was very high on her tornado tips—highest-quality rubber and slip resistant. She hated it when people called her "courageous." She said it was like calling a one-footed bird brave. You just get through the day like anyone else.

"I wonder what happened to her."

"You could find her."

"How?"

"The Internet . . . "

"Maybe sometime."

"I found *you*, but it didn't take the Internet." It sounded like bragging. He was embarrassed and leaned over and kissed her. "Can I stay tonight?"

"What did you think, I'd throw you out?"

"You could if you wanted."

"That's the silliest thing you've ever said. If you turn over, I'll rub your back." He closed his eyes, reached behind, and touched her leg. She rubbed his shoulders, and his breathing deepened. The last thing he remembered was her hand stroking his head, a sound like wind.

Her finger traced the outside of his ear. He looked like a Russian prisoner, his hair cut so short. Lucy watched his shoulder go up and down with each breath; in her mind's ear, she heard his voice calling from the street. She'd thought she never wanted to see him again. But it wasn't true. Prison had taken something from his face, added something else. All that waiting. That's what it looked like—the restless part of him had shrunk, and the patient part had grown wider. It felt sad.

She'd meant it when she'd written him. It was over, and now, lying beside him, the letter was wrong. How did people know, how did they know what was true? It seemed the older she got, the less sure she was about anything. You had to act as though you knew, and then maybe you really did. *Neutiquam erro.* I'm not lost. No, not me.

When she was in high school, she knew lots of things. She knew she wouldn't turn out like her mother. She knew she'd go to college; she'd study Latin and Greek. Afterward, she'd teach. She was less sure now. But she'd just said it out loud, so maybe it was still true. Until Oz had turned up, she'd known something else: that she'd always be alone.

It was after midnight. There was a rumbling in the air, coming closer. Closer. Sometimes, when she was alone, this sound was a nightmare—the slow-moving street-cleaning machines with their flashing lights and monstrous gliding. But tonight . . . she listened to him breathing beneath the roar and felt safe.

Back in high school, she slept on a second-floor sleeping porch. The screens were rusted and soft and shot full of holes. She patched them with silver duct tape, cut in circles. At night she went to the windows and looked into the boughs of trees. She slept through rain and every now and then, snow. Snow was her favorite, but as soon as it fell, her mother made her come inside. Her bed was an army cot that once belonged to Grandpa Henry. It had an iron bar at the head and another at the foot, and under her were rusted springs, dozens of funnel-shaped springs that clattered when she moved. On top of the springs was a mattress with blue-and-white ticking.

I have three quilts over me, it's the end of November, and the frost is falling everywhere, quiet as an ice wing it's coming onto the porch, settling onto my hair. Out on the sleeping porch, I dream of the white-violet creature. "Who are you?" I ask. Something cold is sitting on my heart. I can't see its face, only the outline of a thin cheek, whitish-purple. Am I awake, asleep? I don't know. The thing turns and my throat opens into a scream; there's no face only, the empty shadows of violet snow. My psychology teacher says that everything you dream is you. Is that what color I am inside? My heart too?

I was born bleached they call it albino but I don't like the word. Ugly word. Ugly, ugly. I read once that laboratories breed albino mice and rabbits because they're more docile—that doesn't apply to me.

Oz says I look like the moon. He's the first person who's ever called me beautiful. I'm seventeen years old. The silver chain he gave me is cold around my neck; I touch it with a finger. I read that Noah was a moon man, like me.

My mother smokes pot and works at Sammy's where they sell cheap things. My mother isn't stupid but she's unambitious. I stopped by Sammy's after school yesterday, and my mother was stocking shelves with Christmas stuff. Flimsy wrapping paper lights cards with chickadees kiss-

ing and little holly bows around their necks, holiday candles that smell cheap—of apple and cinnamon. She doesn't belong there.

At parties after she drank gin and tonic my Aunt Harriet stood on a chair and shook her tambourine and slapped it against her thigh and sang whatever came into her head.

In biology I learned about a bristlecone pine tree called Methuselah that's been alive five thousand years. I'd like to go to that tree. I believe the world would be a better place if we remembered the old things, I don't mean Aunt Harriet the way she is now toothless without her tambourine, or Grandpa Henry, I mean that bristlecone pine and what it has to say. I mean the Latin language—haec olim meminisse juvabit—someday we will rejoice to remember these things. I tried to tell Oz about how people shouldn't forget how to speak ancient Latin and Greek we were in his mother's car stopped at a light and he leaned over the gear shift and kissed me and said, "Don't worry about that, baby, you worry too much." I'm not worried; it's more like I have a responsibility to set it right.

Lucy sat up in bed. She lay down again and put her arms around Oz. He was large and warm and stirred in his sleep. The street-cleaning machine was gone, a dull roar in the distance. She laid her hand over his heart. It beat under her palm, *It's okay now, it's okay.* "Oz?" she said. "Honey?" She knew he was there, but she wanted to be sure. She shook him, and he opened an eye and smiled and closed it again. She felt her own breath lengthen, she heard the wind outside, and then she slept.

29

Beverly closed the bedroom door and climbed into bed next to Horace. He turned toward her. He touched her cheek and moved her hair away from her face. His hand, once soft and smooth, was rough like bark. Something in her stirred. He smelled good; she pushed herself closer. His hand fumbled down inside the covers and came up under her nightgown. He put his hand over her stomach. Her lips reached up to kiss his cheek. When she held his head lightly and kissed his ear, he made a sound in his throat. She helped him out of his pajama tops and drew off the bottoms and pushed them to the bottom of the bed with her toes. He pulled her nightgown over her head and dropped it on the floor, and she slid down and kissed his chest. He smelled of the woods. She sucked one of his nipples, and he made a sound she'd never heard. He slid down next to her and caught her head in the crook of his elbow and pulled her close.

30

Beverly answered the doorbell, and there was Oz with Lucy. His girlfriend looked like a moth that had flown a thousand miles. Her face was framed by white hair, wild and curly. She was thin, like a child who hangs around the outskirts of a circus tent, bringing water to elephants, who lives in the shadow of those huge, doomed creatures with chains around their ankles. Her eyes were pale blue-gray, and her mouth large, but the predominant impression was white. Not a passive white, but something lit from inside. She wore a thin blue dress and sandals, and one arm was wrapped tightly around Oz. Over the other, she carried a small black purse, an evening bag on a black string that rattled with shiny black plastic disks.

"Don't stand out there, come in, come in," said Beverly.

"I'm going to go see what's up with Horace," said Oz. "I think he's out behind the garage."

Lucy stepped into the house. With ordinary people, you can see the edges where skin ends. With Lucy you saw something luminous ending in air. They stood and looked at each other a moment. Lucy smiled.

"Would you like something to eat or drink?" asked Beverly.

"A glass of water?" said Lucy.

Beverly went into the kitchen for it and came back to the

living room. Lucy drank a few sips. Her lips were deep red, her eyes pale. Unsettled, Beverly returned to the kitchen. She took six Oreos out of the cupboard and put them on a chartreuse-green plate. She set the plate down on a small low table next to Lucy and tried not to stare. Lucy reached out her hand and took a cookie.

Beverly said, "I like your handbag." She could feel herself wanting to babble foolishly. Lucy looked at the plate of cookies as though she'd never seen an Oreo before. *Black, white,* her mind seemed to be saying, studying the cookie. She held out her palm and crumbled a piece of black into it. She nibbled on the rough edge.

"We have a dog," said Beverly. "His name is Bob."

"Oz told me," said Lucy. She took another nibble and smiled. "I'm going to help out with the planting if Horace wants me. I have to watch the sun. But it's not a problem as long as I wear sunscreen and a hat. You've never seen anyone like me before, have you?"

"No, I guess not."

"I can tell. You'll get used to it."

Looking at her, Beverly thought, *No, I won't.* "I'm very prone to sunburn too, not as prone as you, I imagine."

"No," said Lucy cheerfully, "I've never met anyone who burns like I do. The two things I have to watch for are sunburn and I don't see well enough to drive. I wear contacts, that helps. My eyes sometimes jitter when I'm tired. It's called nystagmus." She moved her finger back and forth, fast. "But other than that . . . "

Other than that, thought Beverly. She'd already fallen in love with her. It was the damnedest thing—as though she got yanked open. "How did you meet Oz?" she asked.

"In high school. He was a basketball star. I was a nobody."

"I don't think you've ever been a nobody."

"Anyway, we got together." She nibbled another bit of Oreo. "I don't believe in love at first sight, do you?"

"No. Yes," said Beverly. It happened with Horace. And once before that—not the same kind of love—on Vinalhaven the summer she learned to drive. She was coming home on the Pequot Road at dusk, entering a lonely woodsy section after the turnoff to the Round Island Road. As she rounded a curve, she passed a young girl in a white nightgown walking alone in high Queen Anne's lace at the shoulder of the road; she had white-blonde hair and carried a small basket. Beverly didn't recognize her— strange in itself since she knew everyone on the island. She felt some primitive love rush through her. But when she looked in the rearview mirror, the little girl was gone. She backed the car up to where she'd seen her, got out and searched all the way into the woods, and never found a trace. It felt as though the girl was here now, sitting on the couch. It scared her a little.

"Have you ever been to Vinalhaven Island?" she asked.

"Where's that?"

"Off Rockland, on the coast of Maine."

"No."

"I just wondered. I used to spend summers there when I was young. My sister and I have a house on the island. She wants to sell it, but I don't."

"Do you like it here?"

"I'm used to it."

"I mean do you like it here?"

"I have friends here."

Lucy waited.

"No, I don't really like Connecticut. It feels—I don't know—as though a lot of people are barking up the wrong tree."

"Why don't you sell this place and keep that one?"

"Horace wouldn't want to move. He's always lived in Connecticut. It's not so bad. It's better than a lot of places. I don't know why I'm going on about it . . . Do you want to see his trees?"

"First, I want to see what you paint. Oz told me."

They climbed the stairs, and Beverly lined up four of the ocean series on top of a long worktable. "These are the latest."

Lucy looked and finally said, "There isn't any talking in them. More like wind. Is that what you were thinking?"

"I wasn't thinking at all. They remind me of the ocean bottom."

"I don't remember ever seeing these colors together." She pointed to Number Four. "You've been doing this a while."

"Forty some years."

"I wish my mom did something like this . . . you're lucky."

"Where does she live?" asked Beverly, leading the way downstairs.

"In Hamden. She works in a store." Beverly turned to look at her—all the oomph had left her voice.

"Do you see her often?"

"We talk on the phone. Once every week or two."

Outside, the truck was gone, and there was no sign of Horace and Oz. "I wonder where those two went," said Beverly. Another few trees had turned brown over by Bill Yardley's fence, and she picked them up. "You should have seen it when they first came. Not a square inch of space . . . Oh, no, here comes Mrs. Bossy." Mrs. Yimona was coming down the street with her Afghan hound, barking orders. "That woman, I swear, never stops walking that dog. Anyway, these are the trees, the little trouble-makers." She stuffed the dead trees in a brown paper bag and put them in the garbage can.

"I don't get it," said Lucy. "What are you doing with all these trees?"

Beverly shrugged. "They turned up one day; there was a mistaken delivery—Horace is obsessed with them."

"Where'd they come from?"

"The U.S. Forest Service."

"Did you call them?"

"No. Horace didn't want to—so technically, they're stolen goods."

Lucy laughed and got down on her hands and knees. "Funny. They don't smell like pine trees." She sat up on her haunches. "They're . . . I don't know—calm."

"I might feel that way if they weren't all over the place." Beverly picked up a tray and moved it out of the path. "They've kind of taken over."

31

"*Lip*stick?" asked Horace. "Out here?"

Lucy capped the tube—Red!—stuck it in her pocket, and smudged her lips together. "Well, yeah. You put your socks on this morning. This is part of getting dressed."

He looked down at his brown socks, saw several blackflies crawling toward his pant leg, and let them be.

On a log, Lucy laid out Ritz crackers, cream cheese, and a jar of pineapple jam. With a plastic knife, she spread a cracker with cream cheese and handed it to Horace.

"Where's Oz?" he asked.

She pointed behind her to the tent. She and Oz had been making love most of the night. All she needed was the back of his finger on the nape of her neck, and the next thing she knew, she'd slid out of her sleeping bag and was in his arms. Last night, the tent had been a huge bird, moving with them like a wing. Half of her was still there next to him, listening to his steady breathing, and beyond, to the huge, lonesome lake. "Where are we going today?" she asked. "Aggg!" She slapped at her chin without waiting for Horace to answer. "Oz!" she yelled. She spread cream cheese on another cracker, ate it, and turned to Horace. "Have you read *The Hedgehog and the Fox?* . . . Do you want to hear about it? Berlin has this theory that people are either hedgehogs or foxes. Hedgehogs live by a single vision. Foxes like contradictions. Dostoevsky was a hedgehog; Tolstoy was a fox who wanted to be a hedgehog. Dante was a hedgehog." She paused. "Which are you?"

"A hedgehog."

"I'm a fox. Oz is a fox, too, but he thinks he should be a hedgehog."

Horace considered. "Beverly's a fox—definitely a fox."

"I think hedgehogs have an easier time of it," she said.

"How so?"

"They get more done. People respect them more. Don't you think?"

"I've never thought about it."

"Look at you, for instance . . . "

"I've just been fired."

She stopped a moment. "That doesn't matter."

He looked at her quizzically.

"Well, it doesn't." She leapt up and went to the tent. "Get up!" She poked her head in. Oz looked so handsome, his hair frowzled around his eyes, his shoulders sticking out of the sleeping bag. Bob pushed his way in and sat down on Oz's legs.

"Out, dog breath," said Oz. He pulled on Lucy's hand. "You're so beautiful . . . "

She started to lie down next to him and stopped herself. "Uh-uh, time to get cracking."

"Come on, angel. Just for a minute. "

"Uh-uh." She pulled her hand away, kissed him, and left.

Half an hour later, they'd paddled up the lake and pulled the canoe out onto the bank near a small clearing. Oz lumbered out with a tray of trees, and Lucy grabbed another tray.

"I'm doing some of the digging today," she said. "I don't want to be treated like some girlie girl."

"Some girlie girl?" said Oz.

"Stop," she said, shoving him.

She started on a hole near the lake, spaded through the first layer of sod, and kept going. Once she got the spade under the roots, she levered up and pulled more grass away. The soil was dark and studded with rocks. Oz dug a few feet away from her. She was aware of his good smell, the steam coming off his shirt. When she was young, she played *he-loves-me-he-loves-me-not*. Back then, she hadn't really cared about the outcome, but now . . . It scared her to imagine a life stretching before her, next to someone. Like Columbus sailing off the edge of the world. She had things to accomplish that had nothing to do with him. She picked up a clump of sod and shook the roots out over the hole. She added compost, nudged a tree out of its pot, and patted it in place. She spaded more soil around it, poured water around the edges.

The memory of last night. Even now, she wanted to run the palm of her hand down his backbone, under the vertical stripe of sweat gathering on the back of his shirt. She moved to a new hole and began to dig.

Late that afternoon, with fifty-five trees planted, she went for a swim while Oz took a nap in the tent. The sky clouded over, and the wind picked up, riffling the water. He'd been kind of distant toward her today, like they'd come too close last night. She swam a distance and came back to shore and went out once more. The soil dropped from her hands as she swam, was swept from under her fingernails, washed from her cheek. She held her breath and went under. Salty sweat mingled with lake, and a skim of sunscreen floated on the water where she surfaced.

She scrubbed her hair with a towel, dried herself, and got dressed. Her skin had burned even though she'd worn SPF 50 and been mostly in the shade. Among the trees still to be planted, she noticed another two had died, and she heaved them into the middle of the lake. It was better that way. Horace grieved for every one of them. As she walked toward the campsite, it looked uninhabited, and for a moment she imagined herself here alone in the wind, a ghost person approaching a tent. She knelt down, unzipped the zipper, and scooted in. Oz's arm was over his eyes, but she could tell he wasn't asleep. The smell of pot hung in the air. He opened his eyes and went to touch her leg. She moved away from him violently.

"I can't believe you," she said.

"Baby. It's only weed." His eyes were soft and foggy.

"Tell that to a judge."

"We're a hundred miles from nowhere. Angel. You look beautiful . . . I can smell the lake on you." He patted the sleeping bag beside him.

She unzipped her bag, took out her jacket, and backed out of the tent on her knees.

Sitting up, he tried to grab her on the way out. "Lucy. Lighten up."

She shook off his hand. "Don't you dare tell me that. Don't you understand *anything*?" She plunged out of the tent, with him following, untied the boat, and pushed off, paddling into the wind.

Oz jumped in, swam after her a few strokes, and sank into a wave. "Lucy!"

32

"We're fucked," Oz said.

"What do you mean 'She took the boat'?"

"She took the boat." Oz began to laugh, and once he started, he couldn't stop. "She took the fucking boat. We're up shit creek."

Horace went down to the shore and caught sight of Lucy on the far side of a distant point, going as fast as she could. "Jesus . . . Lucy!" he roared. The wind blew her name back in his face. He walked back up where Oz was still chuckling to himself. "What the hell! Get up. What's going on?" Horace set the toe of his boot down on his foot.

"Ow!"

"Stop laughing, damn it."

Oz stood up. "She came in the tent. I just had one stick."

"What are you talking about?"

"Weed. She got mad and said we were done and the next thing I know, she's jumped in the boat." A smile twitched around the side of his mouth.

"Stop it," said Horace. He went back to the shore. Lucy had stopped paddling. Then she started up again, but slower. It was amazing how far she'd already gone. He picked up the tree-watering bucket, filled it with water, and carried it up toward the cooking pit. Oz was sitting on a stump, and Horace upended the bucket on him and walked into the shrubbery.

Close to nightfall, she returned. "I came back," she said, looking at Horace, "because of you, not that—gorilla. You can tell him to sleep somewhere else, I don't care where."

Oz spoke up. "You'd think I'd murdered someone."

"I didn't say you did." She slapped at a mosquito. "You're just a jerk."

"I was unwinding."

"I worked just as hard as you did today."

"So we unwind in different ways."

"I've already told you. We're done."

Horace stood there quietly, watching them. "He's not a bad guy," he said to Lucy.

"You haven't been hanging around waiting for him to get out of prison. You think I'm going to do that again?"

"I'm just saying what I think."

She took the Ritz crackers and cream cheese and went to the tent. She sat cross-legged on the sleeping bag, picked up a cracker, and spread it with pineapple jam. *He's the first person who ever called me beautiful.* She'd felt safer with him than anyone in the world. With quick, rough fingers, she got rid of a tear trailing down her cheek. It might have been a scorpion, that's how fast she swiped it off.

33

Oz lay down by the lake and pulled his sleeping bag around his neck. It was pointless to swat, five more mosquitoes behind every one he killed. A lyric drifted into his head. *Nobody tells you what to do . . . Nobody tells you where to go.* Indignation flared up. But then in front of him was Lucy's white skin in the tent last night, her hair falling over his face. He went all the way down inside the sleeping bag until the ragged sound of mosquitoes grew faint. When he came up for air, they were there, waiting for him. *Fuck off, you little bastards.*

He saw bricks, his hands holding a trowel piled high with mortar. House or wall? Brick by brick, a wall went up, knee level, chest level. No windows, no doors. He lifted his head and said it for Lucy. *Think you're the only one who hurts. I can say we're done just like you can.*

Big baby, he thought. You have no one to blame but yourself. The wind rose in the trees, and he slept. In the middle of the night, it began to rain, and he turned the canoe over and got under it. *Woman troubles,* his father used to say. The rain hammered on the bottom of the overturned canoe. The ground smelled like mushrooms. He remembered the day that he and his father were going to a Yankees' game together, just the two of them, but it turned out to be three. What was his father thinking—a seven-year-old boy is too young to know what's what? Consolata was her name. *This is my kid,* his father said. She was pretty, quick to smile, dark hair, plenty of it, big breasts, fuzz on her upper lip the color of dark honey. *What's your name?* she asked, although he knew she already knew it.

He stared at her breasts.

He's got your eyes, she said. *You're a handsome one.* Gently, she lifted his chin with her hand and smiled into his face. She smelled like flowers, and he wanted to smile, but he also didn't want to.

They sat three-quarters of the way up between home and third plate. Him on the aisle, then her, then his father. Every time she looked over at his father, Oz looked at her. When she looked back, he looked away. She wore hot-pink high heels and beige pants rolled up a couple of turns. On top was a soft white blouse, and the arms of her sweater draped around her neck as though someone was hugging her from behind. His father chewed gum, but he didn't really know how. He tried to look casual about it, but he looked more silly than anything, like someone else—with his golf shirt and chinos and new baseball hat. He bought a beer for the two of them, a pepsi for Oz, and a hot dog for Oz and himself. She drank deeply; foam clung to the fuzz of her upper lip. She leaned over and kissed Oz on the cheek—*you're a sweet boy*—and he was so surprised, he dangled his hot dog over her foot, and mustard fell onto her shoe. He watched it for a while, a big blop of yellow on hot-pink leather, half an inning or so, but she never noticed. Finally, he couldn't keep quiet. *You've got mustard on your shoe,* was the only thing he said to her all day. She laughed, wiped it off with a napkin, folded the napkin neatly, and put it in her purse. She was pretty when she laughed.

In the fifth inning, a foul ball flew into the stadium. It came so fast, one of those freak things. Oz saw it whizzing toward them while his father gazed at Consolata. Too late, his father ducked into the ball instead of away from it. *Blam.* Right in the middle of his forehead. He put his head down and held the heel of his hands over his eyes. His eyes were closed, and a moan passed his lips. Consolata screamed, *He's hurt!* She stood up and wheeled around. *Somebody call an ambulance!* The toes of his father's feet were turned in toward each other, as though they were hurt too. A medic came, but his father said, *I'm okay, I'm okay.* The man held a small flashlight up and shone it in his father's eyes, told him he'd have a good headache, and left. The shiner bulged forth like some terrible thing, growing too fast. Consolata said, *Let's go,* and they walked down the stairs and out of the stadium, his father's goose egg turning deeper red, then reddish purple, deepening to purplish blue.

Consolata cried when she left them that day. *I won't sleep all night.* She kissed his father on the lips, and Oz looked away. He'd only seen his parents kiss once like that, ever. Consolata shook Oz's hand and said what a pleasure it was to meet him. His father watched her walk away, and then he took Oz's hand and turned the corner. He must have known Oz wouldn't say anything because he never asked him to keep quiet.

He couldn't have been more than nine when his father left them for good, speeding out the driveway one night. His mother stood on the gravel in powder-blue slippers. *The bastard*, she said, *the bastard*, and Oz never knew what his father did, although it wasn't hard to imagine. She opened a cupboard in the kitchen and threw a whole set of Melmac plates against the wall. Just about everything in the kitchen was unbreakable and you could see she wanted to break something so bad, so she went into the dining room and picked up the television set and threw it out in the hall. Even though the only thing that broke was the antenna, whatever was inside her was used up and she sat down on the sofa and cried.

Woman troubles. He felt sympathy for his dad wash over him. All he'd wanted was to be alive, to sing that Mick Jagger song he was always singing. *I can't get no . . . satisfaction . . . But if you try sometimes, you just might find, you get what you need.* He'd died driving a forklift. A pile of lumber hit him out of nowhere, like that ball that skimmed over the crowd and singled him out. If he'd been working anywhere else, he'd still be alive. Any number of jobs he'd done before that one—as a window washer, rug shampooer, driveway sealer, driving instructor, installer of suburban hot tubs, car windshield repairman, florist delivery man. Why his father? Why that day?

Next morning, Oz's face was swollen with bites, but he'd be damned if he'd say one word about the night he'd spent. He could feel Lucy's eyes on him every so often, big question marks, the way a deer looks at you from the shadow of the woods. As they loaded trees into the canoe, she said to Bob, "Get out of the way. You're always smack in the middle of everything." Bob wagged the tip of his tail ingratiatingly, and she nudged him out of the way with her foot. He realized she was really talking to him. Then it was, "Poor Bob, you do the best you can, huh, big guy." After they'd been working a couple of hours, she gave Bob a dog treat out of her pocket and patted his head.

He watched from a distance. His pickaxe bit into earth and roots, and the breath went out of his lungs with each lunge. It was a cold, damp, windy day, with gray clouds hanging over the lake and mountain. *She wants me to live a careful, respectable life; I don't do that for anyone.* Rain spat from the sky a few minutes before the clouds returned to their brooding. *You should make compromises for the people you love. For the little things, okay, but never compromise the basics.* He spaded deeper in the hole and threw dirt to one side. Oz looked over at Lucy struggling with a thick root. He couldn't see her face. She had her back to him, and her ass was taut and focused as she pulled. *Goddammit, let up a little.* As though she'd heard him, she straightened up and looked into the hole.

192

She picked up the spade, made one clean swipe, and lifted out the root.

"Hey," he said.

"What." Her back was still toward him.

"Turn around."

She didn't.

"I want to be with you. But I can't do what you're asking."

"Then you don't want to be with me."

"You're wrong." He felt suddenly tender toward her, the way she looked so sure of herself. Adult. Like she knew the rules and he didn't. Only what she really looked like was a little girl.

"Look," he said, "you've got to understand what I'm talking about."

She turned around and faced him. "I never liked pot; it makes me sick."

"Well, what if I asked you to give up Latin? What if I said I don't ever want you speaking that dead language again or reading books by those dead people?"

"Is that what you think?"

"No. I'm asking. Would you give it up for me?"

She considered a moment. "No."

"Exactly."

"It matters that much to you," she said. She took a tree from a pot, nestled it in the hole she'd just dug, tamped earth around it. She looked as though she was about to cry.

"Anyway, I threw the stash in the lake."

"You did?" She stood up.

"I may be a jerk, but I don't lie to you."

She picked up his wrist. "It's not going to work if you buy another bag."

"Probably it's not going to work then." Horace hacked at a hole nearby, and Oz went to give him a hand.

That afternoon, a pair of ravens called hoarsely above them. The birds sat in a white spruce and watched over the digging operations. They wore dark cloaks of feathers, and the bigger of the two swooped low over Bob, who slunk into the shrubs and wouldn't come out.

The three of them worked late until the light shifted, until the shadows grew long, longer, and disappeared. They finished planting every last tree. "Head back in the morning," said Horace, almost too tired to lift his leg into the canoe. "Give ourselves a couple days' rest, and turn it around."

"I don't think I'll be coming back," said Lucy.

"I figured that," said Horace, looking at her steadily.

"What?"

"If you'd like a separate tent in addition to the pay we agreed upon, that can certainly be managed."

The next morning, it poured. They rolled the tents into stuff sacks, ate a hurried breakfast of granola bars, and headed onto the lake, Lucy paddling stern, Oz in the bow. In the truck, the steam came off them in clouds. Lucy said seven words between Millinocket and Boston: "I wonder when the rain will stop." And Oz spoke six words to Bob: "You smell like a dirty yak."

34

Before going upstairs to work on Number Seven, Beverly sat down on the piano bench and opened Bach's *Well-Tempered Clavier* to a fugue she'd been practicing. The way the first voice set out on its journey reminded her of Horace—something hopeful and clear-intentioned. The theme began alone, and a second voice joined the first. Then another. She stopped and went back to the beginning. She loved how the voices wove in and out of each other, became more themselves each time a new part came in. It was in the key of E flat and almost beyond her. She played the beginning again, letting her mind wander in and out of the notes. It wasn't too hard until all the voices were in place; then Bach began throwing in complications. If you could get through that mess, though, the reward near the end was great. Suddenly she was racing toward it. Her head buzzed lightly; she hit the high B flat, Bach's great heart opened, the arpeggio unfolded, and the world exploded in praise.

She was just about to close the book and get to work upstairs when she heard the truck in the driveway. Rushing from the house, she yelled, "You're home!" Horace hugged her, but right away, she felt something was wrong. "What? What's the matter?"

"We're all pretty tired," he said.

She couldn't see Lucy all that well in the half-darkness, but what she saw didn't look good. "You okay?"

Oz disappeared with a load of tents and sleeping bags, Horace at his heels.

"Yeah," she said.

"I don't think you are."

"It's just Oz and me. Otherwise things are fine."

"Otherwise, what otherwise? You've had a fight."

"Sort of."

"When Horace and I fight, there's no *sort of* about it. Are you hungry? Can I get you some crackers?"

"I'd just like to go to sleep if you don't mind."

"The bed's still made up."

Lucy stumbled upstairs while Beverly watched her go. Oz finished unpacking the truck. He opened the screen door, and his big shoulders and legs schlumped into the house. He said a quick good night. *Damn,* she thought. *Somebody do something.* Bob ran in circles around the truck.

"Bob! Come here, Bob!" He ignored her. As she turned to go inside, she grabbed one last bag that Horace must have laid beside the hedge and forgotten. But he'd forgotten himself too. He stood in the dark under the magnolia, looking like the last bogman, turning his hat in his hands. "How'd it go?" she asked.

"Good, good," he said, "we got all the trees in. But those two aren't doing well."

"You're tired."

"I can hardly walk." He moved toward the front steps.

"Want me to do anything?"

"Get behind me on the stairs in case I fall down."

She took him upstairs to bed, kissed him on the forehead, and tucked him in. "I'm not sleepy yet," she said. "I'll be back." She wandered around the house and ended up in her studio, where she uncapped a tube of cobalt violet. She saw it hovering over a sea of blue, horizontally, the way air fills with purple near sunset.

The next morning, Lucy woke in the small back bedroom. A spider hung in the corner over her head on a tangle of cobwebs, and she watched it dully as it swung in the air on a small breeze. The air stirred the white hairs of her left arm, along with a slip of paper Scotch-taped to the door frame. "Trash," it said inexplicably. Remember to take out the trash? This door frame is trash? People moved around downstairs, and the refrigerator opened and closed. Just thinking about breakfast made her want to puke.

She wouldn't go back to the woods. She loved the lake, she even loved Horace, but she couldn't be there without it all starting up again. The drop wears away stone not by force but by its constancy. Oz's body was to blame, the big lunkhead hunkness of him.

Mrs. Mavarones had told her she could come back to the library—600 Technology, 700 The Arts, 800 Literature & Rhetoric, 900 Geography & History. She'd move forward into the future. Huh. Whatever that meant. A wave of nausea swept her. She went into the bathroom to brush her teeth and threw up in the toilet. It surprised her, but she felt better afterward.

Oz was out in the yard with Horace counting trees when she came out.

"Six-forty-six to go," he said.

"Not bad, huh?" Horace asked Lucy. "So what do you think? Shall we get you a tent?" Lucy shook her head, and he went back inside.

"You don't look so good," said Oz, coming toward her.

She rushed into the house and threw up in the downstairs

toilet. When she came back out, she told them she was going back to New London. She'd get a bus. She looked at Oz.

"You're going, just like that."

She sat down on the front steps, and Oz sat down beside her. "When will I see you?" he asked.

"I don't know."

"What will you do?"

She shrugged.

"Is it just the one thing?"

"I need to go home." She went inside to gather her things and say good-bye and came out with Beverly, who wanted to drive her to the bus. As they backed out, Lucy lifted her hand to wave to Oz. She smiled as though she'd see him soon, but the smile faded before he could smile back.

Beverly backed out of the driveway and braked fast as a car swerved out in front of them. They came to a light, and she turned to Lucy. "Horace and I have had our bad times too. Once, I was so mad at him, I locked him out of the house."

"What were you mad about?"

"I've forgotten now." She glanced over at Lucy. "Okay, I'll be quiet. I have one question, though; are you going back to that library job?"

"Yes."

"Maybe you could find something you like better."

Lucy didn't say anything, but she thought, *There's nothing better.*

"Before you go, give me your number in case I have to reach you, will you?"

Lucy wrote it down and thanked Beverly. She opened the door and went swinging through the crowd of people; already, it was as though the past weeks had never been, as though you could see straight through them like leafless trees.

Beverly imagined Lucy settled uneasily into a seat on the bus, her white hair plastered on the scratchy upholstery. She drove home and found Horace fixing the valve on his cooking stove.

She kissed the bald top of his head. "What's going on anyway?"

"I already told you they had a big fight."

"What about?"

He told her the rest.

"She's going back to that dead-end job." He turned the knob of the stove and peered at it. "You don't care?" she asked.

He looked at her. "Of course I do—but there's nothing to be done."

"Not by us, I guess."

"I forgot to tell you—Lois called," he said.

"I feel like going to the bus station and dragging Lucy back."

"She's probably already left, don't you think?"

Beverly went into the living room and blew across the tops of a couple of books in the bookcase. Dust swirled around Austen's *Mansfield Park*. She didn't feel like talking to Lois. Opening the book to a random page, she read, "*It is a pleasure to see a lady with such a good heart for riding!* " said he. "*I never see one sit a horse better. She did not seem to have a thought of fear. Very different from you, miss, when you first began . . .* "

Maybe she *would* try to catch Lucy. No, it was useless. She felt like kicking something.

She picked up the phone, picturing Lois in her little house on the north shore of Boston. Her first feeling, whenever she heard her sister's name, was annoyance, but under that was a love so old and deep. You can't know someone for over sixty years, see them hide under the bed, terrified of the coal man, watch them get caught digging through a closet for Christmas presents, listen to them practice scales on a cheap school clarinet, without loving them. But even the love sometimes annoyed her. Her sister had a dramatic stripe of white through her black hair and was beginning to bend self-protectively inward at the shoulders. Ever since Beverly could remember, Lois had been skittish: over the years, a procession of kind, intelligent men—and at least one woman—had been ready to love her, but nothing had come of any of it. She was lonely, but not lonely enough for anything to change. Beverly dialed, wishing that her goodwill wouldn't dissolve. But before she knew it, she was saying, "Don't make it sound as though that's what I *want* to do. I *don't* want to. You're the one who wants to sell it. Ever since we were kids, you've tried to make me think something was my idea when it was really yours."

"But someone might as well be living in it," said Lois. "It's already been three months. You don't need the money. *I* do." Beverly decided not to say that Lois wouldn't need the money either if she hadn't spent the winter traveling around Spain buying lamps and rugs for an import/export business that never got off the ground.

"Well, if you don't want to sell it, why don't we rent it?"

"How would we do that?" asked Beverly.

"Get rid of the junk inside, and get the word out."

"What do you mean 'we'?"

"I could come up and give you a hand on weekends when I'm not working."

"What if I have other plans?"

"Do you?" asked Lois.

"No." Beverly picked a rubber band up off the floor.

"Why do you always have to be so irrational, Beverly? If you don't have plans, why even bring it up?"

"I'm *not*. You're assuming I have nothing else going on in my life, that I'll take care of everything and give you the money when I've cleaned out the house and sold it, and you still won't be satisfied because I won't have gotten enough for it . . . And in fact, I *do* have plans. I've got an art show coming up, for which I need to finish two paintings. I've also got two more sessions at the prison."

"You needn't get so het up," said Lois. "It was only a suggestion."

"Anyway, what if we rented it out to someone who didn't pay us? We'd be worse off than we are now."

"That's what lawyers are for."

"I don't want to be mixed up with lawyers," said Beverly.

"You're married to one."

"Lois, stop. Let me ask you something. Do you have any attachment to the house at all?"

"No. I'd have to say no. I always hated the island. Why?"

"I loved it."

"What did you love?"

"Do you really want to know?"

"I just asked you."

"The rowboat, the way they measured out nails at the hardware store with those little iron weights, the sound of the bell buoy." Beverly's voice grew softer. "Don't you remember?"

"I was in love with Jimmy Doyle."

Lois had invented any excuse to get off the island to see him. She'd offered to do the big family grocery shopping once a month in Rockland so she could have ten minutes in the IGA with Jimmy Doyle. But one day Jimmy failed to turn up, and after that, all Lois could talk about was how miserable she was. At the time, Beverly thought Lois was being more dramatic than she needed to be, but now, forty-five years later, it occurred to her that maybe Jimmy Doyle really had broken her heart. "I'm sorry, dear, I've got to go," she said. "We'll talk soon." She hung up but forgot to take her hand from the receiver. Horace found her standing there, looking into space.

"Are you using the phone?"

"No." She stood out of the way.

He set his glasses on his forehead, looked into the phone book, settled them back on his nose, and dialed the hardware store.

"What are your hours . . . What's that? Your *hours*. How late are you open? . . . Thank you." He set the receiver down. "Do I mumble?"

"Not particularly."

"Would you tell me if I start mumbling? People don't seem to understand me."

"It's because you speak the King's English."

Horace snorted.

"Lois wants me to sell the house."

"Don't let her push you around."

"I'm not."

"She's pushed you around as long as I've known you."

"I just told you . . . I'm *not*. I don't want to sell it."

"But if you don't ever want to live there, you might as well."

"Renting would bring in income, that's all Lois really wants. I told you, I don't want to sell it."

"Well then, you shouldn't."

"But someone needs to go and clear it out, that someone being me."

"Why can't she?"

"The business she's trying to get started."

He made a sound of derision with his nose. "Well, she should give you a greater share of the income for your work."

"I can't ask my sister to pay me."

"Why not?"

"It's difficult," she said. "The whole thing."

A few days later, Horace packed up another load and drove

out the driveway. Beverly told herself she'd die before she clung and wailed, but she wailed on the inside. Each time, it felt more lonesome to stay behind. She went into the house and saw Bob's empty dog dish and sat down at the table. She poked at a pile of papers that needed sorting. Urban haze had settled over the sky like a wash of yellow thinned with white.

She'd tell Lois no to selling the house. But okay, rent it, she'd do that much, and truth be told, it would give her a good excuse to put in some time up there. The thought of a sea breeze cheered her, and her face cleared as she pictured the red nun channel marker bobbing in the waves and up ahead, Norton Point and Green Ledge.

Something was taking shape in her head, and she poked around inside her purse. She couldn't find the slip of paper with Lucy's number on it. She went upstairs and checked the pockets of various pants and tried to remember where she might have put it. Even though it had been only a short time since Lucy had returned to New London, Beverly had already forgotten her last name. Maybe she'd never heard it. No, she had. What did it remind her of? Air, that was it. It reminded her of air. She stopped and sat down on the edge of the bed. Sometimes when she couldn't remember things, they popped out more easily if she didn't push at them. She picked up the phone and dialed information.

"What city, please?"

"New London."

"What listing?"

"Byrd," she said, surprising herself. "Lucy Byrd." Without thinking, she knew what she wanted to say: "I need your help up at the island. I'd pay the same rate as Horace. The work's not much fun, but the place can't be beat."

Lucy hardly hesitated. "I'd love to," she said. "Mrs. Mavarones told me today that I'm not to read the books."

"How much notice do you need to give?"

"I could be gone tomorrow."

"I need two weeks to finish my work for the show, and I've still got two sessions at the prison. That'll give you time to get yourself together. When you come, bring a couple of sweaters. The nights can be cold. Oh, and get yourself some earplugs. Until you're used to foghorns, they'll keep you awake."

$$35$$

The Turtle Gallery was owned by Ivan and Esther Galamian. They'd been good to Beverly over the years, though they tended to show uncontroversial art to people who didn't wish to be disturbed. Usually, that was okay with her. But as she stood in the gallery alone at ten to seven, the opening due to begin any minute, the small cheeses laid out, the plastic glasses and the bottles of cheap wine—not so cheap it would be notice-able—massed on one end of a table, Esther buzzing about, talk-ing in her high-pitched, nervous voice to the few people already there, her dark hair massed near the crown of her head, Beverly wished she were home. She smiled at no one in particular, trying to make herself feel better, and nodded abstractedly to the other artist in the show, a man she hadn't yet met.

Her work was gathered on two walls. She'd helped hang it that afternoon, and in the evening light coming through the windows, the blues and greens and purples glowed darkly, exactly how she'd imagined them in her head before anything filled the canvases. They felt watery to her, even though there wasn't much of the open, sunny ocean of her childhood in them. *Under the Liquid Planet*, she'd called her half of the show, a title that seemed a little grandiose but the best she could do in the time she had to think about it, in the middle of getting everything finished and framed.

"How do you know what it looks like down there?" The other artist, Kenneth Osheroff, had come up next to her, his plastic wineglass already empty, just a smudge of red in the bottom. His dark hair stood on end, kept there with some sort of modern grease, and his slightly protuberant eyes were set under a high, hard forehead. His nose looked as though it might have been broken. He looked more dangerous than his work: roads receding into the distance, a desolate barn. The only thing equal to the force of his presence were the strokes of the brush, some wildness in them, paint thickly applied. She imagined that soon he'd give up on these landscapes and start painting scrappy smokestacks, urban blight.

"I really don't know much about what's down there," she said. "I've only seen one National Geographic television program about the ocean bottom. I watch very little TV, but I happened to see it. Two Russians went down in a submarine. It was like going into space. They had something called a slurp ring that enabled them to vacuum up organisms on the bottom. There were remarkable things roaming around down there: hagfish, tube worms, these feathery, translucent things called crinoids, quite beautiful . . .

"Forgive me," she said when she realized that he was somewhere else. "Sometimes I go on about things that aren't of much interest . . ."

"No, it's me—I'm sorry, I was remembering something I forgot to do."

"Have you shown here before?"

"No. I live in Stamford."

"Stamford. When I was nineteen, I had a crush on a boy from there. He turned out badly."

"What happened?"

"He became a Baptist. Oh, I hope you're not one."

"I was raised Catholic. Can't you tell I was beaten by nuns?"

"So that accounts for it."

"What?"

She felt as though she could say anything to him. "The fact that your face is wilder than your work."

He stopped. "You can see that? . . . I'll be damned. Can I get you a glass of wine?" The place was beginning to fill.

He came back and handed her a glass, having refilled his as well. "You're not from here, are you?"

"From an island off the coast of Maine. But I've lived here over twenty years."

"Which one?"

"Vinalhaven."

"I've been there."

"You have?"

"I think there's even a painting from there." He cast his eyes around the walls. "No, I'm wrong."

A woman came up to them. "Are you Kenneth Osheroff? I just wanted to tell you . . . "

"Excuse me," Beverly said. She wandered away to the cheese table, where Ivan Galamian introduced her to his cousin, who was interested in her Number Five.

"I like your work," he said.

It always amazed her a little, that something conceived in the privacy of her own head, having no thought of anyone else, should touch some chord in another person. She wouldn't have guessed that this man, bald, white-bearded, a mild version of Carl Jung, would want anything to do with her work.

"It touches me," he said. "I don't know why."

"Me neither," she said, smiling.

"I grew up near the ocean."

"Perhaps that's it," she said. "I can't stay away from water.

With the possible exception of Mars, there's no sign of water anywhere in the universe. And no evidence of life either. The two are completely interconnected."

"I'm going to buy the painting for my wife."

"Maybe you should buy it for yourself."

"I don't buy expensive things for myself."

She could tell that was true. His blue shirt was worn and faded. "I like your shirt," she said. "Colors improve with age, I think. In that painting you're buying, you'll see. In ten years, it'll be different."

A woman came up, dressed in an oversized silk outfit that cascaded over her body like a waterfall. "I met you at your last show, remember?"

"I think so," said Beverly.

"We talked about airplanes, how amazing it is that they get off the ground."

"How did you remember that? That was a year and a half ago at least. Do you remember names too?"

"Pretty much."

"I forget names the minute I hear them. What's *your* name?"

"Deborah."

"Now all I'll need to do is turn around and I'll have forgotten. It's embarrassing. Although I'll probably remember, now that I've told you I'll forget. Deborah."

After two hours, she was exhausted. Four of the seven paintings were sold. Esther Galamian was glowing, but it always made Beverly a little sad to sell her work. After this show, *Under the Liquid Planet* would never be together in one place again. All that effort, dispersed. It wasn't like music, or books, which stayed together in one piece no matter where they went.

"Did I tell you," she said to Ivan, "I'll be away when you take this down? Do you mind storing whatever's unsold till I return?"

"No problem. Where are you going?"

"To sort out my childhood house off the coast of Maine."

"Will you be taking your brushes?"

"Not this trip."

"You've done well this evening."

"You made it happen."

Kenneth turned up again. He'd had a good night too. "I'll think about what you said," he told her, putting on a jacket. His ears had turned pink with wine.

It felt like a lifetime ago that they'd spoken. What had she said? Something about his face not matching his paintings. "Sometimes I blurt things," she said.

"It's been a pleasure. I mean it."

"I've got a question if you've got a minute. Would you ever consider teaching in a prison?"

"A prison? Is that what you do?"

"I taught six classes. My last class is the day after tomorrow, but I'll be away, and they want to run another six. It would mean a lot to the guys. It just occurred to me that you'd be a great person to take over."

"Who are they?"

"You mean, what did they do? Bad things. But I swear it's the best class I've ever taught, hands down. And good for your own work. Can I call you, and we'll talk? You could come Thursday and meet everyone."

He wrote down his phone number for her. She couldn't believe it. Just the way she'd been muscled into it. Kenneth Osheroff would be good at it, that hard head, but something underneath that wasn't blind to despair. He turned to go, and she caught a glimpse in him of a heron: the slow, patient way it waits in the shadow of its own wings and then, quick as a snake, strikes. She'd like to see this man's work in ten years.

36

Across from Beverly, a small black-haired boy lay on the seat of the ferry next to a teacher, his legs drawn up as though his stomach hurt. The crossing was rougher than usual, and the boat rocked from side to side in the deep swells. The rest of his classmates ran up and down the stairs, hitting each other with paper lunch sacks. Beverly stood up and made her way toward the bathroom where Lucy had fled. The sky was patchy with sun but mostly ominous-looking; iron-fisted clouds were slammed across the sky by the same wind that chopped at the waves, that tossed the boat, that made her stagger as she rapped on the steel door of the bathroom.

"Lucy? We're almost there."

No answer.

"Do you need help?"

A muffled no.

She went out on deck. *It was a bad idea*, she said as her hair blew around her head. *Lucy's more a city girl.* Burying Island was off to the left, with its string of rocks off to the south. Up ahead was a nest of orange buoys, half of them standing up in the wind. She leaned out over the edge of the boat, and the wind jammed her hair back against her head. She'd forgotten whose lobster buoys were whose now, even though she used to know most of them. Here was a new one, a bright orange plastic laundry detergent container, the wash buoy beside it green with algae, and up ahead, more laundry detergent bottles. Could be the work of Clifton, always saving a buck.

A gull dove for a fish and left a burst of white spray. They passed a channel marker, and ahead was the place on Norton Point where molten basalt had mingled with light granite magma and created fingers of light and dark. And God, look at the new summer houses sprawled on the rocks at Green Ledge where there used to be just gulls and cormorants. She went back for Lucy and found her sitting inside next to a fire extinguisher. "We're just about there."

Lucy followed her to the door, where they waited for the boat to dock and the cars and trucks to drive off. It was calm, finally, in the lee of the island. "I get carsick too," said Lucy. "It's a pain in the neck."

"We're almost there."

"I didn't tell you, but I left the apartment in New London and packed up everything and took it to my Mom's before I left. After we're finished, I'll figure out where I'm going."

"I never knew what I was doing from one moment to the next when I was your age."

Gertie Philpotts was there at the ferry terminal in her old taxicab. "Where to?" she asked grandly before she saw who she was talking to. She scooped Beverly in toward her pillowy bosom. "Gawd, just look at you!" Beverly settled Lucy in the front seat of the cab where the ride would be smoother and sat herself in back, on a seat that sagged to the floor.

They drove past the oil tanks and over the bridge where Carver's Harbor passes into the pond, the wild water sluicing under the road at the turn of tide, past the library and onto Pequot Road, past Booth Quarry and the turnoff to the school and the old rock wall by Roy and Betsy Ganfler's and good Lord, what had Roy put up now? It looked like a Civil War stockade in the front dooryard. And there was the Round Island Road that met up with the North Haven Road on the other side. She wondered how Jordie Franklin was doing up by the Pumping Station, whether she was still alive. On past the James's big, dark-green mailbox, the boat still for sale: *$7500*, the sign said, faded almost to nothing, been there as long as she could remember. And then they were onto the winding part of the road where she'd once seen the little girl in the white nightgown, trees and thickets on either side, oak and spruce and maple and birch all mixed in together, with a new trailer up a dirt road. On the right, the field opened up, filled with drifts of daisies and buttercups and purple vetch and Queen Anne's lace and the sea roses clumped here and there with their sweet, honest smell pouring through the windows, and one dark brown horse. Her heart quickened. On the right, nailed into a tree, was a sign painted on plywood, SLOW DOWN, and the road turned to dirt, and there was that higgledy-piggledy mess of house and trailer and BEWARE OF DOG sign and lobster traps and rusted hulks of bathtubs and trucks and then glory hallelujah, the little neck of water that ran west of Coombs Hill. Beverly leaned forward and pressed her hand onto Lucy's shoulder. Low tide it was now, with the mud banks exposed, and then the Bradys' old farmhouse came up on the right with a view toward Penobscot Island, and Little and Big Smith Islands, and they kept bumping down the dirt road past the lookout until they rounded a bend by a stand of white pine and red spruce. A meadowlark flew up from a field and even though she heard no song, she heard it in the ear of her childhood, that pure sound that split the air when she'd been out on the cliff. She'd carried mussel shells in her pockets up to a flat table of rock and broken them into bits with hunks of gray granite, had ground and ground the shells between rock until they were iridescent rainbows and patted her cheeks with the powder.

And down one more small hill and up the other side, and they were on a rutted driveway now and Beverly could hardly stay in the car. There on the left was a mowed field which sloped gradually away from the road in the direction of the sea, and over the brow of the hill was the old, white, two-gabled farmhouse without shutters, everything about it so right it was like a first breath, the breath of a new love, to look upon it again.

They climbed out, and Gertie helped them with their bags and said she'd be back tomorrow to take them to the market for groceries, and the trip was on her, she couldn't believe Beverly was back at long last. Lucy dragged a suitcase toward the house, and Beverly followed with a couple of bags. She opened the door with her key and found that the smell of Mrs. Howard, Beverly's mother's childhood friend, was still there. Evelyn had lived here rent-free for several years after Beverly's mother died. Beverly pictured her sitting at the pine table in the kitchen looking into the field with her straight, boyish hair, her fleshy nose and face moles that had always made Beverly feel a little sorry for her. She had big hands, surprisingly soft when she touched you. "She has a heart of gold, does Evelyn Howard," her mother always said.

Beverly flung open the window onto the porch, and opened another window in the little downstairs bathroom with its stamp-sized view of the sea. She started up the stairs and halfway up remembered Lucy. "Wait till you see this," she said, beckoning to her. They looked out the bedroom window, and to the north, way far out, was a spray of white where the ocean broke over a ledge, the sea thrashing under a daytime half-moon, pulling the water up toward itself.

37

The walls had once been painted blue and then yellow, then white, then a lighter blue. In the wearing away of paint, the colors were all mixed together. From the bed, Lucy couldn't see the harbor but she knew it was there from the sound of gulls, with their brawling voices. The sea's watery presence was everywhere; the sky was blue and filled with clouds forming and changing into dogs and lions. She felt different. She tried to think what the word was for it—something that had emptied out of her life but was now pouring toward her, like a tide coming in, whatever it was, this thing she'd forgotten.

She heard Beverly down below, muttering something out loud. Yesterday already felt like a distant memory—the ferryboat, the way the waves had tossed and frothed, the bathroom with its red and white marine paint, the steel door that clanged shut, the ledge to step up and over into that hell where she couldn't stop retching.

Beverly had opened the window last night and tucked her in, the way you'd do for a child. "Sweet dreams," she'd said as she turned to go. This morning Lucy saw something that reminded her of Beverly in the lace curtain that blew in on the wind, muslin stained with rain and summer thunder. And she'd woken up hungry for the first time in—how long? She sat up in bed.

Out beyond the end of the field where the land dropped away suddenly, her eye shot out to blue, to a single lobster boat lifting traps.

She got out of bed and opened the closet in the corner; there was a rusted hanger with nothing on it, and another, which held a blue serge vest, shiny with age. She lifted the hanger from the rod and brought the vest to her face and sniffed. Tobacco. Carrying it, she padded down the narrow stairs in her bare feet and found Beverly in the parlor sorting through a box of playing cards and puzzles. Overhead, the ceiling was hung with streamers of dust pussies. "Whose vest was this?" asked Lucy.

"My mother's father," said Beverly. "Grandfather Kearny. I remember him wearing that thing. He looked like a ratty old lion. Why?"

"Just wondering," said Lucy.

"Would you like it?" asked Beverly. "You can have it."

Lucy put it on over her nightgown. She hugged Beverly, the first time ever—somehow she hadn't been sure before—and went back upstairs. She passed down the narrow hallway and into the little room Beverly had given her. Taking off the blue serge vest, she stepped out of her nightgown. She rummaged around in her suitcase, found a clean pair of underpants and a bra, and a terra cotta–colored shirt and jean shorts, and put the vest over the top again.

On one wall of the bedroom, hanging on a nail, was a black-and-white photograph of a woman wearing a string of dark pearls around her neck. Her hair was pinned up under a white, frothy hat that looked like meringue. In her right hand, she held a bottle of champagne over something that looked like a coffin, draped with the Stars and Stripes. It was hard to figure out what was happening—the launching of a boat? But why the coffin? And why the hint of a dimple in her cheek, and her eyes softly looking to one side, a little sly, as though locked in someone's gaze? The picture was posed: the upraised champagne bottle, the frozen expression on her face. Looking at the woman, Lucy thought that she'd be dead now, that if the two of them had been alive at the same time, they wouldn't have been friends. The woman would have fled from her in terror, the way children did on the streets sometimes. *A ghost! A ghost!* they screamed.

Beverly called up the stairs, "There's nothing to eat in the whole house. I'm phoning Gertie to take us into town. You'll come, won't you?"

She yelled down, "Yes!" From the woods, she heard the sound of a chainsaw. She thought of Oz, saw him crouched down, his hands cupped around a small tree.

38

Beverly's plan was to go room by room, sorting and casting off, like a farmer walking through a field sowing seed, calm and stately, but after only half a day she'd already gotten into sections of the parlor, kitchen, and upstairs bedroom, run out of garbage bags, found a dead mouse in the bottom drawer of the stove, a little pile of its fur fallen from it; turned up a two-page letter from her mother to her father written in their courting days, her mother's smell still faintly in the envelope; and gone out for a short walk down to the harbor and up the hill to a tiny cabin that her father had built, just big enough to sit in, with a view all the way to Stonington. She'd met enough of the past already, and it was a relief to be in open air, skirting the sea roses and edges of thickets. Horace and Oz would already be in the woods, God knows where. She looked at trees differently now, how perfectly they were made for soaking up sun, for sinking into the earth, for manufacturing green out of dirt and air and sun and water. She was sitting now in full sun on the little ledge of half-hewn timber that surrounded the cabin on the water side, protected from the wind that blew from the other side.

In the letter she'd found, her mother's hand was flamboyant and spidery, and in it, she was given to phrases like, "Oh, that I were seeing you before Saturday week!" Beverly's father was from the mainland and Beverly's mother from the island. Beverly couldn't imagine what her hardheaded father must have thought when he'd received this letter that told him in so many words that the brown-haired island girl was his, but he'd thought enough of it to keep it forever. And this alone touched Beverly so much she wanted to weep each time she thought of him tucking it into his breast pocket and then into a bureau drawer and then into a cardboard box. *Love is a many splendored thing,* Beverly's mother had told her, at a time when the colors of her love's prism were shining less brightly, when Beverly's father had suffered failures at work, when it was clear that he was settling into a permanent, gentle abnegation of self. He'd wanted to have his own house construction business and never got past taking orders from someone else.

She headed back toward the house and saw Lucy at a distance, sitting on the stoop outside the kitchen. She'd been scouring out the kitchen cupboards and was now barefooted, playing with a blade of grass. It startled Beverly every time she saw her, the way the light gathered around her head. "I've been at the view," she said, sitting down next to her. "Look at this." She fished in her pocket for her mother's letter and handed it over. Lucy's head bent over the paper, while unconsciously, she slid an extra shirt over her feet as the sun hit them.

"She was very passionate," said Lucy. "Did your mother paint?"

"No, she was very practical. I'm an aberration."

"I don't know anything about that," Lucy said.

"You're more likely to have a good life if you *are* an aberration," said Beverly. "Don't you think? Harder but better."

"I guess." Lucy scuffled her feet against the stone stoop.

Beverly went into the house and climbed the stairs to the second floor where the wind was blowing from the northwest through open windows. Opening a narrow door, she made her way up another set of stairs. The attic was airless, and several wasps gathered in the heat at one corner. Beverly opened the bottom sash and propped it open with a stick. Boxes of letters and photographs were stacked on top of each other near a window that looked out to the sea, three or four generations' worth, dating back to the mid-1800s. She pawed through a few and pulled out a letter that began, "My Dear Sir," turned over a group photograph in which people stood so stiffly, it looked as though they'd stopped breathing. Another photo showed a small child sitting in a big bucket and grinning, her head and feet sticking out. The child was dead now. Perhaps no one in the world would even remember her name. She hated being reminded of how one generation gave way to another, to another, hers being the next. Although it was beginning to dawn on her, it was still hard to believe she'd die one day. More and more, though, it was thrown in her face: a few months ago, she'd woken up, and her knee didn't work right. Now every time she went upstairs, it said, *worn out, worn out.*

Near the wasps were her grandmother's old costume boxes. Beverly hadn't loved her grandmother very much; in her youth, she'd thought it had been a character defect on her part, but now she saw it differently. Her father's mother had worshipped herself. She was a handsome, high-headed woman with a shining dark chignon of hair that turned gray only the year before she died. She'd organized theatrical productions on the island and took the best parts for herself. Through a contact at a theater company in New York, she'd been given a collection of discarded costumes. When Beverly was a girl, she'd spent many hours trying on dresses and whatnot, trailing pools of satin down the stairs and into the sunny parlor, once falling down the length of the stairs in green taffeta.

She opened a cardboard box, took out a bright blue livery costume, and held it up. It was tiny, but she remembered a time when it had fit her. In the top of the next box was a collection of ostrich feathers. Dresses bedecked with rhinestones and gew-gaws. She replaced everything, closed the boxes, and dragged the first box toward the top of the stairs. First she pulled and then got behind and shoved.

She went back for the next box, a bigger one, full of button shoes and riding whips and satin pumps. She pushed it across the floor toward the first box and stopped at the top of the stairs to catch her breath while the sweat ran down her legs. Her grand-mother hadn't been an honest woman. She asked bright-eyed questions of this one and that one—What did you say your hus-band did for a living?—and didn't give two hoots about any of them behind their backs. As a girl, Beverly could feel the deep enmity between her mother and her father's mother after they began living together. One day Beverly banged in the back door and yelled something, and she heard her grandmother say in a stage whisper to Beverly's mother, "Oh, my dear, that accent of hers. You'll have to do something before it's too late."

Now, she went back for the next box, the one with the hats, kicked it to the top of the stairs and muscled the three others across the uneven floor. She pushed on the front one, harder, until it tumbled down to the bottom of the stairs and flung half its contents over the floor. She did the same with the others. She felt as though she'd just pushed her grandmother downstairs. "Shame on you," she said to herself happily. She was clambering over the costumes at the bottom of the stairs, kicking them out of the way, when Lucy panted up to the second floor.

"I thought you'd fallen down the stairs."

"My grandmother's drama boxes." The costumes lay tangled at their feet like lives.

"Look at this," said Lucy, picking up a hat with two curved feathers. "It's gorgeous. And this."

"You can have the whole lot if you want it."

"Are you serious?"

"My grandmother loved theater."

"I hate theater," said Lucy. "There's nothing I like about it—but I love these hats." She stopped. "Can I tell you something?"

Beverly was busy scooping up dresses and jamming them into boxes. "Mmmh."

"I think I might be pregnant. My period stopped."

"Dear God," said Beverly.

Lucy stood in front of Beverly with the mauve ostrich-feather hat in her hand, her skin white as bone. She put it on her head. She was so strange and beautiful, wide-open pale eyes, light streaming from her skin as the feather curved around her cheek. *Help me!* Beverly wanted to cry. *Where's her mother? She should be talking to her mother.*

"I don't know much about it, I've never been pregnant," Beverly said. She looked at Lucy's flat tummy. "You're sure it isn't just the tail end of a flu?" She laid her hand on Lucy's forehead.

"I don't have the flu."

"Are you sure?"

"Yes."

"I can go over to Rockland tomorrow. Rite Aid will have pregnancy tests."

"I'll go." Lucy took the hat off and laid it on top of the box. "But I don't even want to be with him."

"Oz?"

"Yes."

"You don't have to decide today."

"I've already decided." She snorted like a young colt. "In school they always said I was so smart."

39

Oz poked his head out of the tent. The night was still, with a heavy cloud cover. Horace had told him that Lucy was on an island with Beverly. He imagined her forgetting him as fast as she could. He saw her white hair, curly, sticking out everywhere. Arms like a young boy's. He'd never see her again.

They were down to fifty-seven trees this trip. And then they'd head back to Connecticut for another hundred. The planting business didn't make sense anymore. It stopped making sense the day Lucy left. He still liked the idea of it, still liked the trees themselves, but the idea of him putting these particular trees in the ground—why?

He'd never say this to anyone, but he missed prison every so often. Not the pissing and moaning or Wilson's farts shooting through the thin mattress. But the lack of bullshit. People told you what they thought, and if you screwed someone over, you could guarantee it'd come back to haunt you. He missed Irv, a guy he played basketball with. And Raymond, a Passamaquoddy Indian he used to cook beside. Raymond wasn't his real name. *Not even you,* he said to Oz one day; *I don't trust no white person with my real name.* He was large, almost as big as Oz, slow to temper but like a blast furnace when he fired up, a kind of right-eousness that wouldn't shake out of him—they sent him to a penitentiary in New York after he beat up an ignorant kid who called him Tonto. The kid started it. He should have gone, not Raymond.

What to do when this job was finished. No idea. He thought of a summer he'd worked with kids from the projects, the best job he ever had. At the end of the summer, the kids put on a show they wrote with the help of a teacher who volunteered her time on Wednesdays. He remembered a sword fight with cardboard swords, girls dressed like princesses, tripping over the hems of their mothers' dresses. Jeremy Kupel, one of the kids, had cerebral palsy. The only two words Jeremy could say were "hot wheels." He did his hurkle-gurkle walk onto the homemade stage and said "hot wheels" in front of a hundred fifty parents. It was enough to make anyone cry, not happy tears but something better than that. He'd like to do something with his life. He unzipped the sleeping bag, laid the flap to one side in the heat.

Bob dreamt the dreams of dogs, his nose to the ground, smelling spring, leaves matted by snow; he lay down and rolled and rolled with his legs in the air, nosed about in urine-scented grass, scratched clods of earth backwards with his four feet, ran on . . .

Horace dreamt that he and Beverly were in a room together. She had her back to him, and he could see only her mousy-brown curls taking off at the roof of her head. He used this word to himself in the dream, *roof*, as though she were a house. She was standing at a canvas, painting bold black circles onto green, and he watched her and thought to himself, *She's getting better; she's damn good, in fact.*

She disappeared, and he picked up her brush. He felt it in his hand, the way it balanced on a narrow shaft of wood, the way the bristles pulled against paint. The room dropped away. Time disappeared. Suddenly he roused himself and realized he'd painted all over Beverly's canvas. There were streaks of blue all over the moss green.

Beverly came back and saw. "What were you thinking?" she asked. "Did you think I was practicing?"

"Yes," he said, because he had no other way to explain himself.

"I wasn't."

"I've ruined it," he said, and woke into the stuffy tent. Bob was sleeping beside him, snoring, his legs twitching.

He remembered how he'd picked up the brush and dipped it in paint without thinking of her. He was drenched in sweat. *Without thinking.*

40

The wind was fresh and steady. On the upper deck of the ferry, Lucy sat on a wooden bench under an awning. She'd just waved good-bye to Beverly and watched the distance between boat and dock widen, the harbor give way to offshore islands. Across from her sat a man with a button missing on his shirt. Every time she glanced in his direction, he was staring at her. His face was unformed, large and childish. A spot of brown sat in the white of one eye, as though part of his pupil had dislodged. His glasses were mended with black duct tape on one side. Usually she didn't pay attention to people staring, but he was so brazen, she finally said, "Give it a break." At last, he got up and moved away.

A woman on the other side of her said, "You must get tired of it." Lucy didn't know whether to be grateful for the kindness or not. The woman had a wide mouth and long blonde hair gathered into an untidy braid. She wore a loose, cotton tank top, and her arms were muscular and tanned, with a tattoo on her bicep that Lucy couldn't see properly but looked something like an airplane. Next to her was a dark-haired girl with a shy smile and a Band-Aid on one knee; it looked as though it wouldn't take much to get her giggling. "He's been on the island all his life—he doesn't really know better," the woman said. "I'm afraid he's not the sharpest tool in the shed—"

"You live on Vinalhaven? You must know Beverly."

"Beverly Woodruff? Is she back? I'll be damned. I've been here for the last fifteen years. My husband's a fisherman. My name's Sarah. This is Cynthi."

"You lost a tooth," said Lucy to the little girl.

"I got another one that's wiggly…" Cynthi stuck her tongue partway through the hole, and the next tooth rocked.

Someone sitting on the other side of Lucy unwrapped a tuna sandwich, and waves of nausea poured through her. "Excuse me," she muttered, rushing downstairs to the bathroom. She didn't take the time to lock the steel door, just lifted the seat, knelt on the cement floor, and got rid of everything. Behind the toilet was a mop, the old-fashioned kind with the gray strings. Just looking at it made her heave again. And a dirty rag on the edge of a dirty sink. She couldn't stop.

She didn't hear him follow her in, didn't know he was there until she sensed him, the missing-button man. She was still on her knees, when he went to the swinging door and closed it with his boot.

"What do you want?" She stood up and faced him, pulled a paper towel from the wall and wiped her mouth.

"What do you think," he said.

The bathroom was built like a shipping container. Even if she screamed, no one would hear, with the wind and the plunging of the boat. He started toward her, and she looked at him, willing him to stay away. He grabbed her arm.

"Get off!" she yelled. He gripped harder, and she twisted under his arm, struggling to pull herself free.

"Be quiet," he said. "I'll have to hurt you." He was trying to pin her against the wall, grabbing at her with his other hand.

"I'm pregnant. If you hurt my baby, I'll kill you." He was twice as big as she was.

She saw the readjustment begin around his mouth. "You don't look pregnant."

She continued to stare him down, the way you beat down a dog. Suddenly, she wrenched herself free and lurched around him toward the door. When she was clear, some fury made her turn. She gathered herself and slugged him in the chest with both fists balled up together. *Unnhhh!* It completely surprised her. She opened the door and stepped through into the hall. "I don't know if I'm pregnant or not," she said over her shoulder, "you bastard." She was shaking uncontrollably. She went to the lower deck and looked out at the water seething beneath the boat, trying to calm herself; she was more upset about having hit him than anything else. Not the fact of it—the feel of his flesh against her fist. It revolted her. She went to the front of the boat and stood in the stiff breeze for a few minutes, quieting herself.

She wanted to return to Sarah and Cynthi, but she saw him up there with his back to her, leaning against the wall that led to the wheelhouse. She hurried back to the lower deck and hid out the rest of the trip, while some deep misery took root in the pit of her stomach. She heard herself saying, *It'll never be any different.* She didn't feel sorry for herself. It felt as though she'd come up against some ancient resignation she'd been hiding from.

The town came into view, and the swells flattened. A gull cried overhead, human-sounding. She rubbed the top of her arm where his hand had tightened. *Bastard, bastard*, she said in her head. Her friend Gwen had something like this happen to her once. Only it was someone she knew, and she didn't get away.

If she ever had a girl, if she was pregnant with a girl now, she'd protect her so fiercely.

After docking, Lucy watched the man climb the concrete gangplank and disappear into the parking lot before she picked up her purse and walked onto land. The water was murky green in the harbor. Cars and trucks were already moving off the boat, and she clung to the side so they wouldn't run her down. Way up ahead, Sarah held Cynthi's hand and turned right at the top of the hill. Lucy ran and caught up with them. "Sorry," she panted, "I got seasick."

"Too bad, "said Sarah. "You're staying on the island?"

"Yes," Lucy said. With those frank, green eyes on her, she felt awkward. She wanted to tell her the truth and be told, *It's okay, honey, it's okay.* Instead, she asked, "You know that guy who was being annoying—what was his name?"

"Johnny Guptill."

"I just wondered." She wouldn't explain. Not with a little girl hanging onto the bottom of her mother's shorts. She looked down at Cynthi in flip-flops. "Good luck with your tooth. When I see you next, maybe you'll have two big teeth." The tongue came out of the new tooth hole, and Cynthi stared at Lucy and stepped on one foot with her other foot.

41

She had a little over two hours before the midday boat would take her back. She followed the stream of car and foot traffic toward what looked like town, passed a coffee shop, a sign to a museum, and continued up the main street, packed with tourists, past little gift shops, galleries stuffed with paintings of ships at sea, weathered houses, noble hunting dogs, cheerful rubbish.

Half a block down, she found a drugstore and went up and down the aisles until she came to the female section, stocked with various brands of tampons and douches. Tucked on a bottom shelf were the pregnancy tests: Accu-real, Horizon, First Alert. First Alert sounded like a fire drill, and it was also the cheapest, just six dollars. But when she took it up to the counter, it rang up as thirteen dollars, and she said, "Wait, I meant to get the less-expensive one." The cashier told her she'd keep the register open for her; Lucy hurried back, grabbed Horizon, and returned to the cashier. She could feel the woman wanting the story. *Will you be happy if you test positive? Will you keep the baby? Where's your wedding ring?* The woman had poor teeth and smudgy mascara. She put the pregnancy test in a bag, handed it over the counter, smiled, and Lucy left, with an hour and a half to go before the ferry was due to leave.

Signs pointed to an annex of the Farnsworth Art Museum that housed three generations of Wyeth painters, and she found her way to a building that had once been a church. The place felt lonesome, as though the Holy Spirit had fled. Not a person was there, either. And in nearly every one of the Andrew Wyeths, she found an absence, a person not there—leafless trees, bare fields, cold spring days, doors ajar, windows looking onto brown grass. She stood in front of a painting of a sycamore tree that grew in a solitary spot, its long shadows cast over the ground. The trunk was scarred and burled. She liked it, the way the tree had survived.

Her favorite was called *Love in the Afternoon*. A window was propped open with a view onto a wetland, a narrow channel curving toward the sea. No people again, but she could imagine a man and woman, an old brass bed against the wall of the room made up with cotton sheets and a thin summer blanket, arms and legs and skin.

She liked these Wyeth men, the wildness in them, as though coyote blood ran in their veins. Most people had lost their wildness. It was still in Oz. She pushed the thought of him away, but he came back as she looked into another painting of a house and barn surrounded by spring mud.

"Oh!" she said, suddenly remembering the boat. She ran outside and down the street and found the ferry already tied to the pier. She checked to make sure the missing-button man wasn't there and found a seat in the belly of the boat out of the sun, took off her jacket and laid her paper bag and purse on the floor. WHEN UNLOADING IN VINALHAVEN, PLEASE STAY OFF THE CAR DECK UNTIL ALL THE VEHICLES HAVE BEEN OFFLOADED, said a sign. People clattered onto the boat and up the stairs to the upper deck, and the boat began to move. Out the window, big rectangles of granite and thick pylons were massed around the pier;

white smoke from two stacks billowed out of an industrial plant on the shore. On the seat in front of her, a dog looked at her; when she mouthed *good dog*, his eyes brightened, and he got to his feet. The owner turned around.

"Sorry," she said.

The man looked at her as though—*good Lord*. He turned back, and the dog sat down. Behind her, two women talked about an upcoming wedding. "I don't know whether it's right. I'm thinking the turquoise. I don't know." The woman kept saying *I don't know*, as though what she really didn't know was whether she wanted to get married.

Lucy couldn't believe how sleepy she was. Her head nodded down onto her chest, and the boat churned across the water, wave after wave. She startled awake just as she heard herself say, *Don't!*, panic rising like water in a tube. As the first of the Vinal-haven offshore islands came into view, a memory washed over her, held so tight against her rib cage—*Keep away! Don't!* Is that what happened? In fourth grade, Mrs. Hatterly pronounced her name carefully as though it would break—*Loo-cy*. The bell rang for the end of the day, and Lucy picked up her lunch box and walked out of the school. They were waiting for her out there. She didn't see them at first, blinded by the sun, but they followed her down the street.

Freak!—and then one of them took her lunch box and she ran after him and skinned her knees black cinder blood and she was back on her feet leave me alone I didn't do anything to you *Albino Girl freak!* They tore her dress and a piece of asphalt hit her shoulder. She ran across the street in front of a car and it stopped and a man said Get in, get in, girl. Her mother had told her never ride with strangers and she was crying and shaking her head no and he said I won't hurt you and her mother had told her this is what they always said, the bad kidnappers who took little girls away. The car was dark blue. She got in. "They took my lunch box," she cried to the strange man. Her Wonder Woman lunch box! Wonder Woman with the star on her forehead, wearing the red halter top and the blue shorts with stars.

The next day she told Mrs. Hatterly, and her teacher said we don't have children at our school who would do that, you must have tripped, that's what happened to you isn't it, and she shook her head no and Mrs. Hatterly said, I thought so, now go sit down and take out your science workbook. In the book there was a black-and-white picture of a hand holding a thermometer against a rod and it said if we beat a piece of steel with a hammer it gets hot and if we keep beating it long enough the metal will melt.

Before the bell rang Mrs. Hatterly said, See me after school, and she walked her out of the building. Mrs. Hatterly said she wasn't allowed to give any of her children a ride, and she drove alongside while Lucy walked home.

It'll never be any different. Lucy thought of those kids, imagined them now adults; saw herself from a distance—a blank, white projection screen, where people threw their demons. Johnny Guptill. Her hand went to her belly. She imagined something nestled there, no bigger than the stub of a pencil, curled in on itself. Her hamster, Gloria, once had babies, red and hairless. Gloria sat on them, one by one. They came into the world and then they died. Blip, blip, blip. And then a few weeks later Gloria ran through the balcony railings to get away from Oscar, the cat, and plunged to her death. *Gloria in excelsis.* Passed on, people said now of those departed. Lucy preferred "dead." She preferred "crippled," honest words. *Freak.* Say it yourself before someone else does.

The boat passed into The Reach within sight of the island. It was low tide, and the granite rocks around the edge of each small island were fringed with seaweed. The town looked tiny. She was up and into the bow before it docked, and the first passenger off.

Beverly was waiting. "How'd you know I'd be on this one?" asked Lucy.

"Just did."

They walked uphill toward the tanks that sold BOC gas. Lucy stopped.

"What?" asked Beverly.

"On the way over, a man followed me into the bathroom. I hit him and got away." Her teeth chattered uncontrollably, and she began to cry.

Beverly put her arm around her waist. "Did you report him?"

Lucy shook her head. "Nothing really happened." She wiped her nose. "It's okay now."

"Is that what you feel?"

"No."

Beverly squeezed her tight.

"I asked a woman on the boat his name."

"Did she know it?"

"Johnny Guptill. Do you know him?"

"I can't imagine him doing something like this."

"It's because of how I look," said Lucy. It was obvious enough to her.

"Don't make excuses for him. It's not your fault."

"I'm just saying."

"Did he touch you?"

"He grabbed my arm and was trying to get me up against the wall. I told him I was pregnant, and I got away and slugged him in the chest."

"You hit him?"

"Banged him in the middle of the chest."

"Good for you."

Lucy looked around suddenly. "You know what? I left the bag on the boat—my purse too." She turned around and started toward the boat.

"Wait a minute, come here." Beverly wrapped her arms around her. Lucy took a breath and pushed it out. Another one.

By the time they got home, a message was blinking on the answering machine from Lorena, Beverly's old friend who worked at the ferry terminal. "Dindy said she thought Lucy was staying with you. We found her purse on the boat, and a paper sack. You're coming to the annual picnic, right? I'll have Lucy's bag, you can tell her for me, okeydokey? See you, Cassidy."

"Who's Cassidy?" asked Lucy.

"She's called me that for years, I don't know why. Anyway, it's the picnic I told you about."

"I don't want to go."

"Just for a few minutes—we'll get your purse, meet a few people, have something to eat."

"How'd she know I was staying with you?"

"Somebody probably told somebody who told somebody who told somebody the minute they saw you and me step off the boat."

"It's kind of sweet," said Lucy.

"Not really. I need to think what to do. I know the Guptills; I've known the family a long time."

"I don't want you to do anything."

"What if I want to?"

"I'd say, 'Please don't.'"

42

Horseshoes thumped on the grass while two men dug a huge bean pot out of a hole lined with hot coals. The air smelled like hot dogs and salt sea; dogs ran about, drunk on wind, pawing each other's backs, barking. Lucy knew no one except Beverly. It was late afternoon, low tide, with the sun still bright on rocks. Snails dotted the shore, their small shadows visible from where she stood. The smell of second-bloom sea roses filled the air, while Queen Anne's lace and goldenrod filled the stretch of land between the shore and woods. An old man with a wheeze sat at a picnic table wearing his house slippers, while a woman, who looked like his daughter, brought him a sagging paper plate of hot dogs and macaroni salad.

"They're gearing up for the dead cricket spitting contest," said Beverly. "That's Danny Roberts on the starting line."

"Gross." Lucy watched him bend down, pick a cricket out of a bucket, and put it in his mouth. A cheer went up from the crowd. "Go get 'em, Danny."

He spat, and the next man stepped up.

"That's him," said Lucy.

"Where?"

"The next to the last guy in line."

Johnny Guptill stepped up to the line and picked up a

cricket. Popped it in his mouth, concentrated, sucked in air, spat. "Three yards, four inches," yelled the judge. There was a splatter of applause.

"Let's go," said Lucy.

"We're not running away without getting something to eat. *He's* the one who ought to hide his head. I guarantee these are the best beans you'll ever eat." Lucy made a face.

Beverly looked at her. "Have you eaten anything since breakfast?"

Lucy shook her head miserably.

"Well."

"Cassidy!" said Lorena. "You must be Lucy." She stuck out her hand. "I've got everything, your purse . . . and a paper sack." Lucy could tell she'd looked in the bag. "They're in my car."

"I was thinking about something else, I guess," said Lucy.

"I never know where my brain is either, half the time," Lorena said. "You staying long on the island?"

"I don't know." Lucy looked at Beverly. "I don't think so."

"Well, welcome. You know which car's mine, right, Cass? The same old blue Ford. It's open—I put them under the front seat on the passenger's side."

Lucy and Beverly brought their loaded plates to the outskirts of the crowd. "Well look who's here," said Beverly. Coming toward them was a man with hair standing up in tufts around his ears.

"Beverly Woodruff," he said. "What are you doing here?"

"Clearing out my mother's house. We're renting it, maybe selling it."

"Don't do that."

"Lois wants to. I've got some people from Massachusetts coming in a couple days to look at it."

"We'll never see you again."

"Sure you will."

Turning to Lucy, Beverly told her that Gus was a botanist specializing in carnivorous plants. "I should have thought to mention you to Horace," she said. "He's planting black spruce. He told me about a plant he saw, a hairy thing with a throat that bugs fall into."

Lucy turned toward the cricket men. They'd just finished the contest, and Johnny was heading toward the food table. She set her plate down on a chair and walked away from Beverly and Gus, catching up to Johnny halfway to the food table. "Pardon me," she said, "I'd like a word with you." Not only was there a spot of brown in the white of one eye, but she noticed the other eye wandered, more like fled from her across the field.

"I thought you ought to know something." She stuffed her hair behind her ear. "Do you have any idea what it's like to be treated the way you treated me? To be roughed up in a bathroom, to wonder if you're going to be . . . *raped*." Her words rose on the wind. "You *would* have, wouldn't you, if I hadn't gotten away."

"I didn't do anything," he said.

"Don't lie to me!" she cried.

He hung his head.

"What did you follow me for?"

He poked the ground with his toe and suddenly looked up into her face. "I wanted to do it to you," he said softly. She tasted bile, felt sick, wanted to get away. Out of the corner of her eye, she caught sight of the wing of a gull as it turned toward the dusky rocks. Something turned in her too, against her will, and all at once, she felt sorry for him. She saw that his life would always be a misery; even when he wasn't miserable, it would only be because he couldn't feel anything because it hurt too much.

"If I ever hear of you messing around with a woman again, I'll make damn sure you end up in jail." It was the worst thing she could think of, jail. She'd rather be dead than go to jail.

He mumbled something she couldn't hear and moved off toward the road.

She walked back and picked up her half-eaten plate of food off the lawn chair, and there was Beverly watching her. "I'm ready to go if you are," Lucy said. She dumped her plate of food in a trash can, and they walked off the field.

"His father drowned when he was in grade school," said Beverly. "They found the boat but not the body. Some people said it was a suicide. They said all sorts of things. Mean things— like he had a lover, faked the whole thing . . . "

"I felt sorry for him, can you believe that? I felt sorry for that bastard."

43

While Horace and Bob scouted out a new site late that afternoon, Oz worked alone near a thicket. He'd planted seventeen trees since they'd left and had the eighteenth hole dug. He'd just turned to pick up a tree, when he heard the sound. And then he saw it.

It was huge, with a raw, skinny, bluish neck and a red flap of skin that hung down under its chin. Its tail was spread like a peacock's, and its wings dragged on the ground. There was a scuffling beyond, near the thicket, and a smaller, drabber turkey disappeared into the undergrowth. As the male turkey turned and saw Oz, his tail spread further. He took a few steps and began to run toward Oz. Fast. His red wattle flapped, and his eyes looked mean. Oz dropped the shovel and ran as fast as he could in the direction of the lake. When he got to the shore, he turned quickly, and the turkey was on him. He plunged—clothes, shoes—and went under. Swimming toward the middle, he surfaced and looked toward shore. It was still there, waiting for him. Wanting to peck his eyes out. The head was hideous, nubbled, snake-like skin, like someone two hundred years old. The Night of the Living Dead.

From the thicket came a series of fast, loud notes, like a cluck, only louder and more definite. "Go back to your honey,"

Oz said. "She's waiting for you. Remember her?" As though he understood, the turkey turned, looked at him once, and ambled toward the shrubs, walking like a chicken, its red wattles swinging.

When the bird was gone, Oz came out of the lake. Laying his shoes on a rock, he peeled off everything else. But when he took off his socks, he noticed dark brown things where the tops of his socks had been. Gross! He pulled at a tick and crushed it between two stones and went back for the others. Five in all. It made him sick, the sight of those writhing legs, the way they'd stuck to him, their bodies fat with his blood. He checked himself everywhere, ran his fingers through his hair, behind his neck. Every puff of wind on his skin felt like a tick.

That morning when he'd woken, he'd felt indomitable. And now—*Big, strapping guy chased by a turkey*. He went back for the shovel where he'd dropped it, and by the time Horace and Bob turned up, he'd collected the remaining trees and was waiting, naked, on a rock.

"What got into *you*?" yelled Horace from the boat.

"I got chased by a turkey."

"You made that up," said Horace, laughing.

"Honest to God. Not only that. I just found fucking five ticks on me."

Bob leapt out of the boat, swam ashore, and shook himself all over Oz. "Christ, Bob, I just got my clothes half dry."

"Found a great place for tomorrow," said Horace.

"Yeah, okay. We're finished here." He couldn't get over it. Chased by a fucking turkey.

44

"What do I do with this?" asked Lucy, opening the bathroom door, a cup in her hand.

"Pee in it," said Beverly. "Just a few drops."

"Once I start, I won't be able to stop." Holding the cup by its edge, Lucy muttered something, went back in and shut the door. After a bit, the toilet flushed, and she came out and handed Beverly the cup.

"Okay," said Beverly, reading aloud. *Remove the Test Cassette and Urine Dropper from its protective foil pouch. Place it on a flat, dry surface. Using the Urine Dropper, drop 4 large drops of urine into the Sample Well.* She didn't know what to wish for as she picked up the small plastic syringe and filled it. The two of them bent over the well and waited. A narrow, deep-pink line appeared, and then another line.

"It says you're pregnant."

Lucy put her hand over her mouth. "I thought so. I thought I was."

Awkwardly, Beverly rocked her in her arms. Most people would say this baby was a bad idea, but she couldn't make herself think so. She smelled the shampoo in Lucy's hair and felt half happy, half terrified for her, this young girl all bones in her arms, a mother-to-be seven or eight months away. Over the top of

Lucy's head, the last light was leaving the sky along a narrow line of the horizon, as though darkness had squeezed all the light into one bright tube of cadmium yellow. Two gulls flew across the harbor into the last of the light.

"My mom's going to go ballistic. She says Oz is a good-for-nothing."

"He's not," said Beverly.

"I know that."

Without a word, Beverly stood up, took Lucy's hand, and pulled her toward the door. The band of light had all but disappeared and the sky was turning deep purple-gray, like the lining of one of the old opera cloaks from the attic. You could almost hear the turn of a wing making its last flight of the day, a gull settle into its every-which-way nest of sticks, a head tuck under a wing. Beverly felt something settle in her, like something she'd swallowed whole. Lucy had her arms folded over her chest and then she didn't, and a sound started up in the low, wet woods on the other side of the road. A barking *hoo, hoo, hoo, hoo, hoo, hooo-ooo-aw!*

"What's that?"

"Barred owl," said Beverly.

Hoo, hoo, hooo-ooo-aw! The night folded them into itself, deepening into moist blackness. Something moved in the dark, a shadow in the weeds. There were voices out on the water, the start of a motor, and the steady *putt putt* of a boat coming in toward land. Beverly held the screen door open for Lucy, leaving Mars hanging just above the horizon.

At the kitchen table, they played Hearts, and Lucy got the queen of spades over and over. The final tally was Beverly: 17, Lucy: 103. Lucy finally wound an elastic around the deck and laughed. "I'm a real ace, aren't I?"

Beverly smiled. "Are you getting enough sleep? You have to get plenty of sleep. By the way, I wanted you to know that whatever you decide to do, I support you a hundred percent."

"You mean get rid of the baby? No."

"I'm glad . . . it's just that . . . I never told Horace how it was . . . you know we never had a child . . . I'll love this baby as though you were my own daughter." She squeezed Lucy's hand between her own two.

Lucy climbed the stairs to bed. She lay down on the creaking springs and thought about Beverly's face, how it looked at the bottom of the stairs, the way happiness and sadness were so mixed together, you couldn't tell which was which. Beverly reminded her of her father sometimes, she didn't know why. They had similar blue-gray eyes. She wondered where he was and whether he'd care where she was. Rummaging in her suitcase, she pulled out a small pad of paper, sat up in bed with her back against the plaster wall, and began to write.

Dear Dad,

I hope this reaches you. I'm on an island off the coast of Maine. If you need to get in touch, the phone is Horace and Beverly Woodruff. (207) 596-1723. I'm helping Beverly sort out the contents of a house where she grew up. I met her through Oz. Remember him? We went to the same school. He's planting trees with Horace north of here.

I'm no longer living in New London. After I leave Vinalhaven, I don't know where I'll be, but I'll let you know.

I hope you're sitting down. I just found out I'm pregnant. Oz is the father, but I don't think we'll be living together. But I'm keeping the baby no matter what. I'm happy, so don't worry, okay?

How's the business going? You said you might be going to Europe and Turkey. Hope you find some good maps. Maybe you're still there. If you get this, don't forget I love you.   —Lucy

She saw him in a back alley of Venice, surrounded by water, digging through old maps. Even though months went by when she didn't hear from him, she liked that he was obsessed. One day, she imagined she'd give in to Latin the way he'd given in to maps. She could feel it tugging at her, the way water grabs your feet at shoreline. But she needed to live out her *quo fata vocant* phase: whither the fates call. She'd told her mother that she didn't need to stay in college. But before all was said and done, she'd be surprised if she didn't go back.

She stared at the ceiling cracks and remembered a picture she'd seen, taken in Germany after World War II: happy-sad like Beverly's face, like her father's face: bombed walls and buildings half standing. The ground was covered with rubble, and a kind of war-filth hung in the air. In the foreground was a baby in a carriage, lying in the sunshine. The baby had a round, healthy face, and Lucy remembered looking at her and wanting a baby of her own. Her mother would have said, *What? Are you crazy? You don't even know how to look after yourself.*

What would Oz say? Maybe he'd never know.

In school, Mrs. Slavin warned her health class over and over about getting pregnant—having a baby was the worst calamity that could befall you. Mrs. Slavin said that no one, *no one* should have a baby before age twenty-four. You had to get your own feet under you. You had to know what love was all about. You had to be financially viable. You had to have your issues sorted out with your parents, you had to have a decent place to raise your child. You had to get the rebelliousness out of you, to gain enough maturity to be able to give something to another human being. Lucy turned on her side. *Mrs. Slavin,* she said to the wall, *I'm twenty-two, so ha.* She felt a kind of ferocity take root, tough as the beak of a gull. *Twenty-two, and I'm keeping it.*

45

Bob dug with his front paws, flinging clods of earth up with his back paws onto the shore of the lake. "What are you doing?" asked Horace.

They had just three more trees to go this trip, and Horace found himself missing Beverly more than he'd missed her all summer. "Oz? Where are you? Oz!"

Oz dragged out of the woods, hitching up his pants. "What." He looked like a savage—matted beard, ripped shirt.

"I was thinking."

"Yeah." Oz looked uninterested. He picked up a hunk of wood and began hacking at it with a jackknife.

"I could use a break . . . You're going to cut yourself like that. Listen, I thought we could surprise them out on Vinalhaven and spend a few days there, come back here after Labor Day when it's cooler and the bugs die down. What do you think?"

"I think you better go on your own." Chips flew from the wood in Oz's hand. He bent over and popped a few blueberries in his mouth from a low-growing plant.

"It's likely that Lucy wouldn't be there if she didn't want to see you again. Have you thought about that?"

Oz stopped.

"Well, would she?"

"I don't know."

"If we're quick, we could get to Millinocket by eight, back home tomorrow afternoon, off the next morning at four, make the noon boat."

Oz dropped the hunk of wood at his feet. "I don't know. Where do you want the last trees?"

"Forget them, let's go."

"I'm putting them in the ground."

"You decide." Horace was already pulling up the stakes around his tent. He looked twenty years younger. *Beverly.*

They arrived home at three. Horace usually avoided the hardware store on Saturdays, but he had to buy a stepladder for Vinalhaven—Beverly had told him over the phone she was standing on a stool, on top of a chair, to reach the high shelves in the kitchen.

In the parking lot of the hardware store, a car nearly backed into him. He pulled the truck into a spot, opened both windows for Bob, and locked the doors. Bob's nose came out the crack, wet, black. When he was a boy, his mother read him a story about how Noah's dog saved all the animals by plugging a hole in the boat with his nose, and that's why, ever after, dog's noses have been cold and wet as the sea. It was no fair, after his kind had saved everyone—Bob wasn't allowed anywhere.

He walked toward the door with the heat surging straight off asphalt; he'd just made it to the cool inside when who should he run into, pulling on a light switch in a display of overhead lights, but Bradford Nolty. *I'll be goddamned.* They shook hands.

"I've been planting trees," said Horace.

"Oh?" said Nolty.

"Volunteer work for the Forest Service on Grand Lake Matagamon. You probably haven't heard of it," said Horace.

"You're right," said Bradford.

"Beautiful country."

"I imagine it is."

Horace studied him. "I hope you won't take this badly, but do you know what your problem is? You don't get enough fresh air. I can see by your face that you think I'm some sort of lunatic, but I'm serious, Bradford; if you don't get more fresh air in your lungs, you're going to be in trouble. You're trying to figure out how you can get away from me as fast as possible, but this is important—I'm not talking about ski slopes. Or picnic sites by the side of the road. I'm talking about off the beaten track. You'd be amazed what it does for you."

Nolty said he'd keep it under advisement and stumbled into the hammer section.

Horace pictured a brown rabbit he'd seen by the lake, eating shoots of grass on a hillock in a downpour, its back slicked down with rain. It shook a wet foot and made a wild dash for cover. It wasn't something that Nolty would ever see.

He left the hardware store carrying the ladder, and for a moment, didn't know where he was. Setting the ladder down and turning around, he saw a fitness gym and a video store, but they didn't look familiar. The heat galloped over asphalt, crackled up through the rubber soles of his shoes. It was Nolty's fault, he thought. He was always thrown off by Nolty. As he passed a hand over his forehead, skin from the last sunburn flaked off. His right ankle didn't want to bend. He leaned over to have a look at it, the way you lean over to look at a flat tire. He had a truck here somewhere. Another wave of something passed over him. What would he do if he couldn't find it? He limped around, faced north, south, east, west, and caught a glimpse of yellow, and suddenly he wasn't lost. He set the ladder in the back and opened the door to Bob, so happy to see him, climbed up into the cab of the truck and turned the key. He wasn't backing fast when he heard the crunch. He turned off the truck, got out, and found that he'd hit a low concrete post. The fender wasn't badly damaged, but he couldn't handle it—he was a tired, stupid old man and needed his Beverly. Oz would have to drive tomorrow.

He drove back home slowly and got out. His legs were tired and shaky. He wanted a nap, but he needed to do this one thing he'd been thinking about first. He went into the backyard, picked out five of the healthiest trees he could find, watered them, and set them in the bed of the truck next to the ladder. If Oz asked what they were for, he wouldn't tell him—he'd tell no one until it was time.

46

While Horace sat in the cab of the truck waiting for the ferry, Oz paced the parking lot, thinking he shouldn't have come. He'd never wanted to in the first place. Lucy would say who'd he think he was, turning up again with no warning. There she was running away from him as fast as she could, and here he was running after her. His mother had chased his father; his father had chased Consolata. Things generally turned out badly for the chaser, he'd noticed.

In front and behind them were lines of rusted-out island cars mixed in with trucks and vacationers, people spilled all over: city guys in boat shoes; children sticky with ice cream; tired, tanned women; island people passing the time with one another. A brown fogbank rolled and undulated out on the horizon, shifting and heaving like an animal. Oz hadn't spent much time next to the sea, and he didn't trust it. No particular reason except that it ate people alive.

A white dog with long, matted hair peed on a patch of weed, ambled up to a trash bin, found a scrap of something underneath, and ate it. As Oz wandered back toward the line of cars, it followed him.

Bob barked up a storm from the back of the truck. "Cut it out," said Horace, his mouth full of sandwich. "It's Oz."

Horace stepped out of the truck and found the white dog. "Where'd *you* come from?" He looked around at the other cars. "Where'd you find him?" Horace asked.

"I didn't." The dog's tail was still, its head low. Every rib stood out.

"He has no collar," said Horace. "Someone'll probably pick him up. They'll give him seven days to be adopted, that's what these shelters do." The dog sat with his haunches on the ground and looked at Horace. "Huh, fella. That's what they do. Maybe you'll be one of the lucky ones."

"Bullshit," said Oz. "He's never been lucky in his life." He walked around the side of the truck and came back. "*I'll* take him." He held out his hand, and the dog sniffed at it from a distance.

"I don't think so," said Horace. "Besides, you don't like dogs."

"I like this one."

"Wait a minute, slow down," said Horace, "you have to plan for an animal." The last of the big trucks rumbled off the ferry, and the foot passengers stood ready with their tickets.

Oz looked at Horace. "So I do my careful planning, and what good does that do this dog? You just said it. He'll be dead."

"Where would he sit?"

"Back here with me and the ladder."

Horace shrugged. "C'mon," he said to Bob. Bob leapt off the back and circled the new dog, his hackles high. The cars around them started up. "Bob, get in," said Horace. He slammed the door and went around to the driver's side while the white dog stood behind the truck. The ferry guy pointed and waved them on. Horace didn't move, and cars drove around them.

"C'mon, boy," said Oz. "Jump in." The dog looked at him.

"Hurry up!" yelled Horace.

"Go on ahead!"

Horace drove onto the boat while Oz walked toward the

ramp. "Come here, boy," he said, patting the leg of his blue jeans. The dog watched him, ears pricked. Oz went down the ramp and onto the boat; whistled and clapped his hands. "C'mon, last chance, get a move on!" The dog began to run. His stride lengthened out, his tail streamed behind. He came to rest next to Oz's knees, panting. Oz reached down and thumped him on the side. The whistle sounded, and the boat pulled away.

The fog grew thicker as they moved away from land, the sea the color of gunmetal. Up on the top deck, fog-sweat collected on Oz's arms, repeated on the dirty white back of the dog.

As the boat rolled, Horace glanced out at the water churning to the right and left of the stern. Behind them, Rockland's foggy wharves were gone, as though they never were. He knew Oz was on the boat, but he hadn't seen the dog get on.

He opened the door of the truck, told Bob to wait, and climbed the stairs to the top deck. Oz stood near the bow, teeth into the wind; the white dog stood next to him. Horace went back to the truck and picked up the rest of his sandwich, climbed the stairs, and held it out to Oz.

"I don't need it," Oz said.

"I mean for the dog." Horace took out the lettuce and threw it overboard.

"Why'd you do that?"

"Dogs don't like lettuce."

"Where's Bob?"

"Down in the truck."

While Oz went to get him, Horace worked out that the dog was a she. "You're a fetching one, aren't you?" She wagged her tail shyly as he bent over and looked into her ears for mites. Patches of fur were missing on her shoulders and rump. Suddenly she stood stiff, hackles up, ears back, as Bob came toward her. He sniffed her underbelly, turned away, and did a little cavort; he sniffed under her tail while she stood still, ears high. The tip of his tail wagged, and he did another little turn about.

"I think she's passed the test," said Horace. "She's a she, by the way."

"Yeah? She's pretty, huh? I mean if she was cleaned up."

"Good dog," said Horace, giving her another pat.

Ahead of them, just visible, was a land of spruce and granite. Small islands dotted the landscape where fishing birds dived into sprays of white water, where rocks had cracked and split along the water's edge and lay like huge turtles in the sun.

"Is that it?"

"Where? Up beyond, yes. It's been a long time since I've seen it."

47

Beverly turned on the vacuum cleaner and turned it off, surprised by the roaring and snarling. She'd forgotten that her grandmother had once set the inside of it on fire. She wasn't sure how, but it had something to do with her not being able to close the door of the woodstove and sucking up the ash and lighting the bag on fire and having to throw the whole thing out in the snow. The old aqua-blue Electrolux was dented where it had bit into the drift; her grandmother never used it again, as though it was the vacuum's fault. She'd belonged in New York, not on an island. Funny how people got stuck in places. Beverly stood with her feet pointing into the downstairs closet, thinking. She'd gotten stuck in Connecticut.

The day was gray and vaporous, heavy with sea. High overhead was a pattern of triangular clouds, like the footprints of gulls. There was the sound of Lucy's bare feet coming down the stairs.

"Have you called your mother?" she asked.

"No."

"How about it?"

"I have to find the right time."

"You'll be relieved when it's behind you."

"I don't know what to say. She'll want to know who the father is. I'll have to tell her, and then she'll say how could I be so stupid? Maybe she'll be so mad she'll tell me don't bother to ever come home again."

"She won't do that."

"I don't know. Give me something to clean today. I want to scrub something."

Beverly looked at her.

"It's okay. I won't hurt myself."

Under the faucet of the claw-foot bathtub, Lucy worked at a reddish-brown stain where water had dripped out of the rusty pipes over the years; she supposed there were ways to remove stains like this one, but she didn't really have a clue. She imagined Grandfather Kearny, lion-man, lying in the tub. She hadn't taken off his ratty old vest since Beverly had given it to her.

She gave up on the tub and began on the floor, but it presented its own problems: the linoleum under the tub was cracked and peeled. Everything smelled like the sea. After scrubbing a while longer, she grabbed an old *National Geographic* and went downstairs to sit on the granite stoop. She turned the pages dreamily, imagining herself first on a rocky outcropping in Iceland, then among horseback-riding Basotho tribesmen. Then in Panama, where dusty, dark-skinned kids gathered around two women in front of a hut. In the arms of one of the smiling women . . . she stopped. A baby, white as white. The article said that one in eighty-five Kuna Indian babies was born albino. *Les enfants de la lune,* they were called. People believed they were angels of mercy: when the flying dog tried to take a bite out of the sun, it was the people of the moon who saved the earth from darkness.

In her heart, *don't say it aloud,* she hoped her baby wouldn't be a moon baby. Like the peal of a bell in a valley, that lonesomeness. Oz said she was beautiful, but he didn't know what it was like to live inside that light, to have a bright day hurt you.

In biology she'd read that one in seventy people carry a gene for OCA, oculocutaneous albinism. People can have normal pigment but carry an altered recessive gene. If both parents are carriers, each of them has a one in two chance of passing on OCA. Together, they have a one in four chance of their baby being a moon baby. But what if one parent is a full moon and the other's a sun? Then the baby's a sun. That was right, wasn't it? Wasn't the only way for a baby to be a moon if both parents had the fucked-up gene? So, if Oz was a carrier, probably there was a three in four chance of moon. But chances are he wasn't.

She knew a baby was in there, but she didn't feel like talking to it today, to something that wouldn't answer. Her mother would say what did she want a baby for, what about college? She'd blame Oz. But it wasn't his fault. She'd tell her mother she liked it here. She'd say she liked the way there were limits to everything—the number of people, the number of things that could go wrong. You could get to know the sounds of birds, owls, things that mattered. Not sales representatives, people who wanted her to join their winning team. So, ruin her life.

"Give me a hand, would you?" Beverly called out a second-story window. "I'm trying to get these books down." Lucy found Beverly upstairs tottering on a little round stool, reaching up to a high shelf.

"Trash novels. Look at this." Beverly handed one down, opened to an illustration. A man was climbing down the side of a building with a woman in his arms. *Priscilla fainted in his arms,* the caption said. Beverly laughed and stopped suddenly. "What's that?"

"What?"

"Someone just drove in."

"I don't think so." Lucy looked out the window and said, "Yes, you're right." There was a truck stopped in the driveway, a familiar yellow one. The thinnest dog in the world leaped over the tailgate, followed by . . . Oz? She didn't think. She ran down the stairs and down the steep bank out of sight behind the tangled thicket of sea roses and crouched on the shore like a savage.

"What are you doing here?" Beverly yelled out the window to Horace. She rushed down the wooden stairs, clattering her shoes.

"Surprise," Horace said, grinning, hugging her.

"You're all hot." She took his hand.

"You've got a big smudge." He licked his thumb and wiped her cheek.

"You wouldn't believe the stuff I've gotten rid of," she said. "Lucy's been a terrific help . . . Was it Oz's idea to come?"

"Mine," he said, looking pleased. "Oz wanted to keep working."

"How are things at the house?"

"A bunch of trees were dying when we got back. Hockness said he'd take care of things until we got back—we'll have to leave again tomorrow."

"Why tomorrow? Stay a few days, rest up, give Oz and Lucy a chance to . . . she's pregnant."

"Lucy is? Good Lord."

"What I thought too."

"Good Lord," he said again.

"She wants to keep the baby. Hasn't told her mother yet."

"I believe the other responsible half is rather *persona non grata* at the moment. That's why we're leaving tomorrow—I promised."

Beverly made a face. "You can't leave so soon. You just got here."

He squeezed her hand. "The last trees are waiting."

Oz's dog half ran, half fell down the bank, headed for the shore. She sniffed along a pathway and froze when she caught sight of Lucy. "Hello, girl," Lucy said softly. "Come here." She patted the dirty back and smelled her palm: dog and engine oil. She ducked back behind the thicket of roses. *If he doesn't come by the time I count to twenty, I'm standing up.* She counted twenty and stayed hidden. The dog waded in the water and dug at something with her front paws. She heard a crashing on the bank and then a voice. "What are you doing?" She looked up to see Oz standing over her.

"I don't know."

He crouched down and pulled her in until they were both on their knees holding each other.

"I'm pregnant." She didn't mean to tell him right away. She hadn't even decided whether to tell him ever. When she said it, it felt as though her insides turned inside out.

"Am I the father?"

She nodded. "Who else?"

"Jesus," he said.

She looked down at the backs of her hands, burned from the sun.

"I've always wanted to be a father," he said. "I mean it." She wrinkled her nose. She didn't imagine they'd be bringing up this kid together. "I don't think," he continued, "that raising a kid is as hard as some people make it out . . . "

"Don't you know *anything*?" Her eyes flashed. "Of *course* it's hard! Think about your mother, all the grief you've given her."

"What! What did I say?"

She raised her eyebrows.

"It wasn't my idea to come," he said. "I almost stayed in Connecticut. It was Horace who wanted to, I mean I wanted to see you. You look so beautiful, like a . . . I don't know. A big cake." He laughed and put his arm around her waist and started pulling her toward a patch of grass near the shore.

She resisted and then let herself go. "Who's the dog?"

"I found her. Her name's Daisy."

She touched his lip with a finger and smiled. "Daisy." Out in the small harbor, a gull dropped a clam onto the rocks. The bird went down, picked it up, flew high and dropped it again, over and over until the shell cracked. "Sometimes I wonder if there's really a baby in here." She smoothed her shirt over her tummy. "I tested positive though." He kissed her, touched her breast with the back of a finger. She closed her eyes. "What if it looks like me?"

"If it looks like you, it would be the happiest thing in the world."

She felt it starting all over, a force like wind pushing her sideways.

48

"What are you doing?" asked Beverly, coming around the corner.

Oz dragged an old lawn chair out of the boathouse and threw it into the grass. "Getting your boat for you."

"I didn't think anyone heard me say I'd like to go for a row." She tried to thank him, but he ducked back in and carried out an old electric heater and a bicycle.

"My father used to ride that." She threw a cracked flowerpot toward the lawn chair while he dragged out a couch. "I never liked that horrible scratchy thing," she said. "We can start a throwaway pile." He pulled out a Maytag washing-machine box and a snow fence and dumped them on the couch.

"You'll never guess what this is," she said at the door. She held a tool in her hand, about a foot long, with a wooden handle.

"What?"

"A file for a horse's teeth. And look at this." She held up a brown net, knitted, with two ears sticking up. "We used to put this over Esther's ears to keep the black flies off. Once upon a time, a net factory employed people downtown. My grandfather courted someone who worked there, but she married someone else and had a baby five months later."

"Lucy's having a baby," he blurted out.

Beverly spread the ear net out and folded it together, ear against ear. She looked thoughtful and smiled up into his face. "You're going to be a father."

He smiled back, feeling strange. *Father . . . Father.* You repeat any word enough times and it sounds like it's in a foreign language. He stumbled into the boathouse for another load and realized he was crying. As he shoved the back of his hand under his nose, two big tears fell on his sneakers. He looked around for something to blow his nose on and found a lawn-mower spark-plug rag. Most of the men he'd known in prison had lost their kids; it felt as though it was going to happen to him. Like a disease he'd caught there. But no, he wouldn't say that, not even to himself.

He pushed a lawn mower out, went back for another load. He cleared a pathway for Beverly's boat, and the two of them inched it down to the water.

"C'mon, I'll take you out," she said. "Grab those oars." One was mended with duct tape, and he thought about asking if it was going to hang on, but it looked as though it had been like that for years. Beverly took off her shoes and climbed over the seaweed, and the boat settled down in the water as she got in. He handed her the oars, put one foot in the stern, and pushed off with the other. She rowed toward an inlet. "That's Neck Island over there," she said, "and out at the end is Bluff Head. And this little one's called Mink Island. I've never seen a mink on it, but I did see one over there running behind a rock. Like a liquid cat." She pulled on the oars and breathed hard. They rounded the point of a small island, and there on the shore was a huge house that had been built on a headland with a stretch of green running down to the water. "That's the Murphys' lawn," she said derisively. "I never did understand why people make lawns like that

". . . I've got an idea. I'll take you up to the little beach by Bluff Head. The tide's right."

She was a skilled oarsman, and looking at her, he thought, *She woke up.* She rowed to a small island shaped like an hourglass, and in the middle of it was the beach she promised. She landed and hauled the boat up before he could help her. There were great slabs of rock warmed by sun, and, strewn about, crab shells the gulls had opened on rocks. He picked up a feather and lay down on a cup-shaped rock.

She let him row back. The tide was with them, and they whooshed in through a break between two islands and home. Oz turned the boat over and tied it up. "Do you think I could take it out for a spin sometime?"

"Sure; watch the current, though. It's stronger than you think." She wasn't getting any reaction. "Did you hear?"

"Watch the current," he said.

He sat on a lobster trap while she went up to the house, and tried to remember the names of the islands. Mink. Bluff Head. Calderwood Neck. Daisy found him and rolled in a pile of seaweed and finished herself off with sand. "No, Daisy," he said as she tried to follow him into the house. It turned out he should have stayed out himself—in the kitchen, he walked straight into a scene.

"Oz! Tell him!" Beverly stood by the stove and waved her arms. "He needs a rest. So what if a few trees die? He says you're going back tomorrow."

"I don't know," he said. He couldn't tell whether Lucy wanted him to stay or go.

"What's the hurry?" said Beverly. He left the room fast, and Beverly's voice rose, and Horace's rose louder. Outside, he heard their voices die down and start up again, around and around they went.

That night, Lucy waited for him, and he didn't come. From far off, a handful of stars shone. Nearer, clouds. She held her hand out of the sheets and held it in front of a bright star. The wind sang high against the house. If he came, she didn't know what she'd do. Part of her would put her arms around him, and the other part would push him away. But you can't go on doing that. He didn't come because he didn't want to be where he was half-wanted. Soon he'd be gone for good, and she'd deserve it. Her breath stopped. *I don't know*, she said into the back of her hand. *Tempus erit, something something*, Ovid had written. He was talking about a woman who shut out her lovers and became cold and lonely and bitter.

Beverly had won one more day—Oz would leave the day after tomorrow. Lucy got out of bed and padded barefoot down the hall to his door. She put her ear against the wood and thought she could hear him breathing. She put her hand on the doorknob, felt the blood rush to her ears. She thought, *This is the moment that will decide my life.* She paused, and the owl started up outdoors. It was a sign. She dropped her hand, turned, and went back to her room.

49

In the morning, Beverly came downstairs before anyone was stirring. The air was cool through the open windows, the sun just up. A gull cried, and a boat started its engine far away. Overhead, she felt Horace's heavy, blurry slumber that wanted to go on and on. She drew herself a glass of water; on the wooden floor upstairs was the sound of a dog's toenails and then another set of toenails. They tumbled downstairs into the kitchen. *Me first,* gnawing and jawing at each other and rolling around on the floor until they nosed their way out the screen door. Out the window, a violet cloud gathered over the water. In a minute, it was gone, replaced by bright gray. She'd row out the gap between Coombs Neck and the island, and if she didn't stay out too long, she'd be able to sail right back home on the incoming tide.

She took a sip of water and thought about how she'd wrecked the previous rowboat years ago with her old friend, Lorena, going out when a storm was brewing. The rain and wind came up and they were blown onto the rocks and stove the boat in, and her father said she was damn lucky the wind had turned them eastward or they would have been blown out to sea, and she'd laughed to sweeten her father's anger, but it only made things worse, and meanwhile Lorena had her own troubles, but nothing compared to what came later when she married that Douglas man.

The dogs were back, scratching at the door for breakfast. She heard someone moving about upstairs; quietly, she let the dogs in and fed them, grabbed a jacket, and slipped out the back door. A moment later, she came back, tore an old envelope in half, and wrote, *Gone rowing. Back in an hour or so.* The wind was rising with the sun, but the water in the harbor back toward Smith Cove was still glassy. Beverly slid down the bank, catching hold of trees and shrubs. She opened the boathouse door, took out the oars, dragged the boat over the pebbles, and began to row. By the time she was halfway down the Neck, the world dropped away, and it was just the lap of water on the bow and the brightening sky. She pulled on the oars, and the water parted with a soft swoosh. She was out at the point now, rounding the curve toward Deep Cove, a protected spot from which you could see the whole ridged back of Deer Isle and Stonington, and the light blue of Mount Desert Island beyond, partially clouded over this morning. And to the east, Isle au Haut. In all these years, she'd never been there. When she was young, they were always going to go. Her mother would make egg salad sandwiches the night before, but something always came up: the wind was wrong or an animal was sick. The island became an impossible place to get to, a place she'd almost rather not go now—every life needs a place you can't get to.

The boat had a small leak, and she stopped to bail with a saucepan and heard the sound of a bulldozer far off toward Smith Cove, where Abner Gould and his son were clearing land for a new house. She picked up the oars again. Today, that Massachusetts couple was coming to see the house. The people wanted to rent it summers, or possibly buy it. Already, she didn't like them. She wanted the house to be occupied year-round, for there to be children and dogs everywhere, for the snow to pile up in winter and be shoveled, for embers to stay lit in the woodstove, for a man or woman to come outside on an April morning and see the bitterns and ducks returning. These people from Massachusetts, what did they know about any of that? They'd have drinks on the lawn and fill pastry shells with crab. Over her dead body.

Oz came softly to Lucy before the sun was up, knocked on her door, and went in. Half of Lucy's head was under the sheet. Later, she couldn't remember what she'd been dreaming, only the effort of lifting herself out of it.

"Can I come in?" he whispered. She opened her eyes onto his face. He was wearing a T-shirt and jockey shorts. She held the sheet back while she moved toward the wall to make room for him. Her shirt was dark blue, like midnight.

"What's the matter?" she asked.

"Nothing," he said, slipping in under the covers. He slid his arm under her and folded her in.

"You looked as though something was the matter. Your hands are cold."

"Can I tell you something?" he said.

"Mm-hmm." She exhaled against him and closed her eyes. Her breath was moist at the bend of his arm.

"You look so beautiful . . . "

She waited for him to say what he was going to say.

"There was an older man in jail who embezzled money from his hometown," Oz said. "He loved his daughters, but he never saw them—he didn't want them seeing him in prison. He was one of the loneliest people; but he made friends with a half-deaf man and he ended up protecting him from a bunch of guys who were always beating him up just for the hell of it. It was like he found a son."

She opened her eyes and looked at him. "Why did you tell me?"

"The older man loved him like he was his own son. I don't

know. It's not always easy to love the people you want to love. But I love *you*, and I don't even have to try . . . and I'll love our baby." She put her arms around him and held tight.

"Someone's going downstairs," he whispered.

"Beverly."

"How do you know?"

"The way she walks." She put the palm of her hand over his eyes and ran it down his nose. "How about shutting the door all the way?"

He got out of bed and took off his shirt and jockey shorts. His legs were white and his arms were brown, and he closed the door and came back to her. He climbed in awkwardly, all knees, like a boy getting into bed. His hand was large and raspy as he ran it down her shoulder. It was one of the things she loved about him—he was big enough that it felt as though nothing bad would ever happen. Except all at once it felt as though something bad would. "I'm afraid you'll end up back in prison," she said.

"I won't."

"How do you know?"

"I just know I won't." She heard his voice go hard, but she kept on.

"You can tell me that, you told me that last time. It's easy to say it."

"You don't believe it, do you," he said coldly. The bed was too small to move away from her, but he did. His eyes were on her the way you grip someone hard by the top of their arm. His leg was pushed hard against the footboard at the end of the bed. She was barely touching it, but she felt the anger in his knee.

"If you keep doing what you're doing, you will someday. You *will.*"

"Stop it." He leaned over, picked his T-shirt off the floor, and pulled it on, stood up, got into his jockey shorts.

"Where are you going?"

"I don't know."

"You can't just leave. We're talking."

"Is that what we're doing?"

"You can't leave in the middle of a fight. What if something happened to you and I never saw you again?" He stood over her. "It makes me crazy to hear you say there's nothing to worry about. They're watching you now. Don't tell me there's nothing to worry about. There is. I don't want to lose you, that's all."

He sat down on the bed and looked at her. He touched his finger to the space between her eyes. "You're the stubbornest person I've ever met," he said. "But I'm not going to promise something I can't live with . . . I don't know."

"So how can I be with you if you don't know?"

He kissed her on the lips, smoothed her hair off her forehead. Her body was shaking, and as he held her, it stopped.

"You don't need this on right now," he said at last, pulling her T-shirt up over her head. She wrestled an arm out, put her legs around his waist, and held on.

50

Half an hour too early, the people from Massachusetts turned up. "Godsakes," Beverly muttered, looking out an upstairs window. A man and woman sat in the front seat of a Volvo with the windows rolled up, as though they were surrounded by carnivores.

Horace was packing his bag upstairs in the bedroom. "You're really going, aren't you," said Beverly. He jammed three more shirts in and zipped it up. Down below, Oz stood under a maple tree like an ox asleep on his feet. Lucy was just crossing the driveway to him.

On his way downstairs, carrying his bag, Horace's sock slid off a riser, and his bag rolled ahead of him. He sat down hard and went halfway down the stairs bump, bump, trying to catch himself on something, until finally he stopped. He didn't feel like standing up right away and groaned softly. Bob came running, put his nose under Horace's elbow, and nudged until Horace stood up. Nothing was broken, but everything hurt. He had an abrasion on the back of his hand, and his cheek was grazed. "Maybe we'll start the day over," he said to Bob, and stood up.

Beverly came to the top of the stairs. "Are you okay?"

"Okay."

"Sweetheart, listen to me; I don't want you to go. You're exhausted. You'll kill yourself."

"I won't," he said.

She had a terrible thought: *If he leaves, I'll never see him again.* "If that's the way you want it," she said under her breath. She raced around upstairs, looking for the keys to the truck, praying they weren't in his pocket. She found them in the kitchen next to the sugar bowl and pocketed them.

Oz and Lucy were kissing under a tree as Horace deposited his bag in the truck. "Where are my keys?" he called to Oz.

Oz shrugged.

"*I've* got them," said Beverly, coming out onto the stoop. She heard the sound of a tractor down the road, pictured the head of Giles Sprague bobbing over the tops of his fields, round and round he went, harrowing, planting. Everything felt safe inside that sound.

Horace came after her.

"No," she said, moving in front of the Massachusetts car.

"Darling . . ."

"I'll give them to you tomorrow." He grabbed her wrist. "NO! Lucy! Help!"

The Massachusetts man got out of the car and advanced on Horace. "See here," he said. His wife got out of the car after him. Beverly broke free and stood between them and Horace.

"Leave him alone," she said. "He's done nothing to you. We were having a quarrel. It's none of your business."

"What's up?" said Oz, sauntering over.

"She won't give me the keys," said Horace.

"Good for her."

"Didn't I give you my extra set?" asked Horace.

"No," Oz lied.

"You'll have to stay then," said Beverly. "I swear I'll throw them in the ocean if you come for me again." Oz went to the truck and unloaded his bag, and Horace went muttering into the house.

Beverly turned to the couple.

"Dick and Sheila Clough," the Massachusetts fellow said. "I'm sorry, I didn't realize . . . "

Beverly shrugged. Dick was a big round guy, booming with good fortune, blondish-gray hair thinned out and combed down neatly. She disliked Sheila on sight—dark circles under the eyes, thin, nervous hands, black suburban shoes. They walked single file to the back door.

"You get many mosquitoes here?" asked Dick.

"Quite a few," said Beverly. She wanted them to go away. "This is the kitchen. Pretty much as my mother left it." *Obviously, it's a kitchen.* It looked shabby as she saw it through their eyes— the porcelain sink rough with use, the plaster wall gouged out where someone had installed a stovepipe, a rocker by the window with a faded green seat, pots and pans stacked around. Sheila's heels clicked on the linoleum. Once upon a time in this kitchen, there'd been large silver cans of milk fresh from a cow, dilly beans processing on the stove, hay and horse shit stuck to the soles of boots, a lamb born too early, nothing that Dick and Sheila would know anything about.

They went on to the sitting room with its view down to the harbor, one of Beverly's favorite spots. The room drank in light, reflecting it like water. As far as she was concerned, there wasn't a more beautiful room in the whole world. But she heard Sheila say *sotto voce* to Dick, "It could be wallpapered; that might help."

Beverly turned and faced her. "You know what," she said. "I don't want to sell the house. I don't believe I want to rent it either."

They looked at her. "Well," said Sheila, "we certainly appreciate your time, Mrs. Woodcock . . . "

"Woodruff," said Beverly. "A woodcock is a type of bird that buzzes when it mates."

"I don't think it's for us anyway, is it darling?" said Sheila.

"Island life seems quite a chore, all the back and forth. We were really thinking of something a little more up-to-date."

She watched as they backed out the driveway. They'd want a beige and taupe interior. Just thinking about it made her want to get out tubes of paint—Prussian blue and Chinese vermilion. After they were gone, Lucy came downstairs, trailing soot into the kitchen with her bare feet. She'd been cleaning out an upstairs chimney. "What's with those people who just left?" she asked, hands wrapping around a glass of milk.

"You're tracking soot."

Lucy looked down. "Sorry." She went outdoors, scuffed her feet in the grass, and came back in.

"They came to look at the house, but I told them to forget it . . . By the way, did you see Horace upstairs?"

"I think he went back to bed."

"Did you ever call your mother?"

"No."

"She knows where you are, right?"

"Yes."

"When are you going to call her?" She felt bad-tempered.

"Today?" asked Lucy.

"Is that a question?"

"No."

Beverly opened a drawer in the kitchen full of miscellany, pulled it out, and carried the whole mess to the table. There were bits of string and rubber bands and an old packet of pipe tobacco and bits of yellowed paper. "Do you mind if I ask you something?" She tossed out a can of dried-up shoe polish. "Oz loves you. What are you waiting for?"

"I don't know," said Lucy.

"Do you care for him?"

"I'm afraid he'll get busted and sent back to prison."

"So you've given him a life sentence . . . You know, raising a baby on your own is no picnic. It's hard enough with two."

Lucy threw a tube of glue into the wastebasket. "Don't lecture me," she said. "I know." The refrigerator stopped chugging, and the kitchen went quiet. Beverly finished sorting the drawer, excused herself, and went into the sitting room. She looked out the window, at Bob and Daisy rolling over and over on the lawn, wrestling, grabbing each other's ears. She picked up a pen and paper, and her hands drew a tree falling from the sky. Tumbling over itself, it fell.

51

Horace hadn't been under house arrest since he was a kid. He'd never have come if he'd known . . . Like Toad in *The Wind in the Willows*. It made him sick to think of the trees dying down in Connecticut. He pictured the lake, the woods where they needed to be, a tumult of clouds, rain falling on green leaves, the sound of young birds *scree-screeee*-ing, wanting food. Who'd she think she was? Two could play this game. He could get up in the middle of the night, find the keys, drive off in the truck—no, wait a minute, he'd have to get a boat.

Forget the trees a minute, you moron, a voice in his head said. *You. She loves* you. He stopped. It was true. Why else would she make such a fuss? He came out of the bedroom.

Wearing a pink kerchief over her head, Lucy was scrubbing the hallway. She had a smile that was . . . what was the word? He smiled back. *Luminous.* He went downstairs.

"Horace?" he heard. "Where are you?" He saw Beverly's head go by the kitchen window as she called to him.

He tried to ignore her. He knew it was childish. But curiosity got the better of him, and he went outdoors. She was on the other side of the lilac bush. When she turned and saw him, she fished in her pocket and held out the keys. "I was wrong," she said.

He took them from her and put them in his pocket.

"I still don't want you to go."

"Maybe I won't," he said.

"I'm going to get fish for dinner from Matty. She said Luke would be coming in this afternoon with sea bass. Shall I get enough for four?"

"Sure."

"And mashed potatoes and beans. There's something I want to talk with you about. I've had an idea about the house." She told him what she was thinking.

He had to hand it to her—not what most people would think of doing, but it made an odd kind of sense. "But it's more complicated," she said. "Promise me you won't be upset. I don't like Connecticut, I've never really liked it. I want to move."

"I'm not particularly fond of it either."

"I thought you were."

"I thought *you* were."

"We can go anywhere," she said. The dogs tumbled into the room and knocked over a lawn chair.

"Out!" he said. "Out of here!"

52

In the lower field, Oz was pulling out some of the underbrush that Beverly said needed to go. His clothes were covered with dirt and bits of twig. If he had to make a guess, he'd say that he and Lucy wouldn't make it. He thought of the way her jaw set, the way she both looked at him and didn't look at him when she was mad. But even worse, the way she flew into herself, like one of those swallows that lives under the eaves. Suddenly the sky's gone out of the bird, and it sinks into a hole deep inside a tree and is gone.

He went down to the shore and found the boat tethered up high near the rocks and roses; he dragged it across the pebble beach, took off his shoes, and pushed off. Setting the oars in the oarlocks, he pulled toward Neck Island, the way he and Beverly had gone out together. The boat curved left, and he pulled on the left oar to straighten it out. Then it went the other way, and he pulled on the right oar. It was harder than it looked. The oars chopped at the water, like chopsticks in soup. He wasn't getting any closer to the southern tip of Neck Island, and then he remembered Beverly saying, Don't overlap the oars on the recovery stroke, don't dip them down toward your feet. He sat still a few moments, not rowing at all, feeling the roll of water under him. When he looked up, it seemed he'd lost ground, that he was

281

farther from the point than ever, and he picked up the oars and focused on getting them both to hit the water together. He was rowing into the wind, and if he could get around the other side of the island, he thought he'd make better headway. He turned the boat and heard barking on the shore—Daisy was running up and down. "Go home!" he yelled, but she barked louder and jumped into the water. "Daisy! Go home, Daisy!" he yelled. She turned as though heading toward shore.

He pulled on the oars, managing to get around the side of the island, and made steady progress up the west side. In fact, he hardly had to lift an oar to move along. There were huge rocks along the shore and dead trees like bones, and before he knew it, he was streaking by the little sandbar Beverly had showed him. And for godsakes, there was Daisy again. She'd swum to the is-land, run the length of it, and now she was barking up and down the sandbar as he sailed past. She ran north toward Bluff Head, and before he knew it, he was out there too, and when it was too late, he saw that water was rushing past the lobster buoys, a cur-rent emptying out of the bay faster than he could row.

As he came around the head of land, the water changed to high chop. He tried to keep close to shore, but the tide carried him north and east. He pulled on the oars for all he was worth, trying to turn south and make it back to Coombs Neck. He could just make out the farmhouse, but he was far north of the inlet, getting farther away.

An oar jumped out of an oarlock, and the boat spun around and faced Isle au Haut. He was pissed now and pulled with all his weight, and the oar that had been mended with duct tape came apart. He tried to unpeel the tape and wrap it back around the broken ends, but the tape was too wet to hold. Far away on shore, the trees tossed in the wind while he tossed in the waves. The wind spun him around again, and out of the corner of his eye, he caught sight of something bob—*Christ, it's Daisy*. Her chin sloshed in and out of the waves as she churned along with her paws, breathing hard. The current carried her now, and even in the wind, he could hear the labor of her breathing. A wave leapt over the gunwales, and a gull cried overhead. Daisy was about the length of a football field away as the current drove her north.

Lucy walked down to the shore and stopped in front of Oz's shoes. At first she expected him to walk barefoot toward her from around the corner, but the boat was gone. She looked out. Far away was a fishing boat followed by gulls, but there was no sign of Oz.

She ran up the hill, back to the house. "The boat's gone," she panted to Horace. "I don't see Oz."

"Beverly would know . . . Beverly?" called Horace. She came into the room with a paper bag in one hand, her hair jammed behind her ears.

"We think Oz is out in the boat."

"It's all right; I told him he could take it when he wanted it."

"He's disappeared."

"What's the tide doing?" She looked out the window. "He's probably just around the point."

"Do you have another boat?" asked Lucy.

"No."

"What about the Coast Guard?"

"Maybe he went up Winter Harbor. I don't think he'd have gone far from shore."

"Don't they look for boats?" asked Lucy. "The Coast Guard?"

"No need to panic," said Beverly. "I think he'd have the sense to see which way the current was going. I'll walk over and check the cove."

Daisy was about half a football field away now, wet and wheezing with each breath. She and the boat were being carried farther and farther from shore, and the distant trees were now no taller than a knuckle. "Come on, girl, you can do it." He tried to paddle toward her, but he was pulled away. A wave went over Daisy's head and she gasped and shuddered and went under. In a second, she was up, her paws flailing. "C'mon, girl." It scared him to think what he'd do if she stopped paddling.

Miles away, a windjammer streaked across the horizon. Another wave broke over Daisy's head, and she went down again and came up. She was only thirty or forty yards away, breathing hard, when some light went out of her eyes, and she stopped. Another wave went over her. Oz took off his outer shirt. And then her head was out of the water and Oz was yelling, "C'mon girl! C'mon, you can do it, get those legs going." She started up again, her paws going quarter speed, and the gap slowly closed until she was the length of a lobster boat away, and then the length of three or four oars and then beside the boat, and Oz wrapped his arms around her cold body and hauled her over the side while the boat lurched sideways and nearly capsized. He toweled her off with his shirt, and she licked him weakly on the face, shaking in great spasms of cold. He rubbed and rubbed his shirt down her back, over her belly, down her legs. "Good girl. Good Daisy girl."

The wind drove them farther out. He thought he remembered Beverly saying something about an island five or six miles to the east. It was too overcast to see anything. Anyway, they'd miss him at some point, wouldn't they? And as long as he didn't swamp the boat or fall in . . . A wave came up over the gunwale, and Daisy whined. And then another wave, and soon she was barking nonstop. "Stop it, Daisy!" What went through his mind was what he and Jeremy Bittore saw on their fourth-grade field trip, the small fist of people on shore, the police cars and the man washed up, the sight of that arm bloated to twice the size of a normal man's arm, and how Mrs. MacAlistair had dragged him and Jeremy away before they had a chance to see the whole of It, because it was an It, not a man anymore.

Lucy looked in the phone book under Coast Guard, and it referred her to the United States Government Transportation Department. She imagined the big, radar-equipped boats, clean and swift. She didn't know whether to go for Command Admin or Operations. Command sounded better. She took the phone under the stairs and dialed. She told the woman on the other end that the rowboat had started out from Coombs Neck, but she didn't know where it was now. "It's blowing up for a storm after dark," said the woman. "We'll radio a few folks and see if anyone's seen him."

Lucy gave the woman her number, and in a sudden blurt, she asked, "Do you think he'll be all right?"

"As long as he hasn't gone over," said the woman. "The water's cold enough, you don't last long."

She considered that a moment. It wasn't what she wanted to hear. *I don't want to lose you, that's all.* She came back out from under the stairs and put the phone back on the hook, and there was Beverly. "I called the Coast Guard," said Lucy.

"I couldn't see him in the cove. Let's go down and check the other side."

A lobster fisherman hauled a trap a long way away. The man's back was turned, but Oz waved his arms and yelled, hoping the sternman might notice. The tide winged the boat along now, out, out until the trees on shore became a green blur.

When the fishing boat turned away from shore and began coming toward them, Oz waved his arms over his head. It seemed as though it turned west for a few moments, but then it straightened out and kept coming. It was impossible to see anyone on the boat, and for a moment he thought maybe it was a ghost boat coming for him. He'd heard of boats sailing toward people who were drowning, black-hulled boats like this one; the people who'd been alive one moment disappeared the next, and on nights when a gale drove the rain before it, there'd be the sound of voices crying in the wind and sometimes the sight of sailors turned white and gauzy, twisting in the air over the masts of ships. And here was this boat still coming for him, followed by a cloud of gulls, and he could see the high black rubber boots on the two men and the winch for pulling up the traps and finally, the faces of the two of them, one old and the other young. He waved again and yelled, and Daisy, who'd finally stopped barking, started up again, and then he felt as stupid as he'd ever felt in his life, and it was his own damn fault for thinking any moron could row a boat just because Beverly could. He didn't see how she hadn't drowned long ago.

"I broke an oar!" he yelled when they were close enough.

"Grab a line, and we'll give yer a tow!" said the older man. "Where you headed?"

"Portugal," said Oz. "But I was trying for Coombs Neck."

The older man's face was pushed in like he'd run into a door. He took off his hat to reposition it over his eyes. "You was lucky," he said. "Abel Gurgin radioed in. Asked whether we'd seen you. Told him we heard a dog, but we didn't see you first-off.

"That's Beverly Woodruff's boat, ain't it? Here, tie that line right on there." He looked as though he'd have a good laugh over a beer tonight. The young man just stared.

"You watch in back, Danny, and I'll fire 'er up."

The older guy picked up his radio receiver. "Got him. Yep. Lost an oar," he said. "Don't worry about it . . . We already hauled almost two-thirds." He put down the handset. It was a long while before they were close upon Deep Cove; he thought he saw a figure up on the hill and thought he hadn't and then they rounded Coombs Point and came up against the tide, still pouring out toward open sea. Even the powerboat labored against it.

And then he saw them all standing on the little gravel beach. Lucy was there—and Beverly and Horace and Bob. He'd lost every shred of self-respect, but he could give a shit. They brought him to the beach, and Daisy leaped out. "Can I pay you for your trouble?" asked Oz, turning to the men.

"Don't you worry about it."

He jumped out in knee-deep water, and hauled the boat to shore while the two men took off in a cloud of gasoline fumes.

"Sorry," mumbled Oz in Beverly's direction. "I broke an oar. And Daisy swam out and we were both caught in the current." He glanced at Lucy. Her eyes were shining. "We would have been okay," he said to her.

"It really wasn't such a big deal, right?" said Lucy. "Not life-threatening or anything."

He got her drift. He put his arms around her, and she began to cry.

"She's been in a state," said Beverly.

Lucy's tears turned into great wet hiccupping sobs.

"Baby, don't, it's okay. Okay . . . Okay."

53

Beverly and Horace walked a little distance away and sat on a flat rock. "God," said Beverly. She was quiet a moment, sitting up close to him. "I hope she doesn't throw away a good chance to be happy." Horace stirred the sand at the base of the rock with a stick while waves rolled in. "One in twenty is supposed to be a big one," he said.

"I wasn't talking about waves."

"Well, either it'll work or it won't."

She wobbled her knee impatiently back and forth against his. "You might *talk* to me about it."

"I don't know what to say, except I know someone else who can be mighty stubborn."

"Who would that be?" She glanced over at Oz and Lucy, kissing.

"You're forgiven, you know," he said, putting his arm around her.

"There's nothing to forgive."

"I beg your pardon? I was a prisoner on this island. The Birdman of Alcatraz. Napoleon on St. Helena."

She laughed. "Why don't I feel sorry for you?"

"You're a hard woman."

"You know what I feel like doing?" she said, jumping up.

"Burning that pile of junk. Why don't I get the gasoline, and we can do it right now."

"Whoa," said Horace. "You'll blow us sky high."

"What?"

"You want kerosene."

"That's what I *meant*." She sounded annoyed.

"Why not just take it to the dump?"

"Because," said Beverly. "Burning's better . . . Hey, you two, want to help?"

"What?" called Lucy.

"We're going to have a bonfire."

"I'm hungry," said Oz.

"Can't it wait?" asked Beverly. "Where're the matches? I don't suppose anyone would have matches?"

"I'll get 'em." Oz took off up the bank.

"He's going to find that potato salad," she muttered, "and then we won't see him for half an hour." Lucy sat on a rock looking listless, the low-blood-sugar look. Beverly picked up a stone and threw it into the water. She felt glad, something that went even beyond Oz being safe. *I wouldn't want to be anywhere else.* When was the last time she'd had a thought like that? Oz tumbled down the hill, holding the matches high, his mouth full of food, carrying a piece of peanut-butter toast for Lucy. Beverly set a can of kerosene down on a rock and began yanking bits of the rubbish pile onto the beach. Horace and Oz lifted the couch over together.

"We need to separate out the metal," said Lucy. She pulled a copper pipe and an old refrigerator shelf over to the left of the boathouse, and Oz dragged over a water boiler. They piled lumber onto the couch, and the snow fence, a chair with no back, the snapped oar, an ugly hollow-core door, a swaybacked wooden bookcase that had lost its shelves.

"All right," said Beverly. "Call the fire department." She

squirted kerosene on the old couch and over the pile of lumber and shelving. Oz lit the match and touched it to the cushion. A dull blue flame started up and went out. He tried again with the shelving. It burned unhappily for a few minutes and went out. They stood around looking at the remnants of smoke. "It's rained a lot lately," said Lucy.

Beverly upended the rest of the can on the couch cushion, and Oz struck another match. It flared up brightly and caught on the oar; the snow fence went up, crackling and snapping, and heat began pouring from the pile. "You don't think it'll set the boat-house on fire . . . " said Beverly. She pulled Lucy farther away as the flames grew higher. Oz reached for the leg of the couch and pulled it toward the beach.

"Watch out," said Horace. "Enough heroics for you for one day."

"I'm never getting in a boat again," said Oz.

"Don't say that," said Beverly, "you might love it someday."

"I won't. How you've kept from drowning all these years—"

Sparks flew into the air and settled on seaweed. "I was remiss in not telling you more about tides."

Horace laughed. "I tipped over a canoe when I was courting Beverly. She was sitting in the boat, and I stepped into the stern wrong, and we both went over. Her father happened to be watching at the time, probably saying to himself, 'That damn fool thinks he's going to marry my daughter.' "

"The fire's dying down," said Beverly. She pushed the dryer box into the middle of it, and the flames shot up again. A few minutes later, the pile was smoldering.

"Well done," said Lucy, her forehead and cheeks red from heat, her white hair backlit by sun.

"That's enough for one day," said Beverly. She started back toward the house, turned around, and stopped. "Listen," she said. "This is as good a time as any. Horace and I have been talking

291

over something." She looked at Lucy and Oz. "We'd like to give the two of you this house. We thought it might be a place to get started with the baby."

"We might build something smaller for ourselves in the lower field," said Horace.

"People don't just give away houses," said Lucy.

"If you wanted to sell it later, you could always get something on the mainland," Beverly said. "But my sister doesn't want it— we'd buy out her share—and it's too big for us. We'll have more than enough to live on after we sell the Connecticut house. Here's the thing: We've grown fond of you. And it's not really as generous as it sounds. We don't have any children of our own; why shouldn't we give it to you?"

They looked at her in disbelief. She went into the boathouse and pulled a moth-eaten crocheted blanket made of pastel pinks and blues out of a pile, some double bedsheets stained with motor oil, and a few rotten lengths of clothesline. Clasping the bedding to her bosom and dragging the clothesline, she dumped them on the smoldering pile, kissed the two of them quickly, and headed up the hill. She was already out of breath when she turned and said over her shoulder, "As long as you never sell it to Dick and that awful wife of his, whatever her name was."

Lucy filled a large pot with water at the big sink and turned on the stove. Opening a can of tuna fish, she said to herself, *People don't give away houses.* She felt like crying. At the open door, she called, "Oz?" She saw him down by the boathouse. "Oz!" He looked up. She beckoned with her hand, and he started up the hill.

"What do we do?" she asked, almost before he'd come through the door.

"Say yes," he said.

"We can't. It's too much. They hardly know us. We don't even know if we'll be together." He turned his baseball cap from back to front and set it back on his head as though things might go better that way. He looked at her and smiled with his eyes.

"We *don't* know," she repeated.

"*You* don't know," he said, holding her shoulders. "For Christ sakes, don't you see? There aren't any strings attached. They're not saying to themselves, *We'll give them this if they give us that.* They're not like that."

She dipped her knees, came out from under his hands. "It doesn't feel right."

"Maybe *I'm* what doesn't feel right."

"That's not what I said."

"That's what you meant, though, wasn't it?"

"Maybe."

"If that's true, I'll be off on the next boat." She knew he meant it.

On the counter was a strawberry rhubarb pie he'd made that afternoon. It was perfect: fruit peeking through, a lattice crust woven in and out, the way he wanted to weave his life with hers.

Horace banged in the door. "I've got something to show you."

"I'm in the middle of cooking dinner," said Lucy.

"Before the wind gets too strong. We're going in the morning, this is the last chance." He noticed the pie. "Is that for us?"

Lucy turned off the stove. "Not now."

"Beverly!" yelled Horace. "I've got them! We'll meet you on the lower field."

Oz shuffled after Horace and Lucy. "What's going on?"

"Can't tell you," said Horace, quickening his steps.

The storm the Coast Guard had predicted was moving toward them, dark clouds rolling from the southeast. Beverly ran down the field and caught up with them. "What's happening?"

"Can't say," said Horace.

Dividing the lower part of the field from the upper was a row of old lilacs, tall as trees. On the other side, two spades were stuck in the ground near an outcropping of granite. Beside them was a large watering can and a bag of compost. Placed at intervals on the grass were five good-sized stones, twine wrapped around them like birthday presents. A little tree sat next to each stone. There were five holes dug.

"I'm a sentimental old fool," Horace said, "but I hope you'll humor me. There's one for each of us, and one for the baby." A thin frizz of hair stood up from the top of his bald spot; his neck was misted with sweat.

"Look what you did," said Lucy. Under each rock, he'd folded a piece of paper inside a plastic bag with a few words in his spidery handwriting. *Oz: Wherever you go, your tree will be saying your name.*

Lucy: Amor vincit omnia. The wind picked up suddenly and blew their hair around their heads. Horace took the spade from Beverly to deepen a hole as the first drops of rain fell. By the time the clouds had let loose and they'd planted the trees, there wasn't a dry inch of skin among them.

Lucy came to Oz that night. She listened at his door, turned the knob, and went in. He was sleeping with the crook of his elbow over his eyes as though there were streetlights outside the window. "Sweetheart?" she whispered.

All at once, he startled and opened his eyes. In one motion, he put his arms out and drew her down on the bed.

"We have to finish what we were talking about."

He put his arm around her. "What?"

"The house," she said, lifting her head from his shoulder. "They'll want to know."

"You don't want it," he said, "right?"

She bobbed above a wave of desire, tried to keep her head

clear. "I don't know." She turned and could barely make out the outline of his face in the dark. "Could *you* imagine living here?"

"I don't really care where I am if you're with me."

She put her palm against his cheek. "Yes. Yes to all of it. Yes, if you'll have me . . . I can't believe I said that."

54

By six-thirty the next morning, Oz was running out the
door, carrying a peanut-butter and jelly sandwich in one hand
and his bag in the other. When they saw him coming, the dogs
jumped back out of the truck and ran around the yard. Horace
yelled, "Fifteen minutes to the ferry!" Oz tackled Daisy and
grabbed Bob by the collar.

"They're off," said Beverly, as the truck backed onto the road.

Lucy turned to her. "I told him yes," she said. "We don't want
you to give us the house, but we'd love to live here."

"Just take it. Please. You'd be doing us a favor. When you're
our age, you want to whittle things down."

"We might disappoint you."

"What's that got to do with anything? You don't owe us anything."

"Where will you live?"

"Anything could happen. Horace may kill himself before he
gets the trees in the ground. I don't know. Maybe we'll join the
Peace Corps."

"Can I tell you something?"

"Hush, it's all right."

That night, Beverly cooked a chicken, and Lucy ate close to half of it, along with potatoes and summer corn and string beans. "I'm waddling," she said, getting up from the table. "I'll do the dishes after." She squeezed Beverly's hand and went out to the granite stoop to watch the birds fly home.

She thought of her baby. It frightened her, the idea of a face growing inside her. A chin, eyebrows, cheeks. Brain and spinal cord and nerves and arteries and veins and capillaries and bones and skin. A four-chambered heart. There were so many things to go wrong. She didn't want to think about this.

Her mother's friend, Adele, fell down on the floor without warning one day, and a week later she was dead. She had a thirteen-year-old daughter. She didn't even smoke. She drank, but no one's perfect. Her mother had called up Adele on the phone—she hadn't talked to her in a few weeks—and a woman she didn't know answered. When Lucy's mother asked to speak to Adele, Adele's sister said, "She's dead." Lucy remembered the way her mother had backed up a step, with the phone up to her ear. It was an old-fashioned phone, black, with a heavy earpiece.

"Dead? Not Adele." Her mother put down the receiver. It looked ceremonial, the way she laid it in the cradle. She turned and saw Lucy. "Adele had a stroke," she said. "People don't have strokes when they're forty-two. She's dead. I can't believe it. Adele Alessendrini is dead."

Lucy didn't want to be thinking about Adele, either—about how her mother's face looked when she set the phone down, how she went and lay down on the couch and smoked a joint and pretty soon she was smoking and crying nonstop and about to set the cushions on fire, and Lucy had to put her arms around her and lead her up to her bed.

At dinner, she'd told Beverly that she'd called her mother. But she hadn't. *Hi, Mom,* she imagined herself saying. *I'm pregnant. Oz is the father . . .* you *know, the guy who went to prison, the one you said was a loser? But it's all right. Don't worry.*

You don't say things like that to your mother. On the other hand, Beverly wasn't the kind of person you lied to.

She waited until Beverly and the dogs had gone to bed, and crept downstairs and pulled the phone as far as it would reach, past the refrigerator and out the back door. She could see a few stars in the middle of all the clouds, and she dialed, waiting eight rings before her mother picked up. "I was watching TV," her mother said. As though she'd talked to Lucy earlier that day, as though a month hadn't just gone by without any kind of talk. It was always Lucy who called her mother, not the other way around. The television blared in the background, some kind of battle scene.

"Could you turn it down, Mom? I can't hear you."

Her mother put down the phone, and Lucy heard steps across the carpeted room, and the TV cut out.

"I'm going to have a baby," she said when her mother returned.

There was a long silence. "You're kidding, right?"

"Why would I be kidding?"

"You've just ruined your life."

"No, I haven't. This is my life. This is how it's turning out."

"How far along are you? You could go to a doctor. I could find you a good doctor."

"I don't want a doctor." She knew the kind of doctor her mother was talking about. "We're going to live together. Oz and me and the baby."

"The guy that was in prison, that's the father? . . . *God help us,*" her mother said under her breath. Out beyond the shoreline, charcoal-gray clouds rested against even darker sky. Lucy thought she heard waves breaking.

"I don't believe this," her mother said. "When did you find out?"

She didn't want to tell her how long it had been. "Couldn't you try to be a little happy for me?"

"Why should I pretend to be happy when I'm not happy? Do you have any idea how much trouble it is to raise a kid?"

"I was the kid. I know." Where did they go in this wilderness? They bounced off each other for another five minutes, and Lucy said she'd be staying out on the island for now.

"I suppose you're going to have the baby out there in a farmhouse, with some kind of granola-midwife."

"Probably," said Lucy.

"What if there are complications?"

"I'll take a boat to the mainland."

"And if there's a storm?"

"I don't know, Mom." She heard her mother's breathing on the other end, the rasp in her throat that moved in every summer. "Are your allergies bad?" she asked. All at once she understood that her mother hadn't expected her life to turn out like this; not herself, not her daughter, not the brown plaid couch that sat in the middle of her living room, not the job she went to, none of it.

Her mother's voice softened suddenly. "I love you, baby." They hung onto the phone receivers in two different states, crying without sound.

And then Lucy said good-bye. It broke her heart. She and her mother disagreed about everything, just about, so how come she was crying? It was something that came from so far beyond words. Her mother was the shaggy old bear that bore her, who smelled right, who would strike down anyone who tried to hurt her daughter, just like that. When you thought about this one true thing, it didn't matter what her mother did with her life, whether she watched TV and smoked pot on a couch covered with an old bedspread.

55

Heat rose off the lake in a sulfur-colored mist. Oz stood naked at the edge of the lake looking toward Katahdin, almost gone behind layers of sludge, and thinking of the hulk of a glacier that had scraped its way slowly across the valley. He'd like to sit on that hunk of ice today. They'd only planted fifteen trees, and Horace said that would have to do for the day. Bob lay on the damp sand at the edge of the lake, panting, turned his head and lapped at the water without getting up. Daisy had dug a hole and lay with her hip sagged into it.

A chipmunk ran around for no apparent reason, squeaking and spitting. Fast little herky-jerky movements. Head up and down into the undercover. Angry chattering. Oz touched his neck and rolled the dried sweat off, and then he plunged. He opened his eyes and swam underwater, halfway across the narrow inlet of water, and came up for air. He'd had a headache all day, and suddenly it wasn't there. Daisy paddled toward him, and then she was right on top of him, flailing her paws. He shoved her off, and she swam around in a circle like a beaver, tail out upon the water.

He thought of Lucy's T-shirt, dark blue, midnight next to her skin, and inside, their baby's first watery home. Everyone was happier in water. Way back, that first fish—the one that grew legs and headed for dry land—made a big mistake. Oz grabbed a lung full of air, went under, and swam down the channel as far as he could go, farther, until he exploded to the surface. A deerfly buzzed over his head, and he dived again.

Underneath, he opened his eyes and saw a smallmouth bass, fourteen to sixteen inches long, greenish-yellow in color, dark striations along the sides, like water shot with light. He swam along behind it and looked up, the way a fish looks up at the surface. Weak, patchy rays shone through the water. When he came up and went under again, the fish was still there, sculling. He swam along beside it, thinking how easy it had been to fall in love with Lucy. He'd wanted her and wanted her but never asked himself whether she was good for him. He didn't really care. He came up and went under again, and with a flick of its tail, the bass was gone. Would it be like that someday with Lucy?

He swam back toward shore and got out onto a rock; Daisy shook herself out, trotted back to the hole she'd made, and lay down. *Open his eyes and she'd be gone*. It's what happened to that Afghan guy—wife gone, two little girls gone, freedom gone, country gone, and everywhere people after his ass thinking he's some kind of freaking terrorist. What was his name—Arif—went to prison for working without a visa. He wasn't political, he just wanted to raise his kids here instead of there. Last time Oz knew, Arif hadn't seen his wife and two girls in a year and a half. He had the saddest eyes in the world. People called him "raghead," they called him plenty of worse things, and one day six inmates jumped him and beat the crap out of him. The guards could have stopped it, but they didn't. Oz knew one of the guys that did it— Groley was his name—and he asked him why.

"Look what they did to *us*."

"What are you talking about?"

"Alkeeda," said Groley, "you moron."

"He doesn't know anything about that."

"Sure, he does. They're all in it. What are you, some kind of fucking Islam?" He pronounced Islam as though it rhymed with ham.

Oz couldn't stop thinking of the ones back there. When he sat down just to be blank in himself, their faces rose up in front of him: Jason, long, lean, manic. Hair in a ponytail. Hard to imagine how he'd make it through his sentence alive with the wiseass mouth he had on him. Ed from the Bronx, overweight, funny-sad. His house-building business went sour after he caught his wife in bed with his brother-in-law. He tried to fix the financial mess with a little creative bank fraud and got caught.

He turned over his wrist and studied the raven. Every day he felt lucky to be out. No more electronic bugle call, nurses handing out sedatives. But in some ways, it was easier back there. What do you do with a life? He looked at Horace sitting by his tent, eyes closed, chest sagging in the heat.

Last night, he'd told Horace the news about Lucy. They'd been sitting on logs next to the fire, Horace nodding off after dinner.

"Are you having a wedding?"

"Lucy doesn't want one. That's fine by me. But sometime, I'm going to get her a ring."

"I'm happy for you," said Horace. "Funny, you never know what's around the next corner." He poked up the fire with a stick. As though the wind had heard him, the still leaves of a quaking aspen on the edge of the campsite began to shake.

Altogether, there were just thirty trees to go. Oz already had a place picked out for the last one: lots of sun and a good view of the lake. They'd dig the hole extra deep, put in extra compost. The two dogs would be sitting nearby, quiet for once, watching. Horace would say a few words over it. It would be the 927th tree.

They'd lost seventy-three; not bad. How many of the ones in the ground would still be alive at the end of the summer, at the end of next winter? A year after that? Birds would sit in their branches. It wasn't glamorous, what they'd done. It wasn't brave. No one even needed to know about it.

56

Beverly was just tacking up a sign on a bulletin board in a shopping center, announcing their yard sale on a Saturday in September, when she ran into Madeline, Horace's old secretary.

"Are you moving?" asked Madeline, reading the sign.

"We're finished with Connecticut," said Beverly.

"What's Horace up to?"

"He's planted a bunch of trees since he left the hospital. It wasn't something he really planned to do—"

"For a nursery?"

Beverly hesitated. "The government."

"Oh." Madeline looked as though she wanted to ask more, but something stopped her.

"How about you?"

"I miss Horace. The place sure isn't the same without him. His sort of integrity . . . people think it's old-fashioned nowadays. Don't get me going . . . Where'd you say you were off to?"

"Vinalhaven Island, off the coast of Maine."

"That's a big change."

"Sure is," said Beverly. "You know, Horace always said you were the best secretary in the world."

"You tell him that's not true."

"I'm not going to tell him that," Beverly said.

The day of the sale, Horace moved the truck out onto the street; and at five in the morning, he and Beverly dragged half the contents of their house out into the driveway. Beverly moved a few things back when she realized she couldn't part with them— a small yellow stool she remembered her mother sitting on when she snapped beans in the kitchen, an antique clock whose hands never moved, two paintings she was fond of.

People started coming early, and by four o'clock, it was over—like a forest fire—what people took and what they left untouched. "Who's going to buy those old law books?" she'd asked Horace at dawn. But by the end, they were gone. What was left was a miscellany of flower vases, a Crock-pot, cookie tins, a brass bell her great-grandmother had once used to call her children home with, some faded yellow kitchen curtains dotted with mushrooms, a set of golf clubs someone had given Horace years before and he'd never used, two chairs that needed caning, a rug Bob had chewed on one corner, old picture frames, a selection of piano music too hard for her now, a 1929 set of the Encyclopedia Britannica.

"Load it right into the car," said Beverly. "I'll get it to Goodwill. If the stuff gets back into the house . . . "

"Don't you want this bell?" said Horace.

"All right."

"And what about the Britannica?"

"No. What did we make?"

"Three hundred forty-seven dollars and forty-two cents."

"That's it? For all that trouble?"

A week before they left, Horace was busy packing tools into a box when a green pickup showed up in the driveway. Even before the two men got out, he recognized the insignia on the door—badge-shaped, with a pine tree in the middle, flanked by a big U and an S. He went down the side steps and into the driveway.

"Sorry to bother you, sir," the taller of the two men said. He wore twill pants and a long-sleeved green shirt. On one pocket was a brass badge with the Forest Service insignia, and on the other, a brass nameplate. "Our records show that in April, one thousand black spruce trees were mistakenly delivered to this address. We don't know how it happened, sir, but this is definitely the address on the invoice. The trees were intended for a research station."

Horace took off his reading glasses and settled them on the top of his head. "I've heard about the government losing all sorts of things," he said. "The other day I was reading in the paper about a shipment of ten thousand hammers . . . " Just then, he noticed a couple of black plastic trays leaning up against the garage behind them.

"You never saw any trees?"

"I'm getting old, but it isn't that bad yet."

"Our driver, who's no longer working with us, has been contacted and remembered the delivery. There was an older woman and a dog."

"Look at me," said Horace. "What would I do with a thousand blue gum trees . . . spruces, whatever they were? I don't know how you mislaid them, but you're welcome to come in for a cup of coffee."

They thanked him and turned to go.

"Just out of curiosity," asked Horace, "what was the research station going to do with them?"

"Inject them with various diseases, subject them to environmental stressors. Extremes of heat, cold, moisture, and drought. An array of industrial pollutants. Study what kills them."

They backed out the driveway, and Horace fetched the plastic trays and tucked them inside the garage. He'd hardly come back into the kitchen before Beverly found him. "You old devil—you lied yourself silly."

"Did you hear what they said?"

"They were going to murder them."

They moved to Vinalhaven on a day when great sheets of water fell from the sky. Beverly went ahead in her car with Bob, and Horace took a moment in the backyard with the black walnut. "You're a good old fellow," he said to the dripping limbs over his head. "Take care of things."

He and Beverly arrived in a caravan off the ferry, the rain just beginning to let up as they put the key into the lock of their six-month winter rental on School Street. Every day, Horace went to the building site. They'd designed a house half the size of the old one, nestled in the lower field, with a small studio on one side for Beverly. That winter, snow fell over the harbor, over the fiberglass hulls of *Becky's Dream* and *Nothin' Fancy* and *Daly's Grind*, over the sloping fields and the roof of the grange hall and the steps of Gigi's Restaurant, *Where the spirits meet the sea*. It took the builders four months from the time they finished the frame to when it was habitable.

Now in the season of stubborn mud, the back of winter nearly broken, Horace sat in his grandfather's chair, parked beside one of the many windows in the new house that still needed trimming. Beverly was in her new studio, working on a painting the town library had commissioned.

He thought suddenly of Bill Yardley scampering down the street in Connecticut in the dusk. Their old life seemed further away than the moon. Across the field, the lights in the old house went on one by one. Lucy would be sitting in the kitchen with her feet propped up. The light from the overhead kitchen bulb would shine over her hair and onto her white eyelashes, and shadow over her cheeks. Her ankles had been swelling the last few days. The midwife said sometimes it was a sign of toxemia: drink water, eat protein, prop up her feet was what she was supposed to do.

She'd be going into labor any day. Horace could feel the baby waiting for its time, lying in its cramped repose. He was nervous as a cat. Heaven help her. Last night, she and Oz and Beverly went to the Lamaze class in town. They'd asked him if he wanted to go, and he'd said maybe next week. "But if I went, would it mean I'd have to be there for the birth?"

"What do you mean, *have* to be there?" asked Beverly. "Don't you want to be?"

"Not really."

Beverly muttered something he couldn't hear. Maybe next week he'd go. It was the last week of class. Men were supposed to do this kind of thing now. Back when he was a boy, no one would have thought to invite a man to a birth. As it was, there'd be three people there, four counting Lucy. That seemed plenty. His stomach turned over just thinking of it.

They'd left for the class carrying pillows and a mat, and when Beverly came home, she said Lucy had practiced two kinds of breathing. Beverly pointed to a nail in the wall, the focal point. Her eyes glazed over, and she breathed slow in and out, big Zen breaths for early labor. And for later when things got worse, a big breath in and out and then shallow panting. *Uhuh, uhuh, uhuh, uhuh.* It excited Bob. Horace tried it and felt his head go light as a balloon. He kept it up and began to hallucinate: Men unloading boxes onto a dock from a big, rusty ship.

Outside the window in the blue-black darkness, pockets of old snow shone here and there. Soon the peepers would start up in the swamps. *Wheeep? Wheeep?* their voices going slow on cold nights and faster on hot ones, so fast they'd sound like sleigh bells. He got up and went to the door, and Bob bolted out, ran to the first slushy snow patch, and rolled around. Horace stepped out and closed the door behind him. He wished to make something for the baby. He thought of a wooden chest, a seafaring chest. It could be for toys, and later it could hold important things. He'd use curly maple. He'd need tools. A plane, a saw, a set of chisels. Hinges and a hasp.

Bob crashed around in the undergrowth of the bank, and the Pleiades disappeared behind a cloud. Horace took a deep breath. He tried panting, Lamaze style, felt his senses take leave of his head again. The men got onto the ship with the big rusting hull. It was headed out of the harbor, moving slow. And then he saw a tiny white head, crowning. Clear as a moon. You want to reach for a baby's head when you see it; you want to protect it.

57

In her dream, Beverly saw firemen standing up on an old-fashioned fire engine, their black hats slanted down the backs of their heads. One held a cord and rang the bell. *Clang, clang, clang.* Her eyes opened onto the dark, and she suddenly realized the phone was ringing. Running toward the sound, she rammed her toe hard against the edge of a metal toolbox. "Ow, ow! Someone's calling!" she yelled backward toward the bedroom.

"Hello?" she said.

"Beverly?" Oz's voice shook. "It's coming. Her water broke. I called Jenny."

"Is that Lucy making that noise?"

"Daisy's howling."

"Open the door, and I'll call her . . . Wait, I'll be right there." She burst into tears.

"Lucy's got the hiccups," said Oz. "Is that normal?"

"I don't know. I'll be right there." She cried a little more and hung up.

Horace stood in the kitchen in his underwear. "Shall I make you some tea?"

"No, no. It's coming. I think I may have broken my toe." She looked down. It was swollen to twice its size. "My baby toe." She started to cry again. "I have to get hold of myself."

"Do you want a Band-Aid?"

"I don't care about my toe." She laughed, a little hysterically. Tears ran down her cheeks.

"Sweetheart," he said, taking her by the shoulders. "Take a deep breath and have a drink of water."

"Later," she said. "I have to get dressed."

"Now." He gave her a Kleenex for her nose. "Blow."

He brought her a drink of cranberry juice and got her to breathe slowly, long enough that she stopped crying. She put a sneaker on one foot and a flip-flop on the other, and set off across the field. She stopped and cried once more on the way over, and continued across the crusty snow. Daisy came toward her in the dark with a single *woof*, and she said, "Go find Bob. Where's Bob?"

She felt shy all of a sudden when she came to their door, as though maybe they wouldn't want her there and she'd just be in the way, an old nincompoop who didn't know anything, not even if it's normal to hiccup, and why don't you just go home and go to bed and wait for the news in the morning? But when Oz opened the door and she saw his face, she never wondered again where she ought to be.

Lucy was in bed, propped against pillows. She looked calm, almost queenly. So white, as though light poured out of her. It was just after two in the morning. Beverly kissed her hair, felt tears rising, and pushed them down. Oz sat on the bed next to Lucy, wringing his hands. Lucy hiccupped vigorously, and suddenly her eyes went somewhere else. "Five and a half minutes," said Oz. He turned to Beverly. "Why do you have two different shoes on?"

She waved her hand. "It's nothing. I stubbed it."

"I'll get you some ice," he said. She let him. He didn't know what to do with himself. He came back with it in a paper towel, bent down and laid it over her toe.

"Ow." She took the paper towel from him. "I think you should call Jenny again."

"She said don't call back until they're five minutes apart."

"Go ahead, call her. And call the restaurant and leave a message that you're not coming to work in the morning."

While he was gone, Lucy said, "If he gets too . . . you know, will you take him outside? . . . *Hic* . . . He told me he gets dizzy at the sight of blood."

Beverly imagined him going down like a column. "Did you tell Jenny?"

"No."

"Want me to call your Mom?"

"No . . . *Hic* . . . not now, she'd just worry."

When the contractions grabbed hold, she went alone to a windy ridge. People talked about pain. It wasn't pain. Pain was sharp-edged like metal. This was a big, savage discomfort like a large thing burrowing in among your bones, trying to move them aside. Her feet scrubbed under the covers. Like a wildness you can't get out of, that you want to run from but you can't because it's in you and the only way out is to get rid of it but it's never going to stop arcing against your tailbone until you feel you have to get out of bed and crouch on the floor and shriek like an animal. *Huh, huh!*—and somewhere in and around you, a sense of majesty, no that's not the word, well for a moment majesty, but then something pitiless and indifferent that will crush you in its fist, devour you the next wave or the one after or the one after that, each time stirring deeper cresting higher until a big one knocks you sideways.

She still had the hiccups, and in between contractions they made her laugh, but they kept on through a double-crested contraction, and then she stopped laughing and lost her focus and wet the bed and there was a scurrying and she opened her eyes wide and looked up at Oz; his face was so scared she squeezed his hand, and told him it's okay, baby, don't worry. Beverly laid a cool washcloth on her forehead and Jenny said you're doing fine, almost fully dilated. Don't push, but before she got the all-clear something broke inside her and she tumbled into a fierce desire, a tidal wave at her back, you can't tell me not to push I can't stop it. "Pant," said Jenny. And she tried to remember what she'd learned and couldn't, and she heard Beverly panting beside her, that was how you did it, and she began panting *uhuh, uhuh, uhuh.* Good, good.

She shook now, every part of her rattling with cold, and she heard Oz asking what's wrong, honey, what's wrong, and she shook and panted and flung his voice away.

And a voice said, *Push,* and her eyeballs burst, her ears flew from the side of her head, roaring. She took a huge breath and pushed again. *Keep going,* they yelled, *keep going,* but she stopped. She couldn't do it anymore. I see it! Beverly cried. Push! Push! Don't stop! She was too tired and there was nothing left, and then along came a wave that carried her. They were cheering, you can do it—you can do it—up over this last rise—push, and she did, now pant! and all at once she saw Jenny with her hands on either side of the baby's head and then there was a crash—Oz had fallen over the rocking chair.

The baby—a girl! "She's a girl!" cried Beverly.

The baby opened her eyes. She wasn't crying, just looking.

Lucy couldn't see properly, or get hold of the words. "Sun or moon?"

"Moon," said Oz squeezing her hand.

Jenny suctioned out her nose and mouth and laid her on Lucy's stomach. The baby's eyelashes were wet, like a bird that's gone through a storm. Lucy ran her finger over one tiny white eyebrow, and they looked into each other's eyes. *I'd give my life for you*, she thought. But how could that be; she didn't even know her. *Didn't even know her, but it was true.*

58

Horace had been looking at the *Scientific American* for several hours when he realized he'd been reading the same paragraph over and over. The article had to do with growing new human organs, and he was stuck on the three-dimensional scaffolds of biodegradable polymers. Normally he liked reading things he couldn't understand, but this article was irritating him.

He stood up and began to pace. Daisy and Bob were asleep on the floor in the bedroom. He looked out the window, and more lights were on over there than before. And an extra car. He wondered whether he should put on his shoes and go over, but he'd only be in the way, and he didn't want to see her suffer. They'd call when there was news. Why was it necessary for it to be so damned—what was the word? So damned . . . strenuous. No. *Wrathful.* Yes, that was it. It seemed to take so much pain to keep the human cycle going.

He wandered into the kitchen. He felt that he ought to do something. He'd never made biscuits, but he remembered his grandmother cutting dough into shapes and baking them for breakfast. Somewhere in the kitchen were the tin cookie cutters she'd used, the only thing left of her. He racketed through the drawers and finally found the cookie cutters in a cardboard box under the kitchen sink.

He got out *The Fannie Farmer Cookbook* and opened it. Stumbled over the floor on the way to get a bowl. *Pick up your feet.* What time *was* it? Five in the morning. He thought of Beverly when she left the house, how she'd gone out the door with a shoe on one foot and a flip-flop on the other.

He measured out flour and salt and baking powder and stirred them around in the bowl. *Rub in the butter,* it said. He didn't know what that meant, but he rubbed the butter around in the flour and kept rubbing until it was pretty well mixed, and then he poured in milk. The cookbook said he was supposed to mix it with only a few strokes, but after three or four turns of the spoon, the flour was still coming out of the bowl onto the floor, and he kept mixing and adding milk until it looked like the white flour paste his mother used to make. He added more flour and got his hands into the act, and the dough made him into a web-fingered man until he sprinkled flour onto his hands and rolled the excess off into the bowl. He upended the bowl onto the counter, rolled the dough into a ball, and patted it out. He set the oven to 425 degrees, pressed the tin down on the dough, and . . . out came a rabbit. And hearts and stars.

The biscuits came out of the oven perfect and brown, except for a few rabbits that lost their tails when he loosened them with a spatula. He piled the biscuits up and tucked the towel around them to keep them warm.

The first light was beginning to show in the sky when he opened the refrigerator and took out the butter dish and a jar of half-eaten raspberry jam, and put them on the tray along with the biscuits. And a box of tea. He took off his slippers and put on his shoes and coat. "Stay," he said to the dogs.

All at once, he wished he'd gone to Lamaze class and been there in that lighted house all the time for whatever happened. He picked his way across the crust of snow, sinking in every so often. It was hard balancing everything on the tray; he walked slowly so he wouldn't go down with the whole thing.

From outside their house, he heard a crash, silence—a cry. He put the tray down in the snow and listened again. He heard nothing at all now, but he believed he'd heard it, and he looked into the top of the sky where he could just see the Pleiades, and he thanked something, a deity if there was one, with all his heart. He stumbled backward, righted himself, and reached in his pocket. He was trying to find something. There were keys in there, some loose change. The trees, the stars, the dark sea blurred in front of his eyes, and his hand touched something damp. His handkerchief. Pulling it out, he held it to his eyes and wept.

59

Horace sat in a chair by the kitchen window. Her name was Lily. Only three hours ago, she wasn't here. Lucy and Oz napped in the bedroom next to Lily's bassinet, and Beverly dozed on the living room couch. He still wasn't used to the sound of her—each time she cried, he felt desperate. There she went. Beverly tiptoed into the bedroom and picked her up.

"Here, you hold her," she said to Horace. If she'd asked, he would have said no, he didn't know how. *Three hours old.* But now she was in his arms in her little yellow blanket, bald except for fine wisps of snowy white hair, no bigger than a cabbage, and what did you do with a baby?

"Just support her head," said Beverly.

"Like this?" He wasn't breathing. Beverly sat down next to him. The baby wailed against him, her nose pushed up against his chest. He brought her down so she was lying on her back in his lap, facing him. She looked into his eyes, and it seemed to him that she looked surprised. She stopped crying.

Her eyes were the palest blue, with a tinge of lavender. Light streamed out beyond her head, but maybe it didn't. He was so tired he couldn't trust himself.

"Hi, Birdie," he said, not knowing the name would stick. "Woodruff's the name."

She looked at him through the mist in front of her eyes. "Little foggy eyes," he said. "Foggy blue . . . How'd you get here? Tramp steamer? It's a hard world, you know. Tough road ahead . . . *You* don't care, do you?" He unwrapped the blanket from around her. "Good Lord, look at your little birdie legs and your little birdie toes . . . Beverly, look at her toes."

"I heard she was born," said Lorena, standing in front of the potatoes in Carver's Harbor Store. Her eyes shifted. "I'm sorry. Blind and retarded, I heard."

"Who said that? There's nothing wrong with her," said Beverly. "She's two weeks old and the most beautiful baby that ever was. You know better than to listen to gossip. Why don't you ask before you go spreading things around?"

"I didn't."

"I'm surprised at you." She turned from her, so mad she forgot half of what was on the list. And by the time she came in the driveway, the tires were spitting gravel. She dragged the grocery bag in the back door. "Of all the ignorant . . . " Bob poked his nose under her elbow.

"Stop it, Bob. Get away."

"What?" said Horace.

"They're already at it."

"What?" He was lying on the bed, reading a book on amateur carpentry. Generally, the technical problem of making joints was related to the nature of wood. As cells take in and give off water, they expand and contract. The movement perpendicular to the grain of the wood is often much greater than the movement parallel to the grain, so when end grain is joined to long grain, the differential can cause the joint to fail. He'd just turned the page and found the several kinds of joints . . . "What? What's the matter?"

"Lorena said Lily was blind and mentally retarded . . . Horace, did you hear what I said? No. You didn't. She said Lily was blind and slow."

"Well, that's a lie."

Beverly slammed the milk into the door of the refrigerator. "They're gossiping about her."

"They can't."

"What do you mean? The place is already full of it."

"Why not write something in the island paper and tell them about her? We'll say she looks different, but she's not deficient. I'll write it."

"You're not serious."

"I am . . . And another thing. I've decided I'm going to use dovetail joints. I figure I'll need four to a side—for a total of sixteen. What do you think?" Right then, he was considering his chisels, how he'd work them to get the joints right, but something told him, stop. Just stop. He gazed at Beverly, as though he'd just fallen over her. It seemed he was looking at her face for the first time—her bushy eyebrows, her gray eyes that had been snapping a minute ago and were back to themselves. "Want to come outside?" he asked.

"I'm still putting away groceries. I'll be out."

He filled the watering can at the outside spigot and carried it to the little spruces. In time, he thought, the wind would have its way with each of them. They'd grow twisted, green on one side and bare in the face of the wind. In time, the snow would weigh down the bottom branches, and they'd root and make new trees. He poured water onto Birdie's tree and onto each of the others. He saw Beverly step off the granite stoop. In time—a lump caught in his throat—he and Beverly would leave the earth, but for now, she was here, he was here. She took his hand.

Next door, Lucy lay Birdie down in her bassinet. She felt no awe and wonder today, not even any particular fondness, just exhaustion, her brain circling doggedly like a goat on a tether. Birdie stuck her thumb in her mouth. Her cheeks sucked softly against it, stopped, started; her breathing lengthened. Lucy stepped into the kitchen, dropped to her hands and knees and crawled toward the door, not to wake her, not to wake her, *please, just ten minutes.* When she reached the threshold, she rose to her feet, opened the door softly, and stepped onto the granite stoop. The air still had the memory of winter in it, but the sun was lukewarm with early spring. She closed her eyes and drank it in. Far off, she heard voices on the water, the cry of a gull, and closer, a rustling in the dry grass at her feet. She opened her eyes. A brown bat lay on its side, a webbed wing barely moving, like a beetle trying to right itself. She went closer and peered into the black, feral eye; she couldn't see a wound anywhere, just a great torpor like a creature in a refrigerator. She picked up a stick and tried to roll it over and get it on its feet. It clung briefly to the stick and dropped its hold. Its fur was mouse-brown and glossy, dark on top and lighter underneath, with round black ears and a black snout, the mouth turned up in a kind of—well, a silly grin really. But it was scary, not funny. The two dogs had been playing in the lower field and tumbled toward the house. "No, Daisy! Get away, Bob! NO!" Daisy turned as though to leave, feinted right, twirled, and pushed at the bat with her nose. She ran in circles while Bob barked, and they both came in, nudged at it, batted at it with their paws. "No! Bob!" Lucy ran into the kitchen and out again, upended a stew pot over the bat, and chased the dogs off. Scooping underneath with the stick, she tried to get the bat right side up and into the pot without injuring it.

Oz pedaled his bicycle up the driveway, back from his cooking job at the restaurant.

"I don't know what's the matter with it," she said.

Oz leaned over, went to touch it, and his hands drew back.

When he had it by its two wings, it moved, and he dropped it. The bat scrabbled on the ground and lay still.

"You've killed it!" cried Lucy.

He stopped and looked at her. "Do you want me to help you or not?" He picked it up again, laid it in the pot, and put the top on. "I think it's hibernating—it'll probably come to when it warms up."

Birdie wailed inside, and Lucy disappeared with the bat in the pot and came out crying with Lily; she saw her life stretching before her: sleepless in her twenties, her thirties, arguments, chasing dogs, no time to think, only running, running. It had only been two weeks . . . "I don't know what to do," she said to Oz, weeping.

"You don't have to do anything."

She offered Birdie her breast; but the baby was crying so hard she kept bumping herself off. "Shhh, shhh," said Oz, stroking her cheek. The milk let down, and at last there were great choking gulps.

"You're such a mess," said Lucy, looking into Birdie's eyes. "Yes, you."

Oz opened a paper bag and held out a container. "I brought soup. Wait till you taste it." He expected it would be all right. The bat would stagger out of the pot and flap into the trees. Birdie would grow up.

"Look," said Lucy. The small hand pumped in and out like a tiny bellows, breath in, breath out.

ACKNOWLEDGMENTS

An Unexpected Forest was born on a windy day in a small A-frame house in Pubnico, Nova Scotia. Many thanks to Nicole d'Entremont and her family for giving me time to write in that solitary spot, and to the Allen family, Susan, Fred, Warren, Sally, Kathy, Andy, and Peter, for writing time in Bartlett's Harbor on North Haven Island in an equally beautiful place.

Thanks to Edith Allison, Jody Meredith, and Ken Rice for helping me learn about bog-loving plants, to Eliot Stanley for his description of a bass, to Aileen Winter Mostel for a close look at pigeons, and to Beth Porter at the USDA Forest Service. I'm grateful to Sid Quarrier for his tour of Vinalhaven by sea, and to Roy Heisler and the Vinalhaven Historical Society.

Portions of *An Unexpected Forest* were written while teaching Sudden Fiction at Portland Adult Education, and at the Maine State Prison, Bolduc Correctional Center, and the Maine Correctional Center at Windham. I wish to thank my fellow writers whose integrity and spirit were an inspiration. A special thanks to Mary Blum, Pascal Poe, Diane White, Chris Kelly, and Brent Elwell who made my work at the prisons possible; and to the Maine Humanities Council for funding the writing workshops at three prisons.

To Kate Kennedy and Alisa Wolf for reading draft manuscripts of *An Unexpected Forest*, my deep thanks for their friendship, generosity, and clear-sighted suggestions.

To friends and family who have encouraged and supported me in so many ways, a big thank-you to Julie Bowman, Ruth Bowman, Jonathan Gaines, Mary Hillas, Dee Kelsey, Barbara Kerner, Shannon Koller, David Kuchta, David Moltz, Alan Morse, Sena Naslund, Tamiko Onidera, Louisa Packness, Barbara Potter, Ruth Riddick, Susan and Charlie Russell, Patty Ryan, Karen Stimpson, Shelagh Willet, Susan Williams, Finnegan Wetterau, and Elizabeth Young. Special gratitude to my mother, Margaret Brooks Morse, who taught me to care about the wild places on earth, and to my daughter, Catherine Seager, and to my son, Alan Seager, and daughter-in-law, Georgia Seager, who've brought me so much joy.

A special thanks to my agent, Jane Gelfman, for her unflagging spirit, wisdom, and advice; and to the staff at Down East Books for their attentiveness and good work. And blessings to John Wetterau, fellow writer in the wilderness, all my heart and soul could ever ask for.